DREAMING
THE
DEAD

A NOVEL

CYNTHIA PEARSON

Blue Canary Press
Pittsburgh, Pennsylvania, USA

ISBN: 978-0-6152-1393-4

Printed in the United States of America.

For my mother

Chapter 1

My hand found the pen by the bed and I wrote with half-closed eyes:

Bonnie calls — happy to hear her voice! She says that O.J. Simpson is outside her house. He has brought her a new car but she knows that if she goes out there, he will run her over with it. She tells me to call 411. I try to do that but can't hit the right buttons. Then I think that 411 should be 499, or 911. Trying to figure this out wakes me up.

Ordinarily, getting the notes down would be enough for the moment, and I would let myself tumble back down into sleep. Later, when I was awake enough to know what day it was, I would write in the date of the dream, and any associations that came to mind. But — wait! I was talking to Bonnie! An adrenaline rush of recognition and alarm hit me, just as it had every morning since my friend died so suddenly and shockingly.

I was now wide awake. I lay in bed, wondering about the dream. If Bonnie were alive, I would have called her later in the day to tell her about it. But Bonnie was dead, dead for over two weeks. I blinked, trying to shut out the picture that seemed to have become my default screen ever since the moment I came upon her crumpled body at the bottom of the concrete stairs at Diamond Head.

We had come to Honolulu for the 1999 conference of the International Association for Study of Dreams, and we planned to spend our free afternoon on the hiking trail that led to the apex of the famous volcano. After sitting in conference presentations for three days, both Bonnie and I craved physical activity. Here we were in paradise, and we were spending most of our time indoors. Not only that, but my body mass is so eager to spread out that if I avoid exercise for more than a couple days, it will start to take over the world.

My slim friend, however, was less interested in watching her weight that day than in enjoying the outdoors. Dr. Bonita Taylor may have been one of the world's foremost experts on the subject of nightmares, but that day she was indulging a newfound enthusiasm for geology. She was so excited that she seemed to talk continuously from the moment we caught sight of the looming black formation through the windshield of our rental car.

Leaving the brilliant Waikiki beach behind us, we turned left and began climbing. The tropical foliage stopped dead and we found ourselves surrounded by charcoal colored rock. "Looks like we keep climbing until we're actually inside the caldera," Bonnie bubbled excitedly.

"What's a caldera?" asked Leo, who was sulking because he'd wanted to go parasailing but had been outvoted. Leo had accompanied me to Hawaii, an unusual arrangement for a divorced couple, but certain challenges had brought us together recently. Now we were sometimes partners again, sometimes affectionate old friends and perpetually cautious lovers.

"A caldera is really just a big crater, formed when a volcano explodes or when a volcanic cone collapses." Bonnie had turned around in the front seat to talk directly to Leo and me. Her husband, Frank, an M.D. who directs their sleep disorder clinic, was at the wheel. "Diamond Head was an important military site during the Second World War and it's still military property, but it's also a state park," Bonnie told us. "We'll be driving into the bottom of a bowl, then we hike up to the top of its rim. The view up there is supposed to be spectacular." She turned to face the front just as we entered a narrow tunnel, which seemed very dark in contrast to the bright sunlight. "Oh, wow, here we are."

Beyond the tunnel lay the bottom of the caldera, an expanse of scrubby vegetation surrounded on all sides by the inside walls of Diamond Head. "Actually," Leo said, "this looks more like a giant pie pan pressed into the top of a burnt mountain." Despite the dramatic idea of being inside a volcano, this area was uninspiring, scattered with low buildings surrounding an asphalt parking lot. We parked the car and slathered on sunscreen as Frank reminded us not to miss our ears and chided us for not wearing hats with brims as he did. We locked our purses in the trunk, and Leo toted the two-liter bottle of water we'd agreed to share. Passing up the entrepreneurs selling bottled water from their coolers, we soon came to the trailhead. Just beyond it were more entrepreneurs, these renting flashlights. "You need them in the tunnels. Only two dollars."

"Tunnels?" I asked, eyeing the people coming back down the trail. Some of them did carry flashlights.

"Yes, there are tunnels, and steps."

"I did read that they built tunnels during the war, for lookout posts," Bonnie told us. Reasoning that one beam could light the way for all of us, we rented one flashlight and set out on our trek. A concrete sidewalk soon gave way to a rock pathway that switched back and forth toward the top. The entire ascent was only three-quarters of a mile, but it grew more and more steep.

The intense sun, Leo's bad knee and Bonnie's narration kept us at a leisurely pace. Bonnie explained that all the Hawaiian islands were formed by underwater volcanoes spurting out puffs of land. This island, Oahu, was among the oldest, but the farther east and south you went, the younger the islands were. Leo asked if the volcanoes on the younger islands were higher and firmer, but Bonnie ignored him. "The youngest one is the big island, Hawaii, which is still being formed. That's where there's a national park where you can witness active volcanoes."

"Good lord, Bonnie, are we going to have to pause for a pledge break after you tell us all this?" I laughed. "I had no idea you were this much of a volcano nut."

"I wasn't until I started reading up on Hawaii before the trip. But it's just so fascinating! This volcano, for example, is called a tuff cone. They think there was just one violent explosion about 150,000 years ago that created all this..."

I tuned out the reportage when other hikers needed to pass by us. We stepped aside for a Boy Scout troop and several impressive joggers, who seemed to have made Diamond Head part of their fitness routine. As the trek got steeper and we slowed down, more people passed us — a German-speaking family with a baby in a backpack, an older African-American couple. This was slightly humiliating for the laggard Leo, but I noticed at least one other hiker who seemed to slow down as much as we did, a wiry Asian man with a fanny pack. "Look at that Leo," I had said reassuringly during a water break. "He looks ten years younger but he's as slow as we are."

When the trail took us into the first dark tunnel, we all sighed with relief to be out of the hot sun. Frank shone the flashlight well ahead, so that we all found our way easily, in spite of feeling blinded by the plunge into darkness after the bright sunlight. Our joy turned to dismay when the tunnel ended and we turned into the sunlight to find ourselves confronted with an astonishingly steep set of concrete steps. A child in the party ahead of us had halted and was throwing a tantrum — she did *not* want to climb those stairs. People coming down the steps tried to encourage her, "You're almost there!" but she was not buying it.

"How many steps are there?" Leo wondered out loud.

"Ninety-nine, I counted," shouted a descending boy who seemed to be racing beyond the reach of a mother who couldn't keep up.

The little girl was persuaded to continue after her mother pulled out a cell phone, made a call and announced, "Daddy wants to speak with you." We watched the girl pull herself together and start up the stairs and then we drank more water and scanned those 99 steps. Frank asked, "Anybody else here want to have a good cry?" but none of us wanted to quit.

There was concern for Leo's knee, but Leo, a self-proclaimed "hydroholic," insisted that as long as he had water he was not worried about his knee. The rest of us shrugged at this typical Leo non-sequitur, and started up the 99 steps. At the top, another tunnel began, and Frank led us panting through it, and then up an even darker spiral staircase to a bunker. This had been an observation post during the Second World War, and we had to stoop low to emerge back into the light. In a few more steps, we were met with a panoramic view of Waikiki beach to the west, the island of Molokai to the south, and Mount Tantalus behind us. Best of all, it was wonderfully windy. All four of us were drenched with sweat.

My memory of what happened after we reached the summit is cloudy now. It seemed we stayed up there a while, and I remember nodding happily to the other survivors of the trek — the little girl, the Asian man — but then the memories fast forward, to the trip back down the dark spiral staircase, going slowly because of Leo's knee, and Frank waiting for us with the flashlight when we came through the tunnel, and then, at the top of the 99 steps, squinting, putting my sunglasses back on, starting down, looking for Bonnie, and then seeing her yellow T-shirt at the bottom of the steps. She was lying down and at first I started to laugh, thinking she had beaten us down the steps and was acting like she'd collapsed with the effort. But then I saw that the Asian man was rising from a crouch next to Bonnie, saw that he was cupping his hands to his mouth and calling up to us, "She has fallen! I get help!" He hurried into the next tunnel as I yelled, "Oh God, Frank!"

Frank and I almost fell over each other rushing to the bottom of the steps, but time and space seemed to telescope and it took forever to reach Bonnie. She lay crumpled and still on the hard concrete, her head bent at an impossible angle. "Oh God, her neck is broken!" Frank cried, dropping to his knees and pressing his fingertips to the artery below her jaw. "No pulse!"

Then I was grasping Leo, controlling an urge to scream but unable to resist sobbing as Frank tried to administer CPR to Bonnie's broken body. The very attempt told me the situation was hopeless. Even I knew that a person with a broken neck couldn't be rolled over and compressed. The effort was clearly futile, but Frank frantically kept at it, making Bonnie's heart beat and making air pass in and out of her lungs for the next twenty minutes, even as the mother with the cell phone came up to us and called for help, even as the park rangers arrived with oxygen and first aid kits.

Chapter 2

My training in psychology tells me that flashbacks to moments of panic and crisis are a common reaction to trauma. They manifest in people who bear witness to unbearable things — survivors of violent crime, natural disasters, wartime atrocities, highway pile-ups. If those flashbacks become pervasive, the condition is called "PTSD," posttraumatic stress disorder, but like so many clinical labels, the name seems to rob it of significance. Wide awake now and filled with the sorrow of the truth, I rolled onto my back. Warm tears rolled into my hair. There's the naming of things like stress disorders and grief processes, and then there's the living of them.

Unfortunately, psychological sophistication doesn't immunize anyone against suffering, as much as I might wish it with every reminder that brought Bonnie's death back to consciousness. I knew that the day would come when the sense of shock and grief would abate, but only in its own good time.

I turned toward Leo, who was snoring softly in the dim light. It had been my policy not to have him stay with me for more than a weekend, but ever since Diamond Head, I needed his company. He responded to my touch, and automatically offered an arm. I rested my head on it and nestled against his side. The snoring stopped.

"Sad again?" he said in a deep, drowsy voice.

"Yep," I said, holding my breath against a sob.

"Anything I can do?"

"Nope." I exhaled. He gave me a sympathetic squeeze. "Actually," I sniffled, "you're doing it."

He kissed my head and was snoring again within the minute, and my breathing gradually slowed to normal. This was the way every day started — waking, remembering, weeping, and then getting on

with it. It's the way it is with grief. I let myself doze until the alarm
went off.

It was hours later when I read over what I'd written that morning
and dated it. Where was it that I read about dreams of the dead, about
the types of messages they seem to be sending to their survivors? Was
it in the IASD magazine? A book review? Or was it an article in the
journal, *Dreaming*? I set out to find it in my office.

Since I'd lost my fulltime job at the college, my home office was
jammed with the books, journals and files that used to be
accommodated in my campus office. Two years ago, I had been on the
tenure track at Grenville, a small college tucked into one of the oldest,
prettiest neighborhoods of Pittsburgh. What Grenville lacked in size
or competitiveness, it made up for in tradition and ambiance.
Millionaires from the industrial revolution had left the college a
number of gracious mansions along their shared private road, and
with them came the landscaping of the well-to-do — large shade trees
that flamed with color in the fall, grassy hillsides that turned white
and invited sledding in the winter, ornamental shrubs that bloomed
pink in the spring. I had been gaining eminence as a researcher who
had every reason to expect to win the tenured spot of a retiring
colleague, until I was implicated in a crime, and a scandal.

Despite my success in exonerating myself, the incident had stirred
up too much unfavorable publicity for me to be offered tenure, or
even a respectable extended contract, and when the school year
ended, I moved out of my Grenville office for good. In the fall, I
would be teaching only as an adjunct, a fancy name for a part-timer,
at three different colleges. One of them could lead to a full time
position, but there were no guarantees. Meanwhile, pension benefits
were a thing of the past, my medical insurance would run out soon,
and part-time teaching would bring in a third of what I had been paid
to teach the same courses as a fulltime professor. I had other irons in
the fire and I was very glad to have the support of Leo and my
friends, but this summer my situation was as tenuous as it's ever
been.

And now my only permanent workplace was my home office,
bulging with computer equipment, books and boxes of files. Every
shelf and surface was covered. I headed for the stack where I kept the
publications of the dream association and scanned the journals. I
found "Dreams and the Rehabilitation of Coma Victims," "The Dream

as Narrative in Medieval Epics" and my own "Dream Incubation: A Universal Tendency," and a wealth of other articles that reflect what I love about IASD — it's a forum for every imaginable facet of dream study, from the biochemical to the artistic to the therapeutic to the "Twilight Zone," adventures in lucid dreaming, shamanic practices and the like. But there was nothing here about dreams of the dead. Then I remembered.

It was in Patricia Garfield's book, *The Dream Messenger: How Dreams of the Departed Bring Healing Gifts.* I'd read it when it first came out, then lent it to a student who returned it just as I was moving out. "So," I thought, "it must be in one of those boxes that I haven't unpacked yet."

There were several of them stacked against the far wall, and when I lifted the lid on the top one, I recognized the contents of the bulletin board from my college office. On the top was a card that Bonnie had sent me back when things were looking bleak. On the front was that famous picture of a kitten hanging on for dear life to a horizontal pole, with the caption, "Hang in there!" Inside, Bonnie had written:

"Don't ever let this incident rob you of your dedication to dreams, your sense of dignity, or even a night's sleep. Come see us at the clinic whenever it's convenient. We can use you here. Love, Bonnie"

It was one of the kindest things anyone did for me during that turbulent time. I was deeply grateful to have such a friend and tacked the note above my desk, where it served as a touchstone during my transition. Indeed, I was to start consulting at the sleep disorder clinic with Bonnie and Frank after we all returned from Hawaii. Now I would wait for some sign from Frank that he felt up to making decisions about my working there. He certainly was not there yet.

Before my mental default screen could take me back to Diamond Head again, I reminded myself of my task and was pleased to find my quarry in the next box I opened. The book's cover features Hermes, the Greek god who served as messenger and guide, in his winged helmet. When he escorted the dead to the afterworld, Hermes was known as the psychopompos, the soul conductor. Garfield had gathered a thousand dream accounts of people who felt they had communicated with someone who had died. I scanned the table of contents. The respondents' dreams were categorized by the messages conveyed. There were chapters called "Please Forgive Me," "Goodbye" and "I'll Always Love You." But none of the headings seemed to match my dream of Bonnie, which I would have characterized as, "Help Me Out." I flipped to the index, hoping for some kind of match, or at least a synchronicity.

Dreams have taught me to pay attention to meaningful coincidences, or synchronicities, as C.G. Jung labeled them. One of the earliest happened when, as a college student, I had a dream of about childhood friend and was then astonished to receive a letter from her the next day. At the time this was "only" a coincidence by my rationalistic view, but the more I recorded my dreams, the more I found such links of time and meaning without a cause and effect relationship.

So I have learned to appreciate synchronicity in dreams, and in waking life. It is like a checkmark that says, "Here, pay attention." And the synchronicity that occurred while I scanned the index of *The Dream Messenger* was the entry: "Simpson, O.J." I leafed to the page, searching for some link to my dream. Garfield was referring to testimony at the notorious trial, in which O.J. had confided to a friend that he had dreamed about killing his ex-wife. I checked the name of this chapter. It was, "Avenge My Murder."

Chapter 3

"Murder?" I said out loud. I closed the book and tossed it back into the box. "That's ridiculous!" I got up from my chair and stared at the box, then gave it a little kick. I paced into the kitchen, where I extracted a bottle of water from the refrigerator and washed the idea down my throat.

I knew from long experience that most of my dreams are like poems, full of metaphoric rather than literal value, and that I would be better off looking at this one from a symbolic perspective. And then I realized that the past was coloring my present, that another death was encroaching on the current one.

A few years earlier, one of my dreams got me into a lot of trouble after a colleague, Rob Bellarius, was found murdered. When I realized that a dream I'd had on the night of his death may have had pertinent content, I shared it with authorities. Unfortunately, instead of following up on my insights, the police then regarded me as a prime suspect in his murder. How else, they reasoned, could I know what I knew?

It didn't matter to the police that I had published papers and contributed to academic books on the subject of dreaming, and served on the board of the International Association for the Study of Dreams. Indeed, if I hadn't done the work I had, I might never have recognized the connections between my dream and Rob's death. But the police didn't see it that way.

Thus, I found myself in a waking nightmare that might have been comical if it hadn't been so damaging. As a suspect in a murder case, my professional and personal history came under scrutiny. The police learned that Rob and I had been lovers some years before, and that my husband and I had had broken up around the same time. And when they also discovered that subsequently, Rob had become my rival for tenure at Grenville, they felt they had a motive. To them, I fit the profile of "jealous woman turns to murder" and they proceeded accordingly.

I stepped back into my office, reopened the box and dug until I found what I knew was in there. It was a note that Rob had written to me before I left Leo. I'd kept it in the bottom of my desk until I'd had to move out, and when it came time to discard the detritus of past years, I couldn't bear to read it, but I couldn't bear to part with it either. I opened the card impulsively and looked at the picture on the front, a flurry of birds in flight. Inside, the message was still short, still sweet. "There's a whole world out there, right now, that we can be enjoying together. Come with me."

I let out a sigh. Rob had cost me so much that I never wanted to forget that special time, when it all seemed worthwhile. I'd been bonkers with excitement then, especially after suffering through an eroding marriage for such a long time. Leo's and my first years together were happy, but then he got promoted and became more distracted just as the demands of new parenthood, and our daughter's illness, took their toll. After her death, the situation went from bad to worse. Leo threw himself further into his work and became impatient and critical. For relaxation he drank, and with TV remote in hand, slipped into his own world, night after night — unless I protested, at which times he would lash out at me. For a long time, I chalked up his behavior to stress and grief, and I tried to puff up the marriage. But gradually, I stopped trying to interest him in going on a vacation, or celebrating our anniversary, or having sex. And I knew that he no longer loved me.

I wanted to try therapy, but Leo said that he didn't need to go because I was the one with the problem. So I went alone, and did gain insight into my own history and some of Leo's too. Because drinking seemed to be a significant factor in our problems, the therapist directed me to Al-Anon, but none of my experiences were as harrowing or desperate as those of the others in the group. Leo never beat me up, got arrested or disappeared for days at a time. He just drank a six pack of beer every night, watched TV and shut me out of his life. I wished someone could just tell me how to fix what was wrong, or even declare absolutely that the situation was hopeless, but no one could.

Into this chaos stepped Rob and the promise of a new life. He wasn't the sort of guy I would have cast as a lover. In fact, when I first got to know him, when he was a new grad student and I was a doctoral candidate at the university, I'd assumed he was gay. Later, after we had tumbled into a love affair, I'd told him this, and we had laughed uproariously between the sheets. "I don't remember exactly why it was I thought you were gay. I think it was because I heard you lived with a guy..."

"But lots of students live with other guys!"

"Who everybody knew was 'light in the loafers.'"

"Well, he <u>was</u> gay, but he was also my cousin."

"And, you had an earring on — which side was it? The one that used to mean somebody was gay," my voice went up in an embarrassed question, "at least, it used to, didn't it? When I was a kid?"

"Way back then? I wouldn't know about that — it was before my time." The age question was a joke between us too. I was eight years older than Rob, something I pointed out to him the first time he kissed me. I had been astonished and pleased all at once, and had stepped back. I gasped, "But I'm old enough to be your..." well, not his mother, but someone a lot older, like... "your babysitter!" This made both of us laugh, but then Rob had replied, "That may be, but I don't find that a compelling argument. I had a crush on my babysitter." And then he had paused, and said seriously, "Please." And that, for some reason, was so touching to me, so deeply affecting, that my defenses collapsed then and there. Being wanted was so novel and so longed for that I thought my heart might burst out of my chest and hop across the floor.

That wasn't the beginning of our sleeping together, but it was the beginning of my falling in love with him. I have been over this a million times in my mind, that I hadn't been so much in love with the man as in love with his admiration for me. I had been living without appreciation for so long that I was in no condition to give sober consideration to the consequences of falling in love. That's why they call it "falling." People stumble, plunge and disappear down the trap door of love.

And so it was for me, although the first heady weeks and months seemed magical, as if an invisible guide were directing me into a new land of love and pleasure and promise. When I announced to Leo that

I wanted a divorce, his initial reaction was silence. Was he shocked? Sorry? Did he even care? Finally, he asked, very quietly, "Are you going to tell me why?"

I had imagined saying, "Because I'm the only one who cares about this marriage," or "Because you love watching television more than you love me," or "Because I can't live without warmth and affection," but what I ended up saying was, "Because I think I'm in love." Then I burst into tears. I was ashamed and embarrassed to make such a declaration to someone who wouldn't, couldn't, get it, whom I hadn't been able to move to passion for years and was now officially giving up on. The discovery that passion still existed, that I could still experience it, seemed a great gift to me, but of course this was not something Leo would understand or appreciate. I realized I shouldn't have told him at all, but then he asked, "Who?"

And when I told him it was Rob Bellarius, he barked with genuine surprise and said, "I thought he was gay."

The affair ended abruptly, one night when we were having dinner in a tavern near the university. The place was filling up, or rather the bar was, when an acquaintance of Rob's stopped by the table. Rob introduced me to Hal, an attractive, athletic man who looked like he'd had a few. He lingered at the table, talking too loud about old times and old friends whose names I didn't recognize. Rob seemed uncomfortable but unable to discourage the guy. Hoping to drop a hint, I excused myself to go to the ladies room. When I returned, the men's conversation had grown heated, and it took me a long stunned minute to take in what was being said. "You're such a hypocrite, Rob. And you are such a slut." This had been said deliberately, and for my benefit. "See ya," Hal said to me, with a mock wave, and turned back into the crowd.

It didn't take long for the situation to disintegrate. Rob, it turned out, did sleep with men "sometimes." But that didn't make him gay, not as far as he was concerned. I felt that I had slipped down a rabbit hole. "Rob, if you are a man who sleeps with other men, then you're gay."

"But gay men don't sleep with women, Willa. I am not gay. I love women! I love you, Willa."

Although the word "bisexual" came to me then, I couldn't get my mind around the idea, not for days. Rob argued intently for tolerance — he'd been afraid of my reaction, had not wanted to be secretive about his past but feared losing me, and had been with only me since our affair began. That's what he said, anyway, and I wanted to be persuaded, to recoup our happiness. But I couldn't go back to the way things had been. I felt that I didn't really know him, and I certainly didn't trust him. The little cloud on which we'd climbed together and which had borne me away from my marriage disappeared, and I fell to earth.

I had saved this note from Rob because he'd written it back at the beginning. It was an invitation I'd accepted with joy, and I never want to forget how it felt to be so alive, and so in love. I still don't. I placed the card back in the box and replaced the lid. I wished the rest of the story could have been as safely, and secretly, tucked away.

Years later, when Rob's body was discovered in his apartment with his skull shattered, I was not only shocked, but certain that a nightmare I'd just had was significant. In it, Rob and I were being chased down a dark street by a street gang that threw rocks at us. It never entered my mind, when I called homicide and offered my input, that I could come under suspicion.

I was fortunate in my friends, however, especially Victoria Golombiewski, my friend since grade school. Vicki grew up to be a lawyer, and was quick to recognize the peril in which I had inadvertently placed myself. "Why didn't you call me about this first?" she had groaned after I mentioned going to the police with my dream. "Why?" I had asked. Within twenty-four hours, Vicki faxed me clippings about a trial that had taken place a decade earlier. In a Midwestern city, a divinity student had been charged and convicted of murder. He became a suspect when he reported to authorities a dream he'd had on the night a young woman in his neighborhood had been brutally murdered. It had been a very disturbing and detailed dream, and the young man had come forward in the hope that it might provide some clue to help the authorities capture the killer. Unfortunately, the police turned their suspicions on him. Never mind that his wife could testify to his presence in their bed that night, or that there was no physical evidence to tie him to the crime. This young father had already served seven years in prison, and continued to protest his innocence.

It was thanks to Vicki that I was able to dodge the legal bullets when they started to fly. And it was because of Leo that I was able to hold myself together. When he learned how much trouble I was in, he offered his support. Consequently, and in no small part due to the collapse of his second marriage, Leo had become not only an ally, but a kind and attentive friend. It was through our combined efforts that I had escaped indictment, but the ordeal had taken its toll.

The case caught the attention of the press. Local news reports were picked up by wire services, and these were followed by calls from curious producers on tabloid television shows. Apparently, the combination of sex, dreams and murder were just the sort of thing viewers would love. After hiding for days, I finally took Vicki's advice and seized the opportunity to defend myself. A feature on "The Dream Lady" aired on *Personal Files* in which I defended both my innocence and the study of dreams. Within a week, however, I learned that I would not be offered tenure at Grenville, a college too small to afford scandal. Within a month, an ex-con was charged with Rob's murder. The motive, police concluded, was "homosexual rage," and the murder weapon was a rock, a geode that I had given to Rob years ago. My dream had been more accurate than even I might have guessed.

I shook my head and clutched my water bottle. I was not going to have anything to do with any suspicion, notion or whiff of murder, ever again. And, I had been at the scene when Bonnie died. Her death had been ruled an accident and no one had any reason to question that. Even to raise a doubt would only make trouble, for Bonnie's family and for myself.

The fact is, I reasoned, that everyone has dreams of people who have died, and that doesn't mean that a message is being conveyed from beyond the grave. And even if I *was* hearing from Bonnie somehow, that didn't mean she had been murdered.

But I did feel that I should find a way to honor the dream. Whenever a strong dream makes an impression on me, I make it a practice to act on it somehow. Settling back down behind my desk, I decided to act on this one by calling Frank and seeing how he was doing. Uncertain where to reach him, I first tried his home, but got a voicemail message. On an impulse, I dialed him at work.

"Three Rivers Sleep Disorder Clinic, how may I help you?" I recognized the voice of Janet Harper, a former student who had become the clinic's office manager.

"Hello, Janet, this is Willa Nilsson. I was calling to find out if Frank has started back to work yet."

"Oh yes, he's been coming in since, well, almost as soon as you all got back." Poor man, I thought, burying himself in work to avoid having to be at home, where the sadness must seem limitless.

"I'll see if he's free. Can you hold?" Janet clicked back after a two minute wait. "I'm sorry," she said, sounding a little breathless. "He's with a patient right now, but I can have him get back to you later on this afternoon."

"Oh, just tell him I called, and that I'm thinking about him. Tell him Leo and I would like to have him come for dinner sometime soon, and to call when he has a minute."

"Certainly, I will," she said, and then hung up abruptly, just as I thought I heard Frank's distinctive laughter in the background.

Chapter 4

I replaced the phone in its cradle and paused. Was I hearing things? And if I wasn't, what just happened? I sat at my desk and stared at the keyboard, as if the letters on it might spell out an answer. Perhaps Frank *had* been available but was unwilling to take my call. Sometimes that happens when people are grieving — contact with others who are in the same pain can feel like too much pain altogether. So maybe this was an evasion of some kind. But even if that were the case, why in the world would he, could he, be laughing?

My thoughts were interrupted by the sound of Leo's arrival. I could share this with him and see what he thought — that would be a good reality check. Leopold Miller is from a long line of Pennsylvania Germans, or Pennsylvania *deutsch*, and thus is analytical, industrious and sometimes, a hard ass. The latter quality might have been worse, were it not for his hearty "black Irish" mother.

Before I could rise from my desk to greet him, Leo appeared in the doorway of the office. He had inherited his mother's dark brown eyes, which complemented the sturdy frame and thick head of hair he got from his father. He's well built, by which I mean he's symmetrical. The right side of his face is just like the left, and the proportions of his body — head to torso to legs — are just right. He lacks buns and has been growing thick in the middle, but standing there in his shirtsleeves, he looked good, except for a worried expression on his face. He had brought in the day's mail and was brandishing something. "I think I'm being stalked," he announced.

Stalked? My mind flew off in a whole new direction, trying to piece together how a self-professed computer nerd could find himself stalked. Especially a computer nerd who claimed to want nothing more than to remarry his first wife. Who could be stalking him? His daffy second wife? Some other woman? A co-worker? "Are you kidding?"

"I tried to break it off, but they won't leave me alone."

"Leo, *what* are you talking about?"

"Potato chips. I've been clean for six weeks, and these were in the mailbox. It's supposedly a 'free sample,' but I don't think so. They're after me and they know where to find me."

I burst out laughing. Leo had been watching his weight by foregoing many of his favorite foods, and none were as sorely missed as potato chips, or "Vitamin P," as he likes to call them. But more importantly, he was trying to make me laugh, and I appreciated it. Leo could be the most difficult and exasperating human being on earth, but when he was good, he was very very good. I went to the doorway, gave him a hug and examined the small cylinder of new, improved junk food. "Yes, this looks suspicious all right. Maybe I should just take custody of these."

"Yes, please. Just don't eat them anywhere that I can see them or smell them. Or hear them."

The phone rang on my desk. As I moved to answer it, I addressed Leo over my shoulder. "Remind me that I want to talk to you about something at dinner. Are you cooking?" I picked up the phone and asked the caller to hold while Leo confirmed that he would, and ascertained the whereabouts of the vegetables he was to grill, and the amount of time they should marinate.

The call was from Charlotte Sweeney, a former student. While she was at Grenville, Charlotte showed great promise in writing, but felt very uneasy about something which she came to share with me, her psychology professor. Charlotte was getting whole stories — characters, plot points, and outcomes — from her dreams. She had only to take notes in the morning and let her imagination do the rest of the work. She feared that this was, in the least, underhanded, and at worst, evidence of instability. I was able to reassure her that she was gifted rather than crazy, and Charlotte was now doing well in a graduate writing program, but today she was calling about a friend.

"Karen's in my narrative writing class. She's older than I am, lives in the suburbs with a husband and a kid. She's kind of quiet, but she has this wry sense of humor that I really enjoy. We've been going for coffee after class, but today she brushed me off. Then I ran into her in the ladies room and saw that she was putting make-up on what I realized was a bruise on her face. I didn't mean to intrude, but of course I asked what happened to her and she said, 'I ran into a door,' and she then said, 'Of course, I was pushed.'" Charlotte took a breath and continued. "She's hinted that her husband is a drinker, and apparently they got into an argument the other night and he shoved her around. I feel really bad about it and I want to help her. Haven't you done work with a women's shelter?"

In fact, I had started a dream sharing group at a local women's shelter three years earlier, and knew it was a good organization. I began to look up the shelter's hotline number, but Charlotte interrupted. "No, I don't think Karen would call a shelter, or a hotline. She's a very private person, and she seems to have a lot of money. I think her husband is loaded — I mean in the financial sense. What I thought you might know is the name of a therapist that would be good for someone in her shoes."

Here it was, again; another stinging reminder that Bonnie was gone. In the past, I would simply have called her. Bonnie was a well known clinician who seemed to be acquainted with every psychotherapist in the city, and she would have given me the name of someone skilled with abused women. Never again, I winced, but this time I caught myself before plummeting into sadness and loss.

"Charlotte, I don't have a name right off the top of my head, but give me a day or two and I'll see what I can do," I told her. "Is there anything more you can tell me? Do you think this has happened before?"

"I'm not sure. We usually just talk about class, so I don't know that much about her personal life. I know she's got a daughter, and that she drives a BMW, so I'm sure she can afford therapy. But she's — I don't know, she seemed sarcastic, but then embarrassed. I had the impression that she may never have discussed this with anyone before, although it did seem like this might be an ongoing thing. In fact, I don't know if she'll get help even if I suggest it. I just think I ought to try if I can."

"Well, your heart is in the right place. These situations can be very sticky, and she might not be prepared to take your advice, but it's worth a try. Let me see what I can find out. I'll call you back as soon as I can."

I hung up and made notes to myself to call the director of the shelter and ask about therapists when, suddenly, my dream came flooding back to me: *talking on the phone with Bonnie*. Perhaps my dream was not a communication from beyond the grave, but a precognitive flash of the day's experiences, featuring a telephone call, a woman in peril, a request that I call for assistance, and the quintessential abusive husband, O.J. Simpson.

Chapter 5

Pittsburgh summers, like Pittsburgh winters, aren't all that dreadful. Both seasons typically feature several weeks of unpleasant extremes with your occasional tornado or blizzard, but the rest of the year is quite tolerable, and I find the seasonal changes exhilarating. But that afternoon, as rush hour peaked, the temperature and the humidity passed into the unpleasant zone. Leo and I ate dinner on the screened-in porch with a box fan rumbling on the floor and drank cold bottles of beer.

Leo no longer drinks much, and when he does imbibe, he limits himself. After his second marriage crashed, Leo had finally sought help for what he now understood to be depression. After starting on medication, he felt better than he had in years, and no longer needed or wanted to drink as he had.

The meal was excellent. Leo had made a marinade of white balsamic vinegar and olive oil and added slices of eggplant, portabella mushrooms, zucchini, onion and a quartered red pepper. After grilling them in the back yard, he arranged them over a bed of couscous.

"This is a perfect summer meal, Leo." I smiled over my fork. I was thinking how pleasant life could be with him, in contrast to how difficult it had been when we were married. Until Hawaii, I believed he stayed on his best behavior when he was with me to prove that he hadn't been such a bad guy after all, but recently I'd been wondering if he had really turned a corner. All I said, though, was, "Thank you for cooking."

"You asked me to remind you to tell me something."

"Oh, yeah — I did." I sighed. "This bothered me, but you might think I'm crazy," I recounted my phone call to Frank, and his incongruous laughter.

"Well, first of all, are you sure it was Frank?"

"You know that kind of Cajun cackle of his?" Frank had grown up in Louisiana, but made it a point to lose his accent when he went north to medical school. Casual acquaintances never guessed he was from the south, unless they happened to hear him when he got excited.

"Yeah, I do," said Leo.

"That's what I heard."

Leo thought for a moment, chin in hand. Then he offered brightly, "Maybe he's fooling around with Janet."

"Leo! Be serious!"

"It's possible. Remember Dan Johnson?" This was an old college buddy of Leo's whose wife died after a long bout with cancer. His friends were shocked when he got married six months later, to a woman he'd met in a caregiver support group.

"And you think Frank and Janet could be playing slap and tickle while she's taking phone calls? That's ridiculous!"

"Well, probably, but it does happen. Did you have another explanation?"

"Actually..." I felt myself sliding away from the idea that had been germinating in the back of my mind. "Never mind."

"No, tell me."

"It's nothing, really. Except maybe paranoia. It's just that I had this dream last night, that Bonnie was trying to get away from O.J. Simpson. And I was thinking about the idea of an abusive husband, and I was wondering — do you think Bonnie was dead when we got to her?"

Leo paused, and then offered, "Well, I know that you don't perform CPR on someone unless there is no pulse and no breathing. That usually constitutes dead."

"Because I thought it was surprising that Frank turned her over. It seemed so rough. I could see that her neck was broken and knew that she shouldn't have been moved."

"You can't second-guess the guy. I think Frank was doing the only thing he could do under the circumstances, and those were horrible circumstances." Leo's eyebrows met in a frown, and he paused before saying, "I think it's wise not to dwell on speculations. It's only caused you trouble in the past."

I caught his meaning and winced. "Willa the Troublemaker" — that had been my father's characterization for as long as I could remember. It wasn't really true, although I was more likely to challenge convention than my sisters. So, when I broke the grandfather clock as a toddler because I wanted to see if I could ride the pendulum; and when as an eighth grader, my desk was moved into the headmistress's office for a week, as an example to other girls who might try studying outdoors via the fire escape; and when in college, I got arrested after leading an unauthorized demonstration for women's safety following a series of campus assaults, my father only shook his head in aggrieved reaction. "You never learn," he would inevitably say, infuriating me and, without my quite realizing it, driving me to learn all the way to a doctoral degree. Eventually the "troublemaker" label faded to a family in-joke, but after my brush with notoriety, I felt the sting of it again. I would avoid a reprise at all costs.

"Tell you what — I promise not to speculate any more. I've learned my lesson." Eager to change the subject, I continued, "And, there was a coincidence later today that seemed to plug into my dream." I told him about the phone call concerning the abused wife as we finished our second beers. Leo was a skeptic when it came to things like precognition, telepathy and the like, but he respected my impressions, and my dreams. He knew better than to write them off.

"So, your dream and this phone call were something of a synchronicity?"

"Yes, and then there was another, a mention of O.J. Simpson in a book that discusses dreams about the dead."

We were interrupted when the doorbell rang and my sister, Trudy, yoo-hooed through the screen door. "I'm walking, wanna join me?" Trudy, a school counselor, was off for the summer and had time for the constitutionals she likes to take, often to the park near my house.

I went to the door to let her in, saying, "How can you stand to walk in this heat?"

Trudy, who had been the star athlete of the family when we were growing up, was fighting the good fight against middle-age spread. She truly was big-boned rather than overweight, but liked to remind us all that Marilyn Monroe wore a size fourteen. With broad shoulders and strong legs, Trudy wore her fine blonde hair pulled back in a don't-waste-my-time-with-fashion ponytail, but she also favored purple, which she believed to be a spiritual color, and elaborate, dangling earrings. It was hard to miss Trudy when she entered a room.

"There's a nice breeze now that the sun's going down. C'mon out and see."

I stepped onto the front step and discovered that it was cooler outside than it was inside. I slipped on my running shoes. Leo declined to join us and we set off toward the park, Trudy starting her customary quick step as I pleaded lethargy and seniority. We slowed to an easy amble.

"I'm glad Leo didn't come," Trudy said when we cleared the house, "because I have to ask you something personal. About sex."

"About sex? We already had that little talk about what happens when the daddy and the mommy want to make a baby, remember?"

Trudy grinned nervously, her blue eyes making a sidelong scan. "I'm talking sex toys. Ever tried them?"

"No, have you?!"

"No, but I want to look into them. I have to do something to liven up our sex life. Ted seems positively bored with me, or sex, or both. And you can imagine what a turn-on that is for me. So we're kinda slowly going down the tubes."

"Well, are you sure this is really a sexual problem? I mean, could it be something else, like problems at work? Could he be depressed?"

"I really don't think so. I think it's being married for a long time, and advancing middle age. You read about this sort of thing in magazines, but you don't ever expect it to happen to you. And frankly, things really have become rather routine. Wearing lacy new underwear used to work, but that ain't doin' the trick any more. So I need to branch out. And I want you to come with me."

"Come with you *where*?" I demanded. "The bondage department at Walmart?"

"There's this shop, the Garden of Eden, that has all kinds of stuff."

"Oh, right! And guys with trench coats and hard-ons strolling the aisles! You've got to be kidding!"

"No, really — this is a women's store. In the suburbs. And they do sell lingerie, but they also have a back room with all kinds of, um, erotic merchandise. They call it the 'the giggle room.'" Trudy fixed her gaze on me and said, "Your eyes look brown — am I freaking you out?"

Unlike my sisters', my eyes are hazel, and change shades ranging from khaki to green to gray, depending on what I wear and sometimes, they claim, how I feel.

"A little!" I admitted. "Where in the world did you learn about this?"

"You know Loretta at work? She lives near the mall where the Garden of Eden is. Her husband got her a Valentine's Day present there, some sheer teddy thing, and it was way too small, so Loretta took it back, and that's how she found the giggle room. She picked up something — she didn't tell me just what — as a joke, I guess, but they ended up finding it pretty sexy. They've been having a great time, apparently." Trudy stopped and turned to me. Her tone was part pleading-little-sister, part worldly confidante. "Please go with me. I don't have the nerve to go alone, but I think I might be able to find something that will snap us out of this."

"Give me a minute here." I started walking again, and this time I was going fast. "Good grief, Gertrude!" I exclaimed, using her formal name, the one invoked only in extreme circumstances. It had been our mother's conceit to name her children after prominent local writers, as literature and local history are her great interests. I was named for Willa Cather, the novelist, because she had spent her early years in Pittsburgh. Our mother was a fifth generation Pittsburgher and a member of the local historical society, and knew an astonishing amount of minutiae about the great and near great who had lived and worked here.

As odd a name as Willa was, I felt relieved to have been spared the fate of Trudy, named after Gertrude Stein. Most people never knew that our oldest sister Marcia was named for Marcia Davenport or that the baby of the family, Mary, was named for Mary Roberts Rinehart. Their names were so common that they seldom had to explain our mother's predilection, or tell about the women who wrote *Valley of Decision* and *The Spiral Staircase*. But then there was Gladys. Although Gladys, Trudy and I often argued over who had the worst name, Glad was the bitterest. It wasn't because Gladys Schmidt was the least well-known of the Pittsburgh authors, but because Glad was often encouraged by our father to behave in a manner true to her name, which she resolutely refused to do.

Our three sisters live out of town now, but we are a close family. I wished some other sister were at hand to take on this assignment.

"How about Loretta?" I posed hopefully. "Couldn't you go with her on your lunch hour or something?"

"No way. It's you or nobody, sister." She threw her arm over my shoulders. "C'mon, it'll be fun. I'd do it for you!"

I was folding. "This ought to be one shopping trip to remember. When did you want to do this?"

"Tomorrow? I'll buy you lunch!"

"Lord, Trudy. Let me sleep on it and I'll give you a call."

Chapter 6

The next morning, I woke up laughing. I reached for my notebook and wrote down what I had been dreaming:

Frankenstein is carrying me in his arms, rescuing me from villagers with torches.

I wrote below:

This was so ludicrous that I understood it as soon as I woke. It's about my paranoia (the crazed villager) casting Frank Conrad as a monster. Moral of the story: I'm getting carried away with this business. Message from deep self: lighten up, Willa!

I was just settling in at my desk that morning to begin organizing the notes on the courses I would be teaching in the fall when Charlotte called.

"I know that this is short notice, but is it possible you'd be able to meet for a cup of coffee sometime this morning?"

Visions of a tall, iced latte danced in my head. I usually skip breakfast unless I can get to a coffee shop. "If it's not too far, I can. What's up?"

Charlotte explained that she'd made plans to meet with her friend Karen that morning at a coffee shop on Shady Avenue, the Latte Lenya. "I think it would be helpful for her to meet you. I tried to bring up the subject of therapy with her, but I couldn't figure out how to do it. But if we, like, ran into you, and I introduced you — she's interested in dreams by the way…"

"Oh, so this is an accidentally-on-purpose kind of a thing? Charlotte, what do you think I'm going to be able to do?"

"Well, nothing, except meet somebody who might benefit from making the acquaintance. I mean, she probably doesn't want to talk to a twenty-three-year-old about her problems, I can understand that. But you're older, and you've done some work with women who have experienced domestic violence — but she doesn't have to know that. We could do this all — like, socially."

I scratched the back of my head and thought. I like Charlotte a lot, but this struck me as a bit devious. On the other hand, I could hear the concern in her voice — Charlotte was a good soul who really was trying to do something helpful here. And, I could have a latte for breakfast.

"Okay, I really do go there a lot, I could go there today. What time?"

We had agreed to meet at eleven when Trudy called. "Well, sistah? Have you screwed up your courage?"

"Yuk, what a way to put it!" I laughed. "I'm going to be at the Latte Lenya coffee shop till 11:30 or so. If you meet me there, I'll go with you. But then you DO have to buy me lunch."

The Latte Lenya was really the first floor of an old house, as are most of the shops on Shady. This was a comfortable place to hang out, a mongrel-retro setting featuring a poster of Lotte Lenya in her villainess role in *From Russia with Love*, a lava lamp behind the counter and Tony Bennett on the sound system. It wasn't very crowded. The lunch rush hadn't started arriving yet, and the morning coffee addicts were already buzzing. I didn't see anyone I knew at the front tables, so I put in my order and then heard my name being called. I turned to see Charlotte and smiled, perhaps a bit too broadly, and said, "Hey hi!"

Charlotte, in jeans and with brown hair cropped short, looked every inch the distracted student as she shrugged off her backpack and quickly introduced her friend. "Willa, this is Karen Morgan. We just got out of a writing class we're taking together. Karen, this is Willa Nilsson. She was my psych professor at Grenville. I think I've told you about her."

"Oh yes, hello," said Karen coolly. Her eyes ran down me and then looked away with disinterest. I took in a woman who looked to be in her thirties, but was probably older. Her appearance didn't look extravagant, but I could tell it cost a lot of money — clothes that were casual but tailored, nails professionally manicured, and medium blonde hair with lighter highlights. I'm an expert on blonde. My sisters and I were all born blonde and then experienced the chagrin of having our hair darken as adolescence set in. Thus the question of whether and when to frost, dye, paint or highlight was an ongoing subject of earnest family discussion. My experienced eye noted that Karen's full mane was an expensive and time-consuming salon production.

"Are you busy? Can you join us?" Charlotte asked me innocently.

"Sure, why not?" I said loudly, raising my voice over the noise of the milk steamer. As we all settled at a table toward the back, I was provided the clinching evidence of Karen's financial circumstances. It appeared that not an ounce of fat rested on her slender frame, no mean feat in a woman over forty, and every muscle was defined, undoubtedly a product of hard labor in a gym, probably with a personal trainer.

I turned to look at the counter. "My coffee's up!" I rose from my seat. "Can I get you something?"

Karen scanned the menu on the chalkboard behind the counter. "I'll have an espresso lemon rind," she said. "If there's no lemon I'll have a Café Americana black."

Charlotte said, "I'll help you," and got to her feet. As we approached the counter, she said, "Maybe this was a bad idea."

"Does she always act entitled and bored?"

"Not really." Charlotte shot a look over her shoulder. "I think she's in a bad mood."

"Well, at least I don't think she's onto our little charade. Let's see if we can make the most of the opportunity."

When we returned to the table, Karen was speaking into the smallest and sleekest looking cell phone I'd ever seen. "I'll be there when I get there," she said, and snapped the phone shut.

"That's quite a phone!" I said.

"This? My husband gave it to me. It's some kind of a prototype," she sighed.

Charlotte tried then to get a conversation rolling. "Karen, Willa's the professor who helped me to get over my writer's — well not block — my writer's willies, I guess you'd say."

"You mean about your dreams?" said Karen. "I wish I could dream my writing assignments!"

"She's kidding," Charlotte confided. "She's amazingly productive. She just finished a story two weeks before it's due."

"What's it about?" I asked, hoping to warm her up.

"A medium," Karen replied without much enthusiasm, "who gets amnesia."

"A medium—like at Lily Dale?" I asked.

"Actually, part of it takes place at Lily Dale," said Karen.

"What's Lily Dale?" asked Charlotte.

"It's a spiritualist community about three hours away, near Chautauqua Lake in New York," I explained.

"Well, what is this, like a town full of mediums or something?" Charlotte was earnestly trying to keep up the conversation.

"Actually, it is," I told her. "But the spiritualists are like any Protestant sort of sect — they sing hymns and have sermons in their amphitheater, and visitors are welcome to attend. What's different about them is that they believe in communication with people after they die. It's an article of faith with them."

"I went there last summer because my daughter... well, never mind." Karen lost some color in her face and shrugged. "But that is where I got my idea for a story about a medium."

"In the summer," I told Charlotte, "you can pay a fee at the gate and attend events throughout the day. Most of them are what they call message services, where different mediums take turns addressing the visitors. They'll point to someone, and say, 'May spirit speak with you?'"

"And then what happens?" Charlotte was intrigued.

"Well, then the medium will deliver some kind of message. She'll say something like, 'I'm getting a vibration of a grandmother, on the father's side. She's holding a flower, does that mean anything to you?' People either nod or shake their heads. Unless you get called on, there's no way to judge how accurate the medium is. To me, the messages sounded like pretty general advice, like 'Stop and smell the roses,' or 'Don't be so hard on yourself.'"

"So it's fakey?"

"It's a sham. You can't talk to someone who is dead." Karen, whose color had returned, looked agitated.

I wiped latte foam from my upper lip. "That's what I thought too, until I got called on. Then I got a message so dead on — so to speak — that I changed my mind."

"Wow, what was it? Do you mind telling me?" asked Charlotte.

"Well, it was really a word that did it, an unusual word that my grandfather used with me and my sisters. He used to call us 'Spindleshanks.' When the medium spoke that word, I really sat up and took notice. It was a major synchronicity."

"What was the message?"

"It wasn't anything dramatic, really. Just that he sent his good wishes, and wanted me to know that I had a fine mind, and could trust my instincts. I wrote it down because I didn't want to forget it."

"So, it was a valuable message?"

"Well, not at first. But I've come back to it a number of times, and I have to say that it has made a difference in my life." I decided not to mention that it also had got me into trouble. Trusting my instincts had led me to think I'd dreamt a clue to Rob's death.

Charlotte said, "It would be confusing advice to me. What does having a fine mind have to do with instincts?"

"Well, that business about the fine mind was just what my grandfather would have liked us to think about ourselves. He was a very positive influence when we were growing up. But I agree, the part about the instincts does sound somewhat paradoxical."

"Most people are torn between their minds and their instincts," Karen remarked with authority. "I think that's true of everyone who's married, for example. Or maybe just all adults in general."

I saw the opening and tried to step into it. "You know what Joseph Campbell said? 'Marriage is not an ideal, it's an ordeal.'" I laughed and added confidentially, "I was married long enough to understand that."

"You're divorced?" Karen asked.

"Yes."

"Raising kids?"

"No."

"That makes a difference."

I nodded at her diamond studded wedding band. "How long have you been married?"

"Nineteen years last May," she replied.

"Leo and I were married for twelve years. He remarried, then divorced again. Lately, we've been spending a lot of time together. I'm still figuring out how being involved is different from being married. It's better though, I can tell you that much."

"Even financially?" Karen's question surprised me. It seemed blunt, even crass.

I chose my words carefully, wondering if we had unexpectedly arrived at the crux of Karen's predicament. "To tell you the truth, I was much unhappier when money was *not* a problem." I wavered for a moment, then decided to forge on. "But every unhappy wife has to decide for herself what her suffering is worth."

I looked at Charlotte, who was biting her bottom lip and regarding Karen, who ran a hand through the hair at her temple as she looked off somewhere in the middle distance. She'd done a good job on her bruise — I only noticed the slight discoloration when she turned her head. Her fingers found the pearl stud in her earlobe and turned it absently.

Charlotte took the silence as encouragement. "Willa, are you still doing dreamwork at the women's shelter?" As I started describing my visits to the shelter, I could see Karen backing away from the subject and from the conversation. "I teach them how to do peer group dreamwork, and once they learn that, they don't need me. But there's a constant turnover, and I do enjoy working with these women. They're being challenged to improve their circumstances and it's an enormous undertaking for them, when they're awake <u>and</u> when they're dreaming."

"I've got to get going," Karen announced, checking her Rolex and gathering up her purse. "It was nice to meet you Willa. Charlotte, I'll be in touch about that assignment." And with that she turned and left the coffee shop on a cloud of distant formality.

Charlotte looked down at her empty cup and muttered, "Well, I screwed that up."

I was touched then by Charlotte's youth, recalling what it was like to have the belief and determination to make things better, and how that used to seem simple. "Hey," I said gently, "you are being a good friend to her. You're concerned and you're doing your best to try and remedy what may be a bad situation. But you can't change people. If she does have a problem, she's probably been having it for a while. You don't know the whole story, and you don't know what all might be involved. I mean, does she drink, is she involved with someone else, is she telling you the truth?"

Charlotte frowned as she considered these questions. "I have no reason to doubt her," she thought aloud, "but of course I have no way of knowing exactly..."

"I don't mean to call your judgment into question," I explained. "I just mean, there's a lot we don't know, that we can't know."

"You've been so nice—can I buy you a biscotti?"

"I'd love that, thanks!" I said brightly. "Carbohydrates would definitely lift our spirits."

While Charlotte was at the counter, I heard an electronic ringing close by. I looked down at the seat that Karen had vacated. There was her fabulous phone, emanating its signal.

Uh-oh, I thought – the superphone has been left behind. But, maybe Karen had discovered it missing and was trying to reach us to see if we had it. I snapped it open, and pressed the likeliest looking button. "Hello? Karen?"

"Who is this?" asked a man's voice.

"I just found Karen's phone and thought I'd better answer. Who's this?"

"This is Cliff Morgan, Karen's husband. Did she leave the coffee shop?"

"Yes, but just a little while ago, not even ten minutes."

"Well, I'm nearby, I'll come and get it."

"Do you know where we are? The Latte Lenya on Shady."

"I know—I'm parking now."

"I'll meet you at the…"

But he had ended the call. By the time I'd walked to the door, he was already stepping in, a big, good looking man in shirtsleeves and sunglasses. Barrel-chested but trim, he'd undoubtedly been an athlete and still took care of himself. His forehead was making inroads toward his crown, but that didn't detract from the overall impression of virility. He peeled off his sunglasses and I held the phone up for him to see. "Yo!" I called.

He looked at me, spotted the phone and smiled. He had a ravishing smile— even white teeth and full lips framed by dimples. "Well, aren't you nice to meet me at the door! Are you Charlotte?"

"No, this is Charlotte…" I gestured for Charlotte, who was still waiting at the counter, to step over.

"Charlotte, this is Cliff Morgan. Karen left her phone behind and he was right here in the neighborhood!"

"Nice to meet you," said Charlotte. "Oops, here's our order."

"Oh, please, let me," said Cliff, and he didn't wait for our consent. He just stepped up to the counter and whipped out a fifty-dollar bill.

"Is this all you ladies want?" he said, gesturing to our biscotti. "Surely, you deserve a reward for returning this lost puppy." He handed the cashier the fifty and said, "Please get these ladies anything they want."

He turned to us. "Or, if you're not hungry now, we can make that a gift certificate."

"Really, this isn't necessary..." I said, and Charlotte was shaking her head, "Really..." she said.

"Oh, of course not, but I appreciate your help. Let me do this for you, won't you?"

He turned back to the counter, winked at the cashier and put a ten in the tip jar.

"Thank you ladies," he said as he retreated, holding up the phone in a gesture of farewell, and pushed his way out the door.

Charlotte and I looked at each other. "Would you like fifty dollars worth of pastries?" I asked her.

"Nooo," she said, looking perplexed.

"How do you want me to do this?" said the cashier. A line was forming, and Charlotte still held the cash she had been about to pay with.

"Good grief—just take the biscotti out of the fifty and give us the change," I said. When we got back to the table, Charlotte began to divide the money and I said, "No, you're a grad student. You keep it."

"But you found the phone," she protested. Then, looking down at the cash, she said, "These aren't ill-gotten gains, are they?"

"I don't know, what does he do for a living?"

"Karen told me he does 'industrial security.' I expected her to say he was a lawyer or a doctor, or somebody who pulls down big bucks. But it sounds like he has a business where he provides security guards. They live in Mount Clair though." This is the deluxe suburb of the city, with two acre zoning, three country clubs and road signs made to look like old English milestones.

"Well, owning a business can be very lucrative," I observed. "And he was determined to treat us, so why don't you take that cash, put it in a jar and start a coffee fund for starving grad students?"

"That's a good idea." Charlotte gave a little nod. "That was really nice of him, wasn't it?"

"Extravagant, and nice," I agreed.

"And," Charlotte's voice dropped to a confidential mumble, "he was so hot, wasn't he?" I had to agree with that too. I don't know what it is about good looks that makes me want to minimize any suspicions I might have about an individual, but I'm as susceptible as the next girl. And he wasn't just yummy looking — he seemed eager to please, if a little over the top, and a nice guy.

Just then Trudy came into the Latte Lenya, wearing a purple scarf and dark glasses. She waved from the door and made her way toward us. Resting my chin in my hand, I shook my head. Trudy, for all her bravado, must have decided to make this venture incognito.

"Charlotte, I'd like you to meet my sister. Ordinarily, you can see her face and head, am I right, *Gertrude*?"

"Call me Trudy," said Trudy. "I'm just trying out my new look. I call it, 'Gypsy Tea Room.' What do you think?"

"Are you a designer?" Charlotte asked innocently, and Trudy emitted her trademark laugh, a snorting guffaw.

"No, no child, just an old married woman trying to bring some excitement into her life."

"My sister is, how shall we say, *peculiar*," I explained over Trudy's head.

Charlotte warmed to the joking, and laughed along with us. Then she rose and hefted her backpack onto her shoulder. "I've got to run — I have another class this afternoon." "Thank you for coming today," she said to me. "I really appreciate it."

"It was good to see you," I said sincerely. "And who knows, maybe you've done something good in introducing Karen and me. You never know."

"See what your instincts tell you," Charlotte proposed cheerfully, then turned and headed to the door.

Chapter 7

The trip to the Garden of Eden took about twenty minutes. Driving to any suburb of Pittsburgh in any direction will almost certainly take you across a bridge. Pittsburgh has more bridges than any other city in America. It has three rivers and quite a few valleys to cross, and its bridges are like staples that hold it all together.

Beyond the bridges lie the suburban tracts where people built homes to get away from the smoke of steel making. Some of them are upscale enclaves where the executives of Pittsburgh's many corporations raised their families, with large lots and houses to go with them. Others are middle class and blue collar neighborhoods with ranch style homes built in the post war housing boom. The complex where we found the Garden of Eden was located in one of the latter.

This mall had originally been of the small, strip variety, a string of stores built in a row. But time and development had expanded this retail outpost into a large warren of parking lots, stores and restaurants that covered perhaps fifteen acres. Trudy and I drove circuitously until we found the Garden of Eden, with a parking spot right in front. I inspected the storefront through the windshield. The display window was filled with women's lingerie, which seemed comforting. Trudy must have picked up on my thoughts. "Hey, this may not be any worse than going into Victoria's Secret!" She poked me with an elbow. "And you were worried!"

"Forgive me, but you're the one wearing a disguise. And I must say that I don't believe I've ever seen anything with feathers at Victoria's Secret." I eyed the full length red robe made of something transparent.

"Br — ock — ock!" crowed Trudy. "You're chicken!"

My response was to tug Trudy's scarf off her head and sprint from the car declaring, "Last one in's a rotten egg."

"No fairs," Trudy complained as she hurried through turning off the car, getting out and catching up to me.

I stood holding the door open for Trudy, who gave up on retying her scarf and draped it around her shoulders. "Just for that, I'm not buying you <u>any</u> sex toys!" Trudy whispered hoarsely as a saleswoman approached us and said, "May I help you?"

Trudy placed a hand on my shoulder. "She wants to see your merchandise, Ma'am."

I shook my head. "We really just wanted to look around, thank you."

The saleswoman, wearing a half-smile that suggested she'd been through this sort of thing before, said, "Well, there's mostly clothing in the front of the store. You'll find our other merchandise in the back." I peered toward the back of the store. There were no men in trench coats visible, and the salesclerk appeared to be an ordinary woman with reading glasses on a string around her neck and just a little bit of cleavage showing under her blouse. "Let me know if there's anything I can help you with." Then she discreetly walked away.

It was easy to lose sight of her, because the store was packed with racks and racks of clothing: diaphanous and lacy robes and nightgowns; teddies; matching sets of bras, panties and garter belts; fishnet stockings, stockings with seams and stockings with lace at the top.

I came to a long feather boa and wrapped it around my neck. "If you got this, Trudy, then I could borrow it."

"Red looks better on you than me," Trudy said. "And I'm trying to think what might give Ted a charge here, not you. Help me out."

The further we progressed, the more suggestive the styles. Soon we came to bras with holes at their tips. I took one off the rack and held the hanger up for Trudy. "How about this? Very *Story of O*, don't you think?"

"I don't think Ted's ever read that. And besides, I don't want to be too obvious about this. I mean, I could run the risk of turning him off."

"I wouldn't think anything here could do that," I grinned.

"Hey, look!" Trudy grabbed another hanger. "Check these out!" She showed me a pair of panties in sheer white, with lace at the crotch — or rather, around it, because there was no crotch.

"Very fetching," I said, inspecting the garment. "But you'd have to be careful how you put these on. I'd end up putting a leg through the middle."

Trudy held the hanger out and frowned. "And it's not at all subtle. I mean, what if he didn't go for this?"

"You could blame the dog. Remember Charlie?" Trudy grabbed my hand in recognition. Charlie, the mutt we'd had as kids, was notorious for attacking underwear, or any pants, that we'd left where he could reach them.

"You could just tell him," I added, looking down at Trudy, who was nearly doubled over with laughter, "'Ted, the dog ate your homework!'"

We were already dabbing at tears as we reached the back of the store, the "giggle room" we'd heard about. It was a revelation to both of us. Cries of "Look at this!" were followed by either whoops of laughter or by silence, as we both read the labels on the packages to try and fathom just what a "Vibrating Pocket Pal" might be, or what one was to do with "The Accommodator."

"Here Trudy, how about this? 'The Rockin' Rabbit,'" I read out loud. "Cock ring with vibrating control."

"How does one, um, propose such a thing?" Trudy asked, scanning the package. "Or do I just try to slip it on while he's not paying attention?"

"Well, you know, men usually experience erections during REM sleep. Maybe you could stay awake some night and as soon as his eyes start rolling around under his lids…"

"I just slip this baby on? I want to excite him, not make him have a heart attack."

"Then, how about this? 'The Pecker Leash.'" I took the package from the rack. "You could take him for walks right along with Boomer. Or maybe, Boomer could walk Ted! Wouldn't that be cute? Maybe you could get them on 'Stupid Pet Tricks!'"

We were weak with laughter before we even found the section with the handcuffs and rubber whips. "Look!" squealed Trudy. "A 'Seven Piece Fantasy Restraint Kit!' Ooops, wait a minute." Once again, we fell silent while we studied the package.

"Wow," I said. "Good thing they're made with Velcro. You could get really bollixed up with these things."

"And how are you supposed to manage all this while you're turned on? I mean, I like to <u>use</u> my arms and legs." Trudy frowned, then added, "Y'know, Ted always likes those hard looking women in movies. You know, like that Ursa character in the Superman movies."

"Ah, yes, the high boots, the black leather."

Trudy was eyeing wide leather collars labeled 'Master' and 'Slave.' "But I don't know that he'd actually like to perform any kind of S&M stuff."

"Or which one he'd like to be," I said. "Maybe you should get both. Then he could choose."

"Lord, I can't even get the man into the sack, let alone into a collar! No, I need something erotic, but not demanding." We continued to scan the racks, until I cried out, "Here, here! Any man would like these!" I handed Trudy a box labeled 'edible condoms.'

"Hmmm, these might be just the thing," Trudy nodded. "Although it doesn't say how you persuade a husband who's had a vasectomy to wear a condom."

"Wait, here we go — edible panties too! You could start with these and then add the other, eh? Once he got the idea."

"Getting the idea is the hard part with Ted, these days." Trudy sighed.

The clerk had drifted to the back and was keeping a delicate distance as she asked, "Is there anything you'd like any help with?"

I turned and said, "What have you got for the sluggish lover?"

Trudy backed away in embarrassment, but I forged ahead. "I've got a partner who seems to have lost interest in sex." I held out my hands to express nothingness.

"Well, I take it you've already tried erotic videos."

I looked back at Trudy quizzically. Almost imperceptibly, she shook her head.

"Actually, no I haven't. Do you have any here?"

"Not to rent. And we don't carry what you might call porn movies, the triple X stuff. But we do sell several instructional videos," she said, slipping behind a counter and pointing to a display inside a case. "And we also carry three of the films directed by Candida Royale."

"Who's that?" asked Trudy.

"She's rather famous for bringing a female sensibility to what used to be called 'stag movies.'" The clerk withdrew one and handed it to me.

"Wow, a dirty movie made by a woman! Trudy, you — I mean I — we must get this!" I exclaimed.

It was expensive, but so was everything else in the giggle room, so we were flushed with success as we made our way to the cash register at the front of the store. There, on the front counter was a display that I hadn't noticed when we came in. It featured what appeared to be statues, or rather, reproductions of statues, of goddesses. There were perhaps a dozen miniature figures, of many different types. I recognized Artemis, with her quiver and arrows on her back, and the Venus of Willendorf, the world embodied in a torso. The clerk noticed my interest and said, "Aren't these wonderful? Here's my favorite."

She handed a three inch figure to me. I'd seen this goddess before, somewhere — with hair or a headdress that looked like a bouffant wig. "She looks familiar," I said, "is she Egyptian?"

"Probably originally, but she's found all around the Mediterranean. She was called Hathor, and Astarte, and later became Aphrodite. In Israel she was called Ashara. She was the goddess consort of Yahweh."

"Really? I thought Yahweh was supposed to be the one and only God." I suspected that this woman didn't know much history, or scripture. Like the first commandment.

"But yes!" she replied. "I recently attended a lecture sponsored by the archeological society where a visiting scholar showed slides of inscriptions from as late as 750 B.C., from Jerusalem, that celebrate Ashara. There was goddess worship throughout the Biblical period."

"Really? That's amazing!" I held the figure and pondered aloud. "So, God was not a bachelor? What a radical idea!"

"To us, yes. And as you might well imagine, religious types are in no rush to accept these findings. To them, this is heresy. But as the archeologist described it, the Bible was a minority report written by radicals, centuries after the fact. But then you have the archeological record, which is like the fossil record. You can't deny the evidence. Goddess worship was alive and well when the Bible says there was no other god than Yahweh." She looked at the figure through her reading glasses. "'Prayers in clay,' that's what the archeologist called the figures they've found in the households they've excavated. Ashara was the power behind fertility and childbirth, and behind the tradition of sacred sexual practices. You remember the temple prostitutes in the Bible?"

I shook my head. I wasn't that attentive in Sunday school, but I was pretty sure I'd never heard any psalms or proverbs about prostitutes.

"That isn't even the right name for them. 'Prostitutes' is a term that religious moralizers used to degrade them. In fact, for thousands of years, sex was believed to be a sacred act, presided over by the Queen of Heaven, whatever name the goddess was known by in that region. There were temples dedicated to sex, and women visited them as they pleased — including married women and those from royal families. Those who lived at the temple were considered sacred women, and their children assumed their mother's name and high social standing. Property passed along female lines, so there were no 'illegitimate' children." The woman nodded to the Ashara figure. "It took centuries to wipe her out, and to make sex a sin and a shame. And now, hardly anyone knows about her. All that remains in the Bible are threats and accounts of violence against harlotry and whoredom."

I would never have expected to encounter such independent scholarship and pro-woman sentiments in a store that stocked sex toys, but it struck me as a refreshing combination. "You know, that's really funny when you think about it," I mused. "Anyone who's had great sex knows that it's holy. How perverse that we never acknowledge it."

"You see why I run this store."

"Yes, I guess I do," I nodded, impressed. "And what an educational experience it has been to come here." I put out a hand. "My name is Willa Nilsson." The woman shook it and said, "Valerie Wallace, nice to meet you. Most customers don't introduce themselves. Newcomers usually feel pretty shy about being here."

"So did I, but now I'm really glad I came."

"Me too," said Trudy, handing over her credit card, having forgotten the pretense that the sex film was my purchase.

"Look at this one, Trudy!" I picked up a reclining figure with huge hips. "A woman after my own heart!"

"Ah," Val nodded appreciatively, "this one is known as the Sleeping Goddess of Malta. No one knows for sure what she represented, but she was found in an underground temple that was carved out before the pyramids or Stonehenge were built. She may have been a protector of sleep, or of the dead. Like so many Neolithic female figures, she's larger than life, you might say."

I inspected the little figure. She lay on her right side, tiny head resting on a pillow, round arms, hips and legs ballooning upward, ending in tiny feet. She looked comfortable, beautiful and mysterious. "Well, I have to get this," I told Trudy, thinking of what I would do with this little talisman. Or taliswoman.

"And I want the one who represents sacred sexuality," Trudy was saying as I reached for my wallet. That's when my eyes fell on a document lying on the counter. It was facing the wrong way, but a name jumped out at me: "Frank Conrad." I tried to be subtle as I craned my neck to see more. This was a database or mailing list, I realized, but why would Frank be on it? There was no "Dr." in front of the name, so maybe it was another Frank Conrad. My heart began racing as I contrived to catch another peek to see the address, but Valerie Wallace cleared the counter so we could sign our credit card receipts.

"Do you have a mailing list?" I asked innocently. "I'd like to sign up."

"Certainly," Val smiled, and reached for the list, but turned it over, saying, "Just write your name and address here." Realizing that I wasn't going to get another look, I decided that it was probably just as well.

Chapter 8

Our shopping trip had been so successful that Trudy proposed we celebrate with lunch at Tripoli, a chic and expensive eatery with waiters in black vests and long white aprons. I didn't protest, reasoning that lunch at such a place was a lot more affordable than dinner, and therefore a bargain.

It was past 1:30 when we got there and we were able to occupy a snug banquette. The waitperson spared us the condescension that abounds at such places, genially served us and then wisely left us alone to talk.

"So, Willa — have you ever watched X rated movies?"

"I cannot tell a lie. Yes, at hotels. Most of them have zillions of blue movies on their systems."

"You were with Leo?"

"Which time?"

Trudy rolled her eyes. "I wouldn't know how you glamorous divorced women manage your sex lives. I'm just a domestic nobody, a loveless wallflower." She clasped her hands to her chest melodramatically, but I detected some real sadness in her voice.

"Hey, this sort of thing happens to everybody. Don't take it as a reflection on you." I patted her hand. "It certainly had a lot to do with Leo's problems."

"Really? All I knew was that he was distant and it drove you crazy."

"Well, it was part and parcel of all those difficult years, adding enormous pressure and disappointment. To some degree, his workaholism and drinking were distractions from sexual problems that he wasn't facing, and certainly not discussing with me. The only message I got was that he wasn't interested."

"Do you think that might be happening with Ted?"

"You're asking me? I was utterly clueless about all of this. It wasn't until Leo married that lunatic, hit bottom and finally went into therapy that he sorted this out." I grinned over my salad. "But I don't think Ted is nearly as thick-headed as Leo."

"But sex is a very — well — touchy subject with him."

"With men, period. Especially if things aren't working the way they used to. But truly, there is nothing to fear but fear itself."

"You mean, fear of not being able to perform like a twenty-year-old, or fear of admitting it?"

"Both, of course," I said, then raised my glass of iced tea to offer a toast. "To better living through chemistry! To Viagra!"

Trudy snorted and shook her head. "What would I do without a big sister to fill me in on these things?" Then she looked up and past me, to someone passing our booth. "Hey, Frank! Fancy meeting you here!"

I turned around to see Frank, looking rather more ruddy than usual, taking us in with a wavering eye.

"Ladies!" he said courteously, and stopped, a little unsteadily. "How nice to see you." He leaned down to give me a peck on the cheek, and only then did I see Janet, the office assistant, standing behind him, looking worried. Frank righted himself and took Trudy's hand. "*Enchanté*, madam," he said, kissing it and then grasping the edge of the table to keep from pitching forward.

Janet moved to help steady him. "Dr. Conrad, I really do think I should take you home instead of back to the office." She looked at me, then at Trudy. "I let him talk me into going out to lunch, but I don't think we're going to get much more work done today."

"Yes, that'd be nice — take me home, tuck me in!" He threw an arm around her shoulder. "But first, I need to see a man about a horse. Would you excuse me?" Frank didn't wait for our permission, but strayed toward the back, craning his neck for a restroom sign. I looked at Janet, trying to figure out what to think of this.

Janet turned from watching him, apparently satisfied that he was out of earshot, and said flatly, "He's a mess."

"Here, take a load off," I said patting the seat next to me.

Janet slipped into the bench alongside me, struggling to keep her short skirt from exposing an unprofessional expanse of thigh. "I'm so stressed!" she moaned as she wriggled.

"Having trouble with the boss?" said Trudy.

"He used to be a wonderful person to work for, but now he's so crazy." She looked out from the booth in his direction, apparently concerned that he might overhear her. "And — I miss her too!" Her voice grew strained with the effort to keep from choking up. "I feel so sorry for him." She blinked and a tear cascaded down her cheek.

Trudy, ever the counselor, dug a tissue out of her purse and handed it to Janet. I swallowed hard, straining to keep from tearing up in sympathy. I didn't want Frank to return to a table of weeping women, especially in his condition. Trudy took charge, using the skills she had honed over years of meeting with troubled, abused, neglected, pregnant and, yes, grieving teenagers at Mount Clair High School.

"We all miss her, Janet, and it's going to take a long time for us to get over it." Trudy had also known Bonnie well, as a member of our dream sharing group, one that has lasted for over ten years.

Janet nodded and wiped her nose. "I wish there was something I could do for him," she said. "It's just so painful." She glanced around the room. "I agreed to come here with him because I thought it would buck him up a little, but now he's had too much to drink."

"He's anesthetizing himself," Trudy smiled calmly. "Has he been hard to get along with at work?"

"Sometimes he's irritable, sometimes he's real quiet, a lot of the time he just seems distracted. It's hard to be around, day in, day out."

"Janet, if it's any comfort to you, all this behavior can be chalked up to grief. And you're right, it is very hard to be in on, day after day. May I make a suggestion?" Trudy asked.

Janet nodded again, blowing her nose.

"Would it be okay if we took Frank home, and you took the rest of the day for yourself? Would the office fall apart?"

"Well, he doesn't have any patients this afternoon." She thought about it some more and added, "I could just call the service and tell them to take the calls for the rest of the day."

"Then, I suggest you do that. You need a break, kiddo." She looked at me. "Men can handle a lot of intense emotions, but not sadness. They don't mind getting furious at an umpire, or terrified of morphing space aliens, but sorrow is just not their bag." She nodded toward Janet. "Here he comes."

Frank appeared at the table, slightly disoriented from his roundabout trip back from the men's room. "Couldn't find you at first," he said jovially.

I spoke up. "We were just talking with Janet, and decided you should give her the afternoon off. That's okay with you, isn't it?"

He cocked his head, considering it, and looked over his half glasses at Janet. "I guess she deserves a little time off," he said without much sincerity.

I turned to Janet. "On your way then!" I said cheerfully. "Have a nice afternoon."

Janet scooted out of the booth but then paused. "I'll see you tomorrow, then," she said hesitantly. Trudy and I both nodded at her, as if to nudge her out the door with our heads.

"Bye then," she said in a cracking voice, and sped to the door.

After we drove Frank home, we lingered until his daughter, Caitlin, came in with groceries. Both of Frank and Bonnie's children were in college, and both had cancelled or deferred their summer plans to be at home with their father, at least until after Bonnie's memorial service. "Dad's having a hard time," she confided after Frank excused himself to take a nap. "He never used to drink during the day."

"Has this happened before today?" Trudy asked.

"No, but he's been drinking more than usual at night."

"Are you worried?"

"Well, I figure it's all part of this — disaster. But this" — she nodded toward the stairs where Frank had retreated — "yeah, this does worry me." Caitlin was normally a vivacious girl, but today she looked pale and tired.

"Of course it does," Trudy spoke comfortingly. "If it's any reassurance, lots of people have these reactions, and they're usually temporary. But there's nothing wrong with telling him that you're concerned, you know. It would probably help."

The phone rang, and we overheard Caitlin take a message from her Uncle Larry, Bonnie's brother. "Well, tell me when to have him call you back this evening. You . . . can't reach him just now."

Caitlin returned with a perplexed look on her face. "This is another thing. Dad's upset with Uncle Larry, for something about Mom's estate."

"He's their lawyer, right?" I asked. I felt a ripple of suspicion start up my back, and shrugged it away.

"Yes, and it seems that Mom had him put money she inherited from her parents in a special trust for Andy and me, and Dad didn't know about it. He thinks Larry put her up to it."

"Why does he think that?" I wondered.

"I'm not sure. She did this pretty recently, I guess, soon after Grandma died last year. Uncle Larry's explanation is that Mom wanted to make sure Andy and I got that money."

"Do you know why?" Trudy asked.

Caitlin shook her head. "Nobody knew anything about any of this until Mom's will was read." She sighed and continued, "But Uncle Larry says it's common for people to put family money in trusts for their kids. Otherwise, if a widower remarried, all his first wife's money would go to the second wife when he dies." Caitlin scratched her head. "I guess I should feel grateful for the money, but it's made Dad hurt and angry, so it doesn't feel right."

"Think of it this way," Trudy offered. "The day may come when you will need to take care of your father in his old age, and now you know you will have the means."

"I guess that's true," said Caitlin. "And maybe Mom was thinking about that too. But," she reached for a tissue, "I really don't know." She blotted her lower lashes and caught two tears. "Everything is so strange without her. I try to think what she would say, or do. And sometimes, it seems like she's still around. Literally — a couple of times I could swear I heard her coming in the kitchen door from the garage. And I'm not the only one. Andy's mentioned it too."

"That's not uncommon either," said Trudy.

Caitlin barked a brief laugh. "Oh good, then we're not crazy."

"No, you're not," I said sincerely. "You're just in the middle of a liminal time."

"What does that mean?"

"It means nothing is normal. 'Liminal' comes from the Latin for 'threshold.' When you're on a threshold, you're in between, not outside or inside. In anthropology, liminality describes the middle, transitional phase of a rite of passage. That includes laying our dead to rest."

"So, when you're liminal, you hear things?"

"Sometimes. People may also see things, or smell things, and often, dream things. When someone dies, especially when the death is sudden, the sense of liminality can last for a long time."

Caitlin sat back on the sofa and sighed. "Andy had a huge dream the other night, about Mom. He said it seemed really, really real."

"Do you know if he wrote it down?" I asked.

"I don't. He said it was too hard to talk about that morning, but I figure he'll tell me about it eventually. I hope he doesn't forget it."

"I think of all dreaming as liminal," I said. "In dreams, we're having direct experiences, usually without any notion that this isn't ordinary life. To me, the dream state really is that — a state of existence, between waking life and other realities that we experience as true."

"Until we wake up and forget them, or blow them off," said Trudy.

"Or don't," I patted Caitlin's knee, "in the case of your mother and me and my sister. Now, before we go, is there anything we can do for you?"

"No, but thanks. We're still trying to finish getting everything organized for the memorial, but we're almost ready."

"Well, you let me know if you need some help, or just want to schmooze," I told her.

"Me too," said Trudy.

"Thank you for everything you've done so far. Everyone has been so kind and generous. We have a freezer full of food."

"A student from Cyprus once told me that when someone dies there, no one in the household cooks for six weeks. The neighborhood tends to the family. That's the way it ought to be," I said as I rose to leave. "That's the way I'd like it to be for you and Andy and your dad. So, stay in touch."

Once in the car, Trudy fixed me with a meaningful stare. "What do you think has been going on here?"

"You mean with Bonnie's estate?"

"I mean with Frank and Janet!" said Trudy.

"Did you think that they were, like, on a date or something?"

"Sure that's what I thought! Didn't you?"

"I did wonder at first, but not for long." I cocked my head with assurance. "I mean, Janet seemed completely sincere."

"Didn't she though?"

"Trudy! You're so suspicious," I exclaimed, even as I wondered about Frank's name on the Garden of Eden mailing list. But maybe that wasn't the same Frank Conrad, or maybe Frank and Bonnie had discovered the giggle room.

"I'm just saying..."

"Well, I'm not," I said, then silently vowed to myself, "And I won't."

Chapter 9

Bonnie's memorial service was scheduled for her birthday. That would make it well over a month since she died, but in the first hours and days of having to absorb the shock of her death, nobody thought that was too long to wait. It gave us all time to collect ourselves and think about how best to memorialize her, and to honor her wishes to be returned to the earth.

Since Frank and Bonnie had discussed how they'd prefer to be buried, that first decision had been an easy one. No crated coffin on the flight back to the mainland for Bonnie; she returned to Pittsburgh as carry-on luggage, in a plastic bag inside a cardboard box which Frank held in his lap for most of the trip. Indeed, it had brought Leo and me comfort too, to hold the box when Frank needed to leave his seat. It reminded me of traveling on a plane with a baby, the handing back and forth, the sense of care and importance. It might have appeared ludicrous to an onlooker, but Bonnie's loss was still too unreal to accept, and the fact that what remained of her was indeed with us, along for the ride and under our care, gave us a sense of a mission to be carried out on her behalf.

Deciding what should be done with her ashes also took time, another good reason for postponing a memorial service. Frank and the children finally agreed to use the ashes to plant the trees Bonnie had always wanted along their front yard. The tree planting was scheduled to take place after a service at the Friend's Meeting House in Oakland. Although Bonnie had not been a practicing Quaker, she'd been active in the peace movement that was based there, and had many friends among the Friends.

The meeting house was originally a Tudor manse, and the main meeting hall where the service was held had once been a ballroom. The carved wainscoting remained, and the hardwood floor, but otherwise, the room was clean and simple, the walls covered in a brown velvet fabric that made it seem both warm and quiet. Rows of wooden chairs quickly filled with a variety of people of all ages: family, friends, colleagues, neighbors. Caitlin and Andy greeted the arrivals, looking pale but resolute. Bonnie's elderly uncle, the last of his generation, hobbled in on a walker. I recognized her brother, Larry, and Frank's sister, and their children. So many people touched by this death, bearing their sadness to this memorial.

Then I recognized Earl Newman and checked an impulse to duck out of sight. Why would he come here, and all the way from Cleveland? Curiosity won out over disdain and I made my way toward him. When he saw me approaching he smiled too broadly, revealing the two large front teeth that earned him the nickname, "The Mad Hatter."

"Earl," I said in tone that was meant to disguise my hostility, "I must say I'm surprised to see you." He was more formally dressed than any other man there, in a dark silk suit and rep tie. Earl had gone to Yale and seemed to regard himself as some sort of Knight of the Ivy League.

"I just felt I had to come to pay my respects," he said somberly. "You know, Cleveland is only a couple of hours away."

It occurred to me then that Earl might be feeling contrite. After all, he had published some scathing criticism of Bonnie's work. Earl was notorious in IASD for his duplicity. A bespectacled WASP type, he behaved the gentleman in person, but reveled in writing contentious reviews and hostile commentaries. I had felt the lash once or twice myself, but on this occasion perhaps I ought to give him the benefit of the doubt.

"Well, it was nice of you to take the trouble to drive down," I said. "I'm sure Frank will appreciate that you came." And maybe he'll even forgive you, I thought to myself as I moved off.

On a table along one wall were photos of Bonnie — baby pictures, grade school shots, her high school year book pose. Here were her graduations from college, all three times; a wedding portrait featuring bride and bridesmaids; and shots of her with both children — at the beach, in Halloween costumes, on Christmas morning. Then I spotted an enlargement of a picture that Leo had taken of Frank and Bonnie together, in Hawaii just a few weeks ago, grinning at the beachside bar at the Royal Hawaiian Hotel. They had actually wanted a picture of their drinks, flamboyant affairs featuring an orchid garnish and paper umbrellas speared in large chunks of pineapple. It was supposed to be a joke — mainland tourists on a tear — but what it really showed was a couple sharing their delight in the moment. It was heartbreaking.

"Holy cripes, what are they <u>drinking</u>?!" It was Maxine, a member of our dream sharing group. A raucous redheaded nurse, Max loves to eat, drink and have fun. It was a great relief to hear her soft Kentucky twang just then.

"They actually ordered Singapore Slings, can you believe it?" I told her, talking through the constriction in my throat. "Nobody could even remember what's in them."

"Well, it does my heart good to see her enjoying herself like that, poor thing."

"To tell you the truth, Maxie, I think I need to pull myself together a little bit." I backed away from the table, making a deliberate attempt to close myself off from my sadness. "I'm supposed to read something for the service and I want to be able to speak without choking up. Distract me, okay?"

Max took me by the arm and walked me away from the table of memories. She's a tall woman, big-boned and well-upholstered, and I felt like I was being borne away by a comfortable sofa. "So, is our gang all here?" Max wondered. We scanned the room, searching for the other members of our dream group. "Hey, there's Joe. He's dressed for the occasion, I see."

Joe Wallace, a middle-aged and unrepentant hippie, had donned a tan sport coat that probably dated from the 1970s, for him a gesture of decorum. Underneath, he wore what I understood to be a statement he was making in honor of Bonnie, a Hawaiian shirt with purple and yellow flowers on a black background. However, this was only partially visible under his long blonde beard. He spotted and joined us.

"Joe, I think Bonnie would be touched that you wore a jacket today," Max said approvingly. "Now tell us about that shirt."

"This is what is called 'aloha attire,' which is how mourners are expected to dress in Hawaii. If I could get one, I would also wear a ginger lei. Bright colors and flowers are important in native Hawaiian funerals. That seemed appropriate for Bonnie."

"A ginger lei?" Max asked quizzically.

"Well, there's a saying in Hawaiian that ginger leaves yellow too quickly: *Awapuhi lau pala wale*. So ginger is a symbol of something that has died before its time."

"That's lovely," I said.

"<u>How</u> do you <u>know</u> this?" demanded Max. This was a question that was often directed at Joe, a man of great and varied learning. He'd started his college education at MIT in physics in the sixties, realized that most of the research there was benefiting arms development, and left. After that he'd studied both history and math formally, and everything else that interested him informally. The upshot was that the man was a walking encyclopedia.

"Oh, I spent some time there in the seventies." There seemed to be no end to the places Joe had been, and the minutiae he knew. The funny thing was, he was not at all pretentious about his learning, or his life for that matter. Just now he was working at the local food co-op.

"What's over there on the table?" he asked.

"It's Bonnie's life in pictures," Max told him. "If you're going, take Kleenex. We're over here recovering from it."

"Hi guys." Trudy came up behind us. "Have you been to The Table?" She was carefully daubing her eyes, trying to catch tears before they trickled down her face and took her mascara with them.

"We were just talking about that." I put an arm around Trudy's shoulder. "I'm trying to keep it together over here for the service. Let's talk about something else for a while, okay? Where'd you get those earrings?"

"At the street fair in Shadyside last year. They make my ears itch if I wear them for too long though." There was a lull as we watched Joe approach The Table and place his finger upon his lips, quietly taking in what he was seeing.

"How about them Steelers?" Max interjected.

"Max, it's baseball season," I said, patting her arm. "But thank you anyway."

"Okay, how about them Buccos?"

I smiled. "Boy, I have missed you guys. Are you all coming to the house for the tree planting?"

"I have to go on duty," said Max.

"I'm due at a meeting," said Trudy.

"Well, let's do this now then — I think we need to resume our get-togethers." In the wake of Bonnie's death we had not scheduled a gathering. It had seemed too hard to meet without her.

"My calendar still has Wednesdays free for a dream meeting," said Max.

"I'm in," said Trudy. "I need this!"

"Me too," I agreed. "I'll check with Joe, but if you don't hear from me otherwise, I'll see you at the coffee house at five next Wednesday."

"Later," said Trudy, nodding to the room to indicate that people were taking their seats for the service. I moved to join Leo, who'd left the circle of Frank and his children, to take our seats behind the family.

When the time came to speak, I took a deep breath and walked to the podium. My voice emerged a bit high with feeling, but I was able to keep it steady as I spoke. "Bonnie and I shared an interest in poetry as well as dreams – we felt that the two have a great deal in common. When I was asked if I would read a poem in Bonnie's memory, Frank and I agreed on this one, by her favorite, Walt Whitman.

The Last Invocation

At the last, tenderly,
From the walls of the powerful fortress'd house,
From the clasp of the knitted locks, from the keep of the
well-closed doors,
Let me be wafted.

Let me glide noiselessly forth;
With the key of softness unlock the locks - with a whisper,
Set ope the doors O soul.

Tenderly - be not impatient,
(Strong is your hold O mortal flesh,
Strong is your hold O love.)"

Chapter 10

The tree planting took place at Frank and Bonnie's home, a corner house on a steep cobblestone street in Squirrel Hill, a neighborhood close to the universities. Few houses here had large plots of ground, which was one reason Bonnie had wanted to plant trees along the front. She had argued that it would be much nicer to look out the window at a row of white birches than at delivery trucks and parked cars. No one had disagreed with her; they had just never got around to doing it. Now it seemed just the right thing to do, to honor her wishes and to dispose of her ashes.

Frank and the children had already dug three holes, and after each poured a portion of the ashes into them, the saplings were set in place. Frank looked wan and panted with the effort as he turned the first several shovelfuls to refill the holes. Then, wiping sweat from his shining forehead, he invited the rest of those gathered to help place the soil onto the bound tree roots, and to say a few words if they wished.

After the extended family, the next up was Joe, who said simply, "I'll see you in the dreamtime, Bonnie." I stood and watched as others came forward and said goodbye, or spoke of a fond memory of Bonnie, and added earth to one of the holes. I lingered at the edge of the group, uncertain when to speak, or show what I brought to bury with the ashes. I watched as Janet, her face streaked with tears, took the shovel and said in a hushed voice, "We all miss you."

Then a young girl I didn't recognize came forward and filled the shovel. As she emptied it, she said, "I hope there are no nightmares in heaven." I watched her return to the group and join a familiar looking woman. It took me a moment to place her, and I was surprised to realize that it was Karen Morgan, Charlotte's friend.

Leo took the shovel, turned the earth and said, "I don't know what I will miss more, Bonnie, your smile or your cooking." Sounds of recognition and some laughter traveled around the group like a breeze. On this note, I stepped forward.

Removing the figure from my pocket, I held it out and said, "This is a replica of the Sleeping Goddess of Malta. I like to think, and I know Bonnie would agree, that she is dreaming." I placed the figure in the hole of the middle tree and scooped dirt onto it.

After the tree planting, the group headed for the house and its air conditioning. Although the sky was overcast, the air was humid and the day had grown increasingly uncomfortable. I looked for Karen and intercepted her on the front steps.

"Karen, we meet again! I didn't know you knew Bonnie."

"Well, I didn't know her very well. But she helped my daughter." She reached behind her to bring the girl alongside her. "Stephanie, this is Dr. Nilsson. She's an expert on nightmares too."

"Actually, just dreams in general — nightmares were Bonnie's, Dr. Taylor's, special expertise," I said, taking Stephanie's hand and shaking it. It felt limp, as if she didn't know what to do with it. She looked to be a tall twelve, wearing both braces and glasses, with wildly curly hair held back in a tight ponytail.

"Dr. Taylor helped Stephanie with her night terrors, didn't she?" Karen said to her daughter. Stephanie shrugged and shifted her weight to one foot, holding one arm to her side with the other. "If you say so, Mother." I couldn't decide if the girl was embarrassed that her mother was talking about her, or just being sulky. Probably both. I can remember how uncomfortable I felt at this age, painfully self-conscious and hard on myself — and even harder on my mother.

"Ah, night terrors — those are supposed to improve with age, aren't they?" I said to them both.

"Well, often they do," Karen answered. "Stephanie's started when she was only three or so, and I had no idea what was wrong then. She'd wake us in the middle of the night, screaming in her bed, and I'd rush into her but couldn't calm her down. Finally, I read an article that said kids with these problems aren't really awake. The next time it happened, even though her eyes were open and she was sitting up in bed, I shook her and said, 'Wake up, wake up!' And, she did! She just looked at me and said, 'Goodnight Mommy' and rolled over and went back to sleep."

Karen smiled at her daughter, but Stephanie was looking off into the street as if she didn't want to hear her mother talking about her. I said, "So Stephanie, were you ever aware of this?"

"No."

Her mother continued, "It did become less frequent as she got older, although she had other symptoms — she would always talk in her sleep a lot. But then, when she was in fifth grade, she went to a slumber party and managed to sleepwalk out the front door and trip a burglar alarm. She scared the life out of her friend's parents. We had more episodes of this, and more night terrors."

"Night<u>mares</u>, Mother," Stephanie corrected.

"Anyway, that's how we came to know Dr. Taylor, isn't it?" Karen asked her daughter. Stephanie looked at me, suddenly sincere, apparently compensating for her grudging remark earlier. "She helped me."

Just then, Joe came past us and I grabbed his hand. "Joe, the dream crew — we're going to meet on Wednesday."

"The dream crew?" said Karen. I introduced Joe to Karen and Stephanie and explained, "We've had a regular dream-sharing group for a number of years, but we haven't met since Bonnie died."

Karen said, "How does a dream-sharing group work?"

"It's very simple," Joe said affably. "First, you write down your dreams, then you meet with other people who do the same thing. Have you ever kept a dream journal?"

Karen shook her head, and Joe looked to Stephanie, who seemed surprised that he was including her.

"I used to, when I was seeing Dr. Taylor." She looked at me.

This was an awkward situation. Clinical propriety demands that a therapist not divulge a relationship with a client. Of course Bonnie was not here to be cautious on her young client's behalf. Instead, her mother had offered — to a woman who was a stranger to Stephanie — the details of the youngster's sleep disorder. In all fairness, I felt I should offer no further explanation to Joe and risk further violating the child's privacy.

I wasn't sure if Joe had picked up on this, but he did continue in his light conversational vein, explaining how ordinary dreamers can benefit from sharing their dreams with one another. "Anyone can do what we do. The system we use was developed by a psychoanalyst who realized that people don't need psychoanalysts to get a lot out of their dreams. All you really need is a few other people." Stephanie's gaze was no longer distant; she was listening, and Joe continued.

"We bring our dream journals to a meeting. Somebody will start by reading a dream to the rest of us." He looked at Stephanie. "You can do this with your friends or classmates, anybody really."

"Then what?" she asked.

"Then everybody asks about the details of the dream, like, what kind of a dog was that, or, was it day or night in the dream, that sort of thing. Usually we all take notes, because dreams can get complicated. Then everyone in the group talks about what they'd make of the dream if they had had it. We even say, 'If this were my dream,' and we use the words 'I' and 'me' instead of 'you.' That's very important. It prevents dream stealing."

"What's dream stealing?" Stephanie asked.

"Well, what if I were to say to you…" Joe gestured to the girl, "Stephanie, let's say you told me a dream about not being ready to take a math test — have you ever had a dream like that?" Stephanie nodded, her brown eyes alert with interest.

"Well, what if you told me about that dream and I said, 'Your dream means that you are bad at math.' What would you think?"

"Well, I'd wonder why that would be, because I do pretty well in math."

"But what if I had said, 'If this were my dream, it would have to do with my fear of math because I always have had trouble with it.'"

"Well, then that's just what you'd think. It wouldn't have to mean it's what's true about me."

"Bingo," said Joe. "The official term for attributing your own feelings to someone else is 'projection.' People do it all the time without realizing it. In dreamwork, it's especially common because for any element in a dream, there is no single, absolute meaning to fall back on. So if we're not careful, we can rob a dreamer of personal insight. That's why it's called dream stealing."

We were interrupted as Earl Newman reached us on his way into the house.

"Are these people trying to convert you, young lady?" he said. "Don't let them lead you astray!" He contrived to smile, no doubt to hide his scorn.

"We're talking about writing down dreams, Earl," I said. "Surely you don't disapprove of that!"

Earl smiled more broadly, exposing his Mad Hatter teeth, and cocked his head genially. "Of course not! We want you all to write down your dreams!"

"Dr. Newman," I told the others, "is famous for his longitudinal research. He's a pioneer in studying dream series throughout the life cycle."

"How interesting!" Karen said, but I was wondering why Earl was bothering with any of this — coming to the funeral, intruding into this conversation, trying to be genial, however lame the effort.

"We were just talking about dream stealing, Earl. You know, when someone takes the meaning away from the dreamer?" I was being sarcastic, but trying not to sound it.

Earl looked puzzled, but then said, "Oh, you mean when you people do your little discussion groups?"

"Yes Earl. Because not all dreamers are recording their dreams so you can code them and then crunch the numbers."

Earl blinked, ducked his head in a gesture of retreat, and continued up the steps.

Joe rolled his eyes and shot me a questioning look. I shrugged. "Never mind me. The guy's created a little karma, that's all. Finish telling about the dreamwork."

Joe turned back to Stephanie. "So then you would talk about what you think about your dream, now that you've heard these different ideas. Usually the dreamer has what we call an 'aha!,' a new perception they wouldn't have had otherwise. It's funny, but I've found that my own dreams seem to be the hardest to crack. I always get more out of a dream that I've shared with other people."

"This sounds fascinating! If you ever take newcomers, I'd love to try it sometime," Karen enthused, and began rummaging through her purse. "Let me give you my number." But she was interrupted by the beep of a car horn on the street.

"Mother, look, it's Van." Stephanie nudged her mother and all turned to watch a black Cadillac come to a stop in front of the house, alongside the cars parked there. "What's he doing here? Did you tell him to come for us?" She sounded tense and exasperated.

"No, but your dad might have sent him for some reason. Let's go see."

We watched as the mother and daughter stepped around us and made their way to the street. We watched them lean over and talk into the half open, tinted window on the passenger side. We saw Stephanie shake her head vehemently, then turn around and walk back toward us. Karen spoke again to the driver, then followed her daughter. She'd caught up with her by the time they rejoined us.

"Well, we have to be going," Karen said evenly.

"Mom!" Stephanie's anger made this come out as a three syllable word.

"We're taking my car," Karen said to her pointedly. The girl shrugged.

"I hope everything is okay?" I said.

"Oh, yes, just an appointment we'd forgotten. Luckily, Van — he works for my husband — was able to come and alert us. I'd turned off my cell at the service and forgot to turn it back on." She started toward the street. "Let's go, Stephanie."

Frowning, the girl reluctantly followed her mother to their car and then flung herself into the front seat.

"Whoa, what was that about?" Joe said, as the silver BMW nosed out of its parking place. I saw the girl sitting rigidly with her arms wrapped tightly against her chest.

"I have no idea," I said, and then noticed that the Cadillac had waited until the BMW had gone past it, then pulled out behind it and followed in its wake.

I insisted on staying to help after most of the others had left the Conrad house, but Caitlin pulled me from the kitchen as I was drying platters that had recently been filled with cold cuts and sandwich rolls.

"C'mon, sit down for a few minutes. Andy and I want to talk to you. Dad too." Mystified, I followed Caitlin back to the living room. Andy, older looking from having put on those famous "freshman fifteen," was sitting back on the couch with two cardboard file boxes in front of him on the floor. The lid was off one of the boxes, and I recognized what was inside — the spiral bound notebooks in which Bonnie had written down her dreams over the years.

Caitlin said, "You know, we've been trying to go through Mom's things, while we're still home and can help Dad. It's hard."

"I bet it is," I nodded.

Andy said, "We've been talking about Mom's dream journals. It's hard to imagine what we would do with them. But they were important to her. We don't want to toss them." He picked up several small boxes containing floppy disks. "But there are so many of them, between her notebooks and the records she kept on her computer."

I strained to focus my mind on what Andy was saying, but was overwhelmed by the alarming notion of what would become of my own dream journals when I die. Dream records are in some ways even more intimate than a personal diary. A daytime journal includes what has been processed through orderly, waking thought, but a dream journal is a collection of extravagant, unfettered accounts, described as they have been experienced, unmitigated by any governing consciousness. As such, their content could be embarrassing, even explosive.

Frank's voice carried into the room then from the front hall, loud and belligerent. "Bull!" he roared. "Earl, if I were you, I would leave right now, before I lose my temper." The kids and I blinked at one another as we heard the screen door close, and Frank slam the main door behind it. When he appeared in the door of the room, we stared at him expectantly.

"God, Dad, what happened?" Andy asked.

"I can't believe that guy!"

"Who?" said Caitlin.

"Goddam Earl Newman. Thinks he can waltz in here and sweet talk me into giving him your mother's dream records."

"So that's why he came!" I exclaimed. "What a nerve!"

"Why would he want them?" Andy wanted to know.

Frank shook his head, too disgusted to explain. "You tell them, Willa."

I sighed and answered, "Earl Newman uses people's dream journals for his research. To collect the raw data he needs for his life span project, he needs to acquire journals that span many years, like your mother's."

"But you don't want him to do that with Mom's journal?" Caitlin asked her father.

"Hell no," Frank said.

"Earl manages to offend people wherever he goes," I told the kids. "His scholarship is highly respected, but he's so determined to promote himself and his own studies that he's hostile to others, including your mother and me."

"What did he have against Mom?" Caitlin asked.

"Let me try and explain it. With the type of statistical analysis that Earl uses for his dream studies, there's no such thing as a metaphor. A car, a tree, a house — they never stand for anything else. Other scholars who use these statistical methods allow that this is simply a limitation of the tool, but not Earl. He's openly critical of people who address symbolism, or just work with their own dreams. As far as he's concerned, the only purpose in keeping a dream journal is for him to use it."

"And he's an arrogant dirtbag," Frank scowled. "He wrote a real nasty response to a paper your mother delivered a couple of years back."

"About the matching symbolism in her own dreams and her clients'," I nodded, remembering. "He's notorious for that kind of conduct — I suppose he thinks it's sporting or something, as if contempt must demonstrate lively academic thinking." But I hastened to add, "You should understand, there's nothing wrong with statistical studies, as far as they go. They can tell us a lot about what people commonly dream about. But there's a lot wrong with Earl."

"Nuts," Frank said with disgust, and shook his head as if to banish the subject from his brain. "Does anyone else need something to drink? I'm going to have a beer."

"I'll get it, Dad," Caitlin offered. "Willa?"

"A big glass of water would be great. Outrage makes me thirsty."

While we waited for the drinks, Frank said, "I <u>have</u> been wondering if someone should be a kind of trustee for Bonnie's journals. And I've told the kids that you would be the best person for the job."

I put my hand to my chest. "Me?"

"The truth is, you understood Bonnie's feelings about her dreams as well as I did, if not better. And if the whole field of journal keeping is going to grow, you'll be one of the people who'll spearhead it."

That was probably true. And of the other journal enthusiasts in IASD, none were as close to Bonnie as I had been. We were all hoping that someday there would be a dream archive, and people could leave their journals to it just as now people could leave their papers and letters to libraries. It would take time, and privacy policies would have to be developed, but technology was quickly making such things possible. Indeed, everyone — save Bonnie now — expected to see this come to pass in our lifetimes.

And just then, I knew that if the tables were turned, Bonnie is exactly the person with whom I would want my own journals entrusted.

"Well, this is really an honor," I said. "But are you all sure this is what you think is best?"

"I really do," said Caitlin, returning with the drinks.

"And I know next to nothing about this, but I agree with Dad and Caitlin," said Andy. "I know this meant a lot to Mom. She always wanted me to write down my dreams, but I hardly ever did."

"Andy, tell her about that dream you had the other day," Caitlin prodded.

Andy flushed. "I didn't write that one down either," he said sheepishly.

"You told me you talked to Mom on the phone," Caitlin began.

"Oh, yeah. I was in my room at the dorm, and the phone rang and it was Mom. Her voice sounded so real."

"I had a dream of talking to your mom on the phone too!" I exclaimed. "Did she say anything?"

"Actually, she was singing, a lullaby she used to sing about the baby in the boat."

Caitlin said, "Do you know it? 'Baby's boat's a silver moon, sailing in the sky?'" She recited from memory, "Sailing o'er the sea of sleep, as the clouds roll by."

"That's the one," said Andy. "I used to get it confused with the three men in a tub, and with those Winken, Blinken and Nod guys. Anyway, in the dream I understood that she was telling me that this is what dreaming is like — going on a long journey every night and coming back every morning — and also, what death is like." He'd been looking down as he searched for the words to describe what he'd experienced. When he looked up, his face showed awe. "It sounds weird to try and explain it, but in the dream, it all made total sense. It felt — " he looked down again — "as if her voice was injecting me with . . .understanding. And she seemed absolutely real, maybe even more real than when she was alive."

"Wow," I said, awed myself. "If that had been my dream, I'd feel like I'd had a profound visit."

"I did," said Andy. "I really did."

When we took our leave, Frank and Andy and Leo toted out the
file boxes with Bonnie's dream history inside. I was thinking, as they
placed them in the trunk, of the boxes already stacked in my office,
full of contents I had not yet made a place for. "Well, the more the
merrier," I thought, grimacing inwardly. What in the world would I
do with all these records? I didn't know, but if it felt right and
brought peace to Bonnie's family to leave these in my care, then I
would, by god, take care of them.

Chapter 11

That night, I dreamt of the silver BMW and the black Cadillac. Although the dream woke me up, I could remember nothing else about it, except that both cars were ridiculously long, longer than stretch limos, the length of city block. I lay in bed and waited for the sleep bus to come by again. This is how I deal with the frustrating problem of waking in the middle of the night. Rather than growing anxious over getting enough rest, I just pretend I'm waiting at the bus stop for sleep to come around again. The Sleep Bus, I call it. Often, waiting becomes dreaming.

I thought about the silver BMW and the black Cadillac. I have a long history of indifference to the trappings of financial success, and disdain for showing them off. On the other hand, I was now confronting personal financial instability. There was probably some connection.

I rolled onto my side. Those cars had something to do with pretentiousness, I guessed, but possibly also envy. Being an academic means never having to say you're sorry for being rich, that's for sure. In my heart, I've wanted to believe that money doesn't matter, but of course it does.

I owe my dislike of ostentation and my determination not to live a life in pursuit of the bottom line to my father. A prosperous businessman in the world, he was a genuine tyrant at home. Our childhood seemed to be a succession of family dinners at which my father bragged about his business dealings, and followed up with castigations of our mother. Somehow, it wasn't enough that he feel like the conquering hero of corporate America; he also needed to make sure that others felt inferior to him. If my mother failed to behave in a sufficiently submissive manner, he became increasingly scornful, criticizing anything that caught his attention, from an undercooked potato to a tardy daughter. Thus our domestic life was one of trying to please Dad at all costs when he was home, and utterly ignoring his dictates when he wasn't.

Since he traveled a good deal, my sisters and I enjoyed an almost utopian childhood much of the time. Our father's earnings provided us with a large and comfortable home, landscaped surroundings to play in, good schools and, when our father was away, a calm and loving mother who presided over it all. Mother defended Dad, when we were old enough to complain about him, by pointing out how well he provided for us. But to me, the means did not justify the end. As a teenager, I converted the hurt we had all suffered into anger. I continued to resent my father's contemptuous behavior, but also began to doubt my mother, who seemed trapped in her marriage by her own desire for comfort and ease. I never believed that the interior decorating, designer clothes and club memberships were worth the sacrifice that my mother made for them. I would forever after scrutinize what money really costs to have.

But that was when I was young and rebellious. Now I thought about those cars and wondered what it would be like to have the kind of financial security they represented. That would go a long way, as those long cars may have pointed out. What would I do if I had Karen's — or rather, Karen's husband's — money? Would I have to look like Karen? That would mean spending hours every week with a personal trainer, and patronizing beauty parlors, which were no temptation to me. But maybe I could read as much as I liked, learn to play the piano again, or devote more time to cooking.

The dream I wrote down the next morning featured the Sleeping Goddess of Malta lying across the top of the piano like a lounge singer. The pianist wore a chef's hat and the song was Frank Sinatra's "My Way." Don't ask me how this duo rendered Frank's classic, but it wasn't a problem at the time. Dreams are like that.

I stumbled downstairs for coffee and immediately settled in at my desk. It was important to do office work early in the day, before the sun rose high enough to heat up the room. On hot days, in spite of a ceiling fan and open windows, I couldn't work past noon. My summer routine features tasks that take me outside the house — and into air conditioning — in the afternoon.

For an hour I made progress, ferreting out and organizing the files on the courses I would be teaching in the fall, establishing the deadlines for submitting the course overview for each and checking to see if bookstores had the most recent edition of each of the required text books. When I was a fulltime faculty member at Grenville, this last task was solved with a single phone call. As an adjunct instead of a professor, I was having trouble getting the attention I needed. College office staffs were often shorthanded during the summer with few student interns, and now, I realized, I had lost status. Adjuncts are transients to permanent staff and faculty. To ensure that my students would have the textbooks they needed on time, I would have to make calls to the college bookstores myself. It all took the better part of the morning.

I was on hold with one bookstore when my call waiting beeped, but I didn't dare take the call and risk losing the four minutes I had already invested in waiting for a representative to be with me as soon as possible. When the sun had risen high enough to begin beaming onto the roof of the office, I remembered to check my voicemail. It was Charlotte, saying, "Good news. Karen asked me this morning for your phone number. I didn't think you'd mind if I gave it to her. Hope you're having a good day. Bye."

The phone rang almost immediately, and I was not surprised to hear Karen's voice.

"Dr. Nilsson, this is Karen Morgan. Charlotte gave me your number. There's something I'd like to talk to you about. Do you have a minute?"

I listened quietly as Karen explained that since the death of Dr. Taylor, her daughter Stephanie had been without counseling for her nightmare problem. The Three Rivers Sleep Clinic had a list of other therapists for the referral of Dr. Taylor's clients, but none of them were experts on nightmares, or even dreams. "After we saw you at the funeral, I thought you would be perfect. Are you taking new clients?"

"Actually, I have no clients," I told her. "I'm a research psychologist, not a clinician. I have no practice."

Karen did not understand the distinction, so I explained. "I have a Ph.D. in developmental psychology, but Dr. Taylor was a clinical psychologist, meaning she was trained to treat people. I, on the other hand, am a scholar and a teacher. The whole idea can be confusing, because many clinical psychologists also teach and do research. Basically, the difference is one of emphasis."

"Oh," Karen sounded disappointed. "So you don't see patients at all." After a pause she added, "But you do help people with their dreams, like you helped Charlotte."

"Well, that is often part of my work as a teacher. But Bonnie — Dr. Taylor — was a licensed, clinical doctor of psychology. I, on the other hand, hold a traditional Ph.D. in developmental psychology."

There was another silence, and then Karen spoke. "Let me ask you something. I understand what you're saying about licensing and so on. But isn't it therapeutic just to learn about dreams?"

I laughed, "I certainly think so!" and Karen's agreement persuaded me to continue. "Did you know that the word, 'therapeutic,' shares some history with dreaming?"

"From Freud, you mean?"

"No, no much earlier. In ancient Greece, for about a thousand years, there were temples where healing took place in the dream state. This was the cult of Asklepios, the son of Apollo, who was the physician of the gods. There were hundreds of Asklepian temples all over Greece. People who were ill or crippled, or suffering from something like impotence or infertility, came to the temples, often for weeks at a time. At the temple were attendants called *therapeutes*, who assisted the pilgrims to be healed in the dream state."

"Were these, like, dream analysts?"

"Partly yes. Their job was to guide worshippers through the process of their dream healing. A person might travel a long way and wait a long time to be summoned into a kind of dormitory where healing dreams took place. Dreamers there slept on beds that were called *kliniks*. That's where we get the word 'clinic.'"

"This is fascinating," said Karen. "But how can someone be healed by dreaming?"

"The Greeks believed that, if prepared through various rituals, the dreamer would be visited and healed by the god, who could appear in many forms — a snake, a dog or a boy. If one of these appeared in a dream — or a vision, if you were too excited to fall asleep — and it touched you, you were instantly cured."

"You know, Stephanie would love to hear about this. She's always loved mythology." Karen added, "Of course, she'd probably believe that this all really happened."

"Well, it was a common practice in its time, and there are testimonials from grateful dreamers inscribed on tablets that are still in existence. One tells how Asklepios appeared to a blind man in a dream and opened the man's eyelids, whereupon the man awoke, opened his eyes and was able to see."

"Do people think these things really happened?"

"Some scholars treat it as flimflam, but others don't."

"What do you think?"

"Personally? I wouldn't presume to judge," I said honestly. "There is so much we don't understand about faith and healing, not to mention the placebo effect. And I know from experience that dreams draw on resources that I cannot begin to explain."

"I wonder," Karen said then, "would you ever consider being, let's say, a dream teacher? Privately? Like a tutor?"

"Do you mean, to work with your daughter?"

"That's what I was thinking. There really isn't anyone else in town here with your expertise in dreaming."

I knew that was true. "I might consider it, but neither you nor Stephanie should expect this to replace therapy."

"Well, of course, we will always consult with the clinic for Stephanie's sleep disorder. It was Dr. Conrad who prescribed her medication and so on." Frank, the physician in charge, was a neurologist who could prescribe drugs at the clinic. This is why he and Bonnie had made such a good team — he could perform the physical assessments and prescribe drugs, Bonnie was the therapist who could work with patients on their psychological needs.

"Well, you see, that's why this arrangement wouldn't work. I'm sure your expenses at the clinic were all covered by health insurance. But nothing I could do with Stephanie would be eligible for reimbursement."

"Oh, that's not a problem. We wouldn't even treat this as a health expense, but as tutoring. Except that, of course, I'd pay you the same fees I paid Dr. Taylor."

The caution that I had been feeling suddenly turned into something approaching exhilaration. Bonnie's rates had probably been in excess of $125 an hour, which sounded great to a woman with a cash flow problem. I said carefully, "Well, that would be satisfactory, but I'll need to think it over. I've never done anything like this before."

"I hope you'll agree to try. I'm sure Stephanie will approve. She has missed her sessions with Dr. Taylor, and she has already met you, and knows that you and Dr. Taylor were friends. I think she'll like this idea."

"And I should speak with Dr. Conrad about her medical background." I really wanted to make sure there were no serious problems that might preclude working with this child. "Would that be all right with you?"

"Certainly. Will I need to call and give them my consent?"

I thought for a second. "It should probably be something in writing. As I say, I've never done this before."

"Well. I can easily call the office and fax whatever they need."

"Okay then," I said. "For the time being, let's take one step at a time. You speak with Stephanie, and I'll — sleep on it."

"Like the Greeks?"

"Something like that."

Chapter 12

When I called Frank's office, Janet answered, and hearing my voice, dropped her own.

"Dr. Nilsson, things are looking up," she confided with a tone of relief. "He agreed to go golfing this week. I just reserved a tee time for him."

"That is good news." I thought Janet sounded completely sincere, but that would be the case whether she was speaking as a loyal employee or a furtive girlfriend. I reminded myself that I'd rather not know what was going on over there, and made a mental note to commend Leo for promoting a golf date among Frank's friends. Frank hadn't touched his clubs since Hawaii.

"Is he available to talk?"

"He's on a consult right now, but I'll leave him a message to call you."

"When you do, you might pull a file for him to have handy. One for a patient named Stephanie Morgan."

"I'll try to do that, although some of our filing is still a mess. Because of our last break-in."

"What break-in? Again?" The sleep lab was located in a medical facility that had its share of theft attempts, although Frank had upgraded the clinic's security after a burglary a couple of years back.

"Oh, yes, this happened just after Dr. Taylor died. The cops thought the thieves probably read about it in the paper and exploited the opportunity."

"I didn't know."

"I don't think you all had even got back to town yet. They acted that fast."

"Did they get anything?"

"The usual — they cleaned out all the drug samples they could find. Some drug addicts must have been feeling mighty sleepy for awhile. Not to mention all the other stuff that the drug company sales reps always leave — like all the antibiotics. Dr. Conrad said there were probably a couple of junkies out there somewhere with raging diarrhea." Janet laughed. "At least I hope so."

"But they messed up the files too?"

"Actually, they seemed to just go into any drawer or door they could find. They jimmied open all the locks, and tossed everything out on the floor — files and notes and patient data all over the place. It was a big fat mess to put back together, I can tell you. "

"Poor Janet! This must have been such a headache for you!"

"In a way, it was a welcome distraction. It gave me something immediate to do, something to concentrate on besides . . . you know."

When Frank called me back, I explained Karen Morgan's proposal to hire me as a dream tutor. "I've explained to her that I'm not a psychotherapist, and she understands that. I told her I wanted to check with you first. I know that treatment records are confidential, but she was willing to give her consent for you to talk to me."

"I see that she's faxed a release here. What is it you'd like to know?"

"I'd just like a heads-up if there's anything about Stephanie's learning more about dreams that would interfere with her treatment."

"Well," Frank began, "to be perfectly honest, I'm a little fuzzy on this one. I did see her once, and prescribed some medication for her to use when she was having bouts of sleepwalking. This was almost two years ago. I can see from her records here that her inoculations were up to date, and that she's a healthy child. Allergic to cats, a little asthmatic when she exercises hard, but otherwise, a clean bill of health. She was primarily Bonnie's patient."

"I see," I said, wondering whether I should ask about Bonnie's files. What happens to the files of patients when a therapist dies? Presumably, they would be destroyed at some point, but probably not until some time had passed — in case data was needed for insurance or taxes, or to inform a patient's new psychotherapist. Before I could decide whether to ask, Frank mentioned them.

"Now, Janet did check Bonnie's office to look for her records on Stephanie, but she came up blank. You heard about our break-in here?"

"Yes, and I was shocked. What a rotten thing to have happen at a time like that."

"By the time I got back to the office, Janet and our part time bookkeeper had done all the work. I hardly thought about it." There was a pause, and he added, "It's amazing how trivial this sort of thing can seem when you're in the middle of a disaster."

Disaster — the same word Caitlin had used about the death of her mother. A sudden calamity that comes from the Latin for "star," as in "ill-starred." A very apt word for the occasion, I thought, and wondered whether it would be better to stick to business with Frank, or talk about Bonnie for a while. I waited for an indication from him.

"What I can tell you is that, from my own medical records, I see no reason why you shouldn't work with this girl."

Business it was. "Okay, good then," I said. "And if I should learn of any more sleep problems, I will make sure I remind them — her and her mother — to consult you."

I hung up with a sense of relief — not only to learn that there didn't seem to be any reason not to take up this lucrative tutoring job, but to have navigated a conversation with Frank without slipping into a new wave of grief. Yes, this is the way it happens. Slowly, very slowly, we get over it.

I was gratified that Karen Morgan wanted me to start seeing Stephanie right away. From a financial standpoint, the sooner the better. I was also glad that Karen felt it was fine for me to tutor Stephanie at their home, as my office was still in no condition to receive visitors.

The drive to Mount Clair is only twenty minutes from my house in the East End, but finding the Morgan home was challenging, once I penetrated the dense foliage and winding roads of the most exclusive suburb of Pittsburgh. The streets with older homes were familiar — I'd had friends who lived here during my teenage years, fellow classmates in the private school we attended. But I'd had little occasion to go there since and was unfamiliar with many of the newer streets.

The Morgan house sat in a cul-de-sac with three others of the same vintage, homes I would call new because they were built within the last twenty years. Each featured massive dimensions adorned with friendly highlights — bay windows, gables, a deeply sloping roof — to make them look less austere. The result, I decided, was too unnatural to succeed, giving the overall impression of a cottage on steroids. I pulled into the driveway of the three car garage, parked, and reached for my book bag.

I had debated what to bring to this first session. I have files bulging with course content on the subject of dreaming, but my initial challenge was to decide how best to tailor all that knowledge for a twelve-year-old. I planned to spend the first session chatting with Stephanie, learning about her interests and, more subtly, her sophistication. Taking a cue from Stephanie's interest in mythology, I'd brought a book that showed the ruins of the temples at Delphi and Epidauros, where the ancient Greeks solicited the intervention of the gods in their dreams. I'd also run off a list of web sites where Stephanie could explore the subject in her free time, if she cared to.

I walked to the front door along a fragrant boxwood hedge, trimmed immaculately. The only people I had spotted as I'd driven through Mount Clair were the landscaping crews that seemed to be at work on every street. Otherwise, except for the occasional SUV driver, the suburb seemed to be uninhabited, like a beautifully maintained cemetery with really big mausoleums. The humidity felt deadening as I rang the doorbell. I smiled to myself: clever of me, to schedule this session during the worst heat of the day and spend it in air conditioning.

Karen opened the large double doors, and I stepped into a showcase. I knew the signs — the parquet floors, the oriental rugs, the wallpaper, the artsy accent pieces. This place had been decorated with a capital D. Memories of my mother, poring over silky fabric samples and carpet colors, rushed through my mind. Decorating was how my mother compensated herself for having such a difficult marriage and as I grew up, I tired of the constant hubbub as decorators and remodelers, painters and paperhangers trooped through our household. The effect, I realized as I stepped in and said all the things one ought to about someone's lovely home, is that I assumed that such exquisite attention to the look of things amounted to a cover-up.

Or was I just thinking that because I knew that the relationship between Karen and her husband was not all perfection?

I was forced into attentiveness by Karen's conversation. She was saying that this was her dream house, then laughed at the correspondence with my specialty. "I never had anything like this when I was growing up," she told me. "My dad left us when I was little and my mom raised me by herself. She worked as a secretary and things were always tight. I got a scholarship to college though. That's where I met Cliff. He grew up in a little town in West Virginia. His father died of black lung. I tell Stephanie all the time how lucky she is, but you know kids..." Her voice trailed off as Stephanie appeared in the doorway to the kitchen, wearing shorts and a T-shirt and an expression of defiance.

"Go ahead, Mom," she said. "Tell me how kids are."

Karen shot me a look of motherly exasperation. "Kids are unlikely to appreciate the finer things in life, unless they've never had them." I thought about this. As one who had grown up with those finer things, I wonder if I'd appreciate them more if I'd been deprived of them. But it wasn't that I didn't like beautiful things. I just don't think they matter more than things like truth and honor.

I looked at Stephanie, waiting to see if she was going to respond to her mother, and when she didn't I said, "Hello again."

"Hi," said Stephanie, shy now.

"I didn't know where you two would like to work," Karen said. "There's the dining room, or the family room, or the den."

"Anywhere is fine with me," I said, directing my attention to Stephanie now. "Where's your computer?"

"In my bedroom," said Stephanie.

"But believe me, you don't want to go in there!" Karen exclaimed. "The maid does her best, but it's always a shambles. I just close the door."

"Where do you think we'd be most comfortable, Stephanie?"

"I guess the family room. It's this way." She gestured for me to follow her through the kitchen.

"Would you like some iced tea?" Karen interceded. "I've got raspberry flavored and green."

"As long as it's unsweetened, I'd love the raspberry, thanks." Did she mean to be distracting me from paying attention to Stephanie, or was I just caught in the mother-daughter crossfire? I moved toward Stephanie and said, "You'll have to show me around."

Stephanie led me into a spacious room featuring an entertainment center fit for a rock star, shelves filled with videos, CDs, and books, and two plush white sofas at right angles skirting a large coffee table. The far wall was lined with French doors that opened onto a flagstone patio dotted with wrought iron furniture and beyond it, a swimming pool, its blue water glimmering invitingly in the sunlight.

"Would you like to be outside?" I asked Stephanie, eyeing the glass-topped table capped with a green canvas umbrella. I was thinking that some fresh air might be a relief from the formality of the house. It was all so oppressively perfect.

"Too hot," said the girl, and I nodded. "You're right. It's so comfortable inside that you forget how muggy it is out there. But it must be great to be able to swim any time you want."

"I used to swim all the time," said Stephanie.

"Used to?"

"After the accident, I didn't want to."

Karen arrived with the iced tea just as I was asking, "There was an accident?"

Retrieving a coaster from a drawer, Karen said over her shoulder, "Stephanie's sister drowned two years ago."

"Oh my," I said. "I'm so sorry."

"Maggie was five years older than me. She taught me to swim," said Stephanie.

"So Stephanie hasn't enjoyed using the pool like she used to." Karen set the glass down on the coffee table and gestured for me to have a seat on the larger sofa. "None of us has, really." She looked out at the glinting blue rectangle. "I've actually thought about just filling it in, but we haven't been able to make a decision."

"Dad says it's an asset," Stephanie said with a note of sarcasm as she plopped herself down next to me.

"Well, it is, I guess," said Karen. "He entertains sometimes, and he likes to grill…" her voice trailed off, as if she'd lost interest in her train of thought. "Well," she said, returning to the present circumstances, "I'll let you two get down to business. I think you'll be comfortable here."

"Oh yes, this will be fine," I said, and then added, "Is this okay with you, Stephanie?"

"Yes, fine," Stephanie said, stressing the second word. Her mother took the hint and left the room.

"Tell me Stephanie, do you have any other sisters and brothers?"

"Nope. It was just Maggie and me."

I was wondering whether I was on some sort of loss-event wavelength. I sometimes go through periods when life seems to dish out instructive experiences that make me feel like I'm taking a course. I've come to think of these episodes in life as "doing a unit." This summer, I decided as I settled in next to Stephanie, I've been doing a unit on untimely death.

"I can't imagine how I'd feel if I lost one of my sisters," I said. "You must miss her a lot."

"I do. It's been hard to get used to. I felt really scared for awhile, and I had more trouble sleeping than ever before. I didn't want to be away from home. I was afraid something would happen to my mom or my dad."

"When we lose someone, especially suddenly, it can make everyone feel insecure and anxious."

"I know my mom and dad feel nervous about me, too. Dad especially." The picture was becoming clear. The sudden death of Maggie had provoked sleep disorders in her sister and hyper-vigilance in the parents. Most likely, it also contributed to the heavy drinking that so often fuels domestic abuse. To make matters worse for Stephanie, the therapist who'd been treating her also died suddenly. I sighed. This was quite a burden for a child, and for a family. You could have all the money in the world and it wouldn't help with this kind of suffering.

But, money could allow you to hire someone to befriend and instruct your surviving child, and so, feeling more purposeful than I had at the outset, I got on with it.

Chapter 13

Concentrating on the early history of dreaming, I was pleased to realize that Stephanie was easy to engage. And she was astute for a twelve-year-old, or at least I thought so. When I described a theory that Stone Age cave paintings could be accounts of dreams, Stephanie grasped that this could only be speculation. She understood that by "history," we were discussing "those things we know about because written records of them survive."

So I began with the oldest recorded accounts of dream interpretation, from Egypt and Mesopotamia, where dreams were important in public affairs as well as daily life. Dream consultants — friends, priests, even gods — were often enlisted to decipher a dream's meaning. This was the case with Gilgamesh, the Sumerian king whose four-thousand-year-old story is considered the earliest epic in western literature. Gilgamesh reported two puzzling dreams to his mother, a "wise god," who correctly predicted that her son would soon meet his match and best friend, the mighty Enkidu.

"Most dream interpreters were women there," I told Stephanie as an aside.

"Good," she said, making me smile.

"All ancient cultures had professional dream interpreters. And dream books were popular too — guides to decode a dream's meaning. Here's a picture of an Egyptian dream papyrus from an archeology magazine."

Stephanie looked this over as I explained *The Egyptian Book of the Dead*. "What we call the soul the Egyptians called the Ba. It was depicted as a bird with a human head, and it could travel between this world and the next. *The Book of the Dead* was buried with mummies. It was meant to serve as a guide for the dead to make their way in the next world. But *The Book of the Dead* was also found in temples, and it included advice and information about dreams — prayers to ward off nightmares and instructions that explained how, for example, to be healed in a dream."

"Like the Greeks!" Stephanie observed. "Mom told me about that."

"Actually, lots of ancient cultures practiced dream incubation, which means sleeping in a sacred place in order to have dreams that will guide you or cure you. It's still a popular practice in many parts of the world."

"Could I do it?" asked Stephanie. "Would I have to sleep in a church?"

"The answer is yes you can, and not really. Anyone can ask their dreams for help, or inspiration, or information. The hard part, once you've asked for the help and had a dream, is figuring out what to make of it. What will turn out to be true, and what not? It's been four thousand years since this papyrus was made, but dream books are still popular. Everybody wants to know what their dreams mean. This papyrus says that a dream of drinking warm beer indicates misfortune on the way. What do you think?"

"I think you need a god to help you have the dream in the first place, and then you need a god to figure it out," Stephanie observed, and I laughed out loud.

"The Greeks were stymied too, you know. Are you familiar with *The Odyssey*?"

"On TV — does that count?"

"Sure — you know the story then. And you know who Homer is?"

"The man who wrote it."

"Well, told it anyway. It didn't get written down for a long while. But Homer talks of a dream as a human form that comes to us in sleep. The Greeks believed that there's a realm of 'dream people' who live beyond the earth, on the other side of Oceanus."

"The river that runs all around the world," Stephanie added.

"Yes, right!" I said. This kid really did know her Greek mythology. "Well, the realm of the dream people adjoins the one that's occupied by the souls of the dead. Some dreams are those souls, and some are dream people. Sometimes a god would send one from the Palace of Dreams. It would go to a dreamer, stand at his sleeping head and make a statement that the dreamer would remember. But, there was a catch. A dream left the Palace of Dreams through one of two gates. One was the Gate of Horn, and if your dream came through this gate, it was true. But it might have left by way of the Gate of Ivory, and if that's the case, it was a false dream."

"How's the dreamer supposed to know which one is which?" Stephanie wondered.

I leaned over and said confidentially, "I wish I knew."

We proceeded to the Bible and the Old Testament stories, of Jacob dreaming of the ladder to God, of Daniel's interpreting the dream of the king in Babylon, and of Joseph's interpreting the dream of the Pharaoh in Egypt. And in the New Testament, I explained, it is through dreams that angels advise Joseph to take Mary as his wife, and then tell him to flee with her and the infant Jesus into Egypt, and then tell him to return to Judea, and then tell him to take the family to Galilee.

"Wow, he really got ordered around, didn't he?" Stephanie observed.

"Hmm, I'd say 'guided' is the better word." I paused. "What's interesting is that dreams are a way for humans to hear from God." I was wondering whether to go into explaining that dreams are often very important during the formation of a religion. In the Old Testament, there are thirteen dreams in Genesis alone, but few are mentioned after Moses is given the Ten Commandments. In the New Testament, dream guidance saves Jesus, but as the early church developed, dreams were declared suspicious, even dangerous, by the clergy. Some dreamers of divine revelation were enshrined in history, but others were burned at the stake. But I decided this particular line of thought was too political for the occasion.

Just then, a low rumble began which I identified as a garage door going up, then down. Stephanie, who had been studying a medieval illustration of the "Flight into Egypt" in my book of Bible history, looked at me through her smudged glasses and said, "Dad."

I continued, "You know, you can find both the Bible and *The Odyssey* on the Internet. It might be fun sometime to do a word search and find all the sections where dreams are mentioned."

We were interrupted when a door into the kitchen opened. I heard Cliff Morgan before I saw him.

"Who the hell's in the driveway?" he called out irritably. "Karen?"

Stephanie rolled her eyes toward the ceiling. Karen's voice floated toward us, "Hold on, I'll be right there."

Stephanie sighed, walked toward the kitchen and said, "Why don't you come see, Dad," in a tone of exhausted patience.

Cliff stepped in the doorway, laid a hand on his daughter's head and said gently, "Hey Steph. Where's your mother?"

Just then, Karen appeared. "You're home early. Didn't you work out at the club?"

"My elbow is still bothering me. What's going on?"

"Stephanie's meeting with her tutor. I mentioned this to you, don't you remember?" She gestured to me. "Willa, this is Cliff, Stephanie's daddy. Honey, this is Willa Nilsson."

"We meet again," I said, smiling and waving from the sofa, but he looked puzzled. "At the coffee shop, remember?"

"Oh, that's right – and thank you for returning my phone!" said Karen.

As if on cue, a cell phone beeped and Cliff retreated to the kitchen to answer it, with Karen following. The kitchen door swung shut and Stephanie returned to the sofa and flopped down.

"Why is she parked in the driveway?" Cliff's voice penetrated the closed door. The accent was on the "why," as if this demanded an explanation. "You're supposed to tell the help not to park there."

"I'm sorry, I should have asked her to park on the road." I suddenly realized that he wasn't on the phone now — he was talking to Karen, about me, or rather, about my poor, decrepit car. Karen was speaking in a low voice, but I was listening closely now. "I didn't realize you'd be home so early, Cliff."

"It shouldn't matter when you <u>expect</u> me," he said. Stephanie and I regarded one another as we listened to glasses being filled with ice and something being poured.

Stephanie muttered a word to herself which I overheard: "Drinky-poos."

I thought about how to get back to business with Stephanie. I checked my watch, saw that our hour had ended a few minutes ago and then Karen came into the room.

"So, how'd it go you two?"

"It was good," said Stephanie, sounding surprisingly positive.

"Good then! Stephanie, I need to talk to Dr. Nilsson for a minute, okay?"

Stephanie turned to me. "I'm going to try that word search right now." One side of her mouth was definitely curved upward in a smile.

"Great. I'll see you next time then."

When Karen and I were alone, she handed me a stack of twenty dollar bills, fresh from the ATM. "There's $160 there. I hope you don't mind cash."

Mind? Hell no, I thought. For this kind of money, I wouldn't mind being called "the help" either. "That's fine," I said, slipping the cash into my bag.

Karen paused. "I want to apologize for Cliff just now. He's kind of a control freak, especially when new things surprise him. And he's been in a bad mood recently."

Karen had no idea that I'd already heard about Cliff's "bad moods." But for $160 an hour, I'd try the high road. "I'll be glad to park in the street," I offered.

"I guess that's best. You know, ordinarily, he wouldn't even have seen you here." She was holding two fingers to her lips, then shifted her hand to hold her cheek. "Frankly, the less he knows about household stuff, the better. He's such a fusspot, y'know?"

I didn't answer because I couldn't think what to say. Karen forged ahead. "He doesn't like it when people come to work at the house. He feels like they're getting into his stuff. If he had things his way, we'd be sealed in here alone with him."

I couldn't contain myself any longer. "But then," I said, "would he do floors?"

Karen's laugh popped out like a surprise. "No, of course not! I'd be here cleaning and cooking full time!" We were lapsing into girl talk, lighthearted but candid. "You know," she continued, hand to chest, as if speaking from the heart, "the only reason he agreed to pay for grad school for me is because writers work at home. That's really his objective. Everybody home on the range." Her glance traveled to the corners of the room, and she shook her head. "He was always like this, but it got worse after Maggie died. After that, though, as anxious as he was to keep us all safe at home, I was just as desperate to get out."

As I drove home, I thought about the phrase, "the help." If it was supposed to be an insult, it was an ineffectual one to pitch at Willa the

Troublemaker. I'd grown up in a household that included help, African-American women who lived in distant mill towns or inner city neighborhoods and rode buses a long way to work and back. Even though they had families of their own, these women were kind to me and my sisters, and we felt a deep attachment to them. As small children, that was easy, but as we grew older and learned about bigotry in the wider world, we were horrified, and ashamed.

So, I decided that I approved of being called "the help." It could serve as a tribute to the women I'd loved as a child, and to the general principle of the work I'd undertaken, to help Stephanie to understand herself better through her dreams. Cliff Morgan's put-down would be my inspiration.

Chapter 14

I came into my house as the phone was ringing. It was Leo, calling from work.

"I'm leaving shortly. If you haven't picked up anything for dinner, let's go out."

"Okay, but nothing trendy. I've got to watch my budget." I was careful to maintain the boundaries of our divorced status. I spent my money and Leo spent his, but he had lots more of it. He's an information specialist, a computer know-it-all whose job was paying better than ever. Before our marriage fell apart, as both of us found success in our professions, we'd enjoyed increasing ease. The divorce had taken us both down a few pegs, but Leo continued to enjoy salary increases. I'd got the house, which was expensive to maintain, but the budget constraints of recent years were nothing compared to my present circumstances.

"How about Indian?" I proposed.

"Sounds good to me. I'll pick up some wine. Red or white?"

"Surprise me."

We drove to Atwood Street in Oakland, one of the many streets near the University of Pittsburgh that are crammed with shabby dwellings that landlords seem never to improve. There is so much demand for apartments from students that it is a perpetual seller's market. To make matters more crowded and complicated, Atwood features a number of restaurants within two blocks, most with terrific ethnic food at reasonable prices.

The Star Garden was aromatic with spices and the lingering fog of dishes served smoking from the tandoori.

"Lord, I am starved," I announced, unfolding my napkin. "Let's throw caution to the winds. Let's have a nice, high fat korma and a couple of breads with lots of carbohydrates!"

"Easy girl," said Leo, as he pulled a green bottle out of its brown paper bag and placed it on the table.

"What is this?" I said, reading the label. "Is this — French?"

"Well, I discovered some specials in the vintage section."

"Well, yum!" I said, then eyed him quizzically. "But why? Are you up to something?"

"No, it was just my turn to bring the wine and I decided to get something nice."

"Good!" I said, exhaling relief and fanning myself. "For a minute there I was afraid you were going to talk about getting married again." I wiped the moisture off the label and read the text aloud in my best French. "Mind you, I would drink this in any event, but I don't want to go there, do you?"

Leo shook his head. "I don't want to go there, either."

"Good," I nodded definitely, but felt more ambivalent than I sounded.

"But I do have a proposition," Leo announced.

"Goody!"

"Not that kind of proposition. Not yet anyway."

An efficient Sikh waiter had arrived with glasses and a corkscrew and was noisily prying the cork out of the bottle. Leo and I stopped talking as he poured the wine.

I sipped. It was rich, cool and buttery. It was expensive, I knew. I sipped again and decided to enjoy this extravagance.

"All right, you've got me where you want me. This is the best wine I've had in a long time," I said. "What's your proposition?"

"Well, it's about my apartment. You know my lease is up in a couple of months." Since the demise of his brief second marriage, Leo had been living in a two bedroom apartment in a restored old manse in Shadyside. It was a nice place with high ceilings and a marble fireplace, on a tree-lined street, but he hadn't spent much time there recently.

I thought I saw where this was going and opened my mouth to speak, but Leo raised his hand in a gesture of "hold on."

"I want to reassure you that this is a monetary proposition. I wonder if you would consider taking on a tenant."

I closed my mouth, opened it to speak, and closed it again. Finally I said, "You want to move in, right?"

"I want," he said, looking above my head for just the right words, "to offer you the benefit of becoming a lessor to a solvent lessee."

"You'd pay me to live in our house with me."

"I'm paying rent now on a place where I haven't laid my head for weeks."

This was true. I screwed up my face, thinking hard. "But you can always go back to your apartment if you want to."

"I never seem to want to, do I?"

"Or if I...need some space."

"Well, that'll be the part you'll have to think about. A tenant is definitely going to be in your space."

I burst out laughing. "Tenant, my ass! You're trying to move back in with me!"

Leo smiled and observed, "I've already all but moved back in with you. But this is a business arrangement. You own the house, I'm offering to pay rent. Think it over."

I took another sip of wine and snuffled into the glass, giggling. This was all so silly, and yet — well, I really, really did need income. And I had become very comfortable with Leo in my life, and in my bed. But so far this had just been a rather luxurious interlude — happy sex with someone who knows exactly what I like, a man around the house who's willing and able to repair dripping faucets, set mousetraps und use a plunger. After years of struggling to care for a house by myself, this was no small consideration.

But I'd decided firmly as our marriage dissolved that I never wanted to have a husband again. A lover now and then would be fine, but after Rob I'd been very leery of investing my heart and soul with a man. Maybe a tenant would be okay, but this wouldn't be just a tenant or just a lover. It would be — returning to cohabiting with my ex-husband. I shook my head.

"Leo, this strikes me as a bad idea."

"I'm not asking you to make up your mind right away. You think about it for awhile. Consider all the aspects. We've been getting along as well as we ever have. We know how to stay out of each other's way. And frankly, my dear," he raised an eyebrow, "you need the money."

He was right about that. My last paycheck from Grenville would arrive soon — my contract ran through August. I expected to resort to savings to fill the gap until I'd built up enough income from new sources, but I was uncertain how soon — or whether — I could attain the same income level. I was already trying to cut costs — cheap haircuts, repairing my eleven-year-old car instead of shopping for a new one, canceling my cell phone. I struggled mightily not to let anxiety about the future dominate my thoughts, but it was becoming a bigger struggle with every week. There was still the possibility of consulting at the Sleep Clinic, but did I really want to work alongside Frank and Janet? I felt my mind slide away from the prospect.

"Plus," Leo was adding, "you get a live-in handyman."

Well, that was true. I was reminded of the etymology of "husband," from the German *hus*, meaning house, and *bondi*, to dwell. The word which now refers primarily to a man joined to a women in marriage used also to mean "steward" and "house-keeper" — one who dwelt in and managed a household. I smiled at the irony — here was Leo, my ex-husband, with a plan to share in the keeping of my house and help me to conserve my resources. He was being more supportive now, more of a husband, than he had been during the last five years of our marriage.

"I will. Think about it, I mean," I said. "There are a lot of things I need to mull over." Like, what if I met someone I wanted to date? What if Leo did? And I'd have to make room for his stuff, although most of it used to occupy the house anyway. I'd have to empty out the middle bedroom. Is that what he'd prefer?

"You'd take the middle bedroom, I imagine. It's bigger."

"That'd be fine. But I'd still like to sleep with the landlady."

I laughed. "We wouldn't put that in the lease, though, would we? Otherwise this might seem like another sort of contract altogether."

"Probably not legal in Pennsylvania," Leo allowed, grinning.

I took my last sip, draining my glass. "And way too much like marriage," I said.

The house in question is a three bedroom brick of no particular character, but beloved because of its location. Carnegie Place is a block-long, one-way residential street that empties out at Frick Park on Reynolds Street. This verdant and quiet corner features a bowling green and beyond it, acres of forest laced with walking paths. Residents of the few streets that border this section seldom sell their houses, and Leo and I had felt lucky to find one just a few doors away. We both loved the park in all seasons, and walking in it was our favorite exercise.

The neighborhood is also rich with history. Andrew Carnegie himself had owned the land that became Carnegie Place and Frick Park was the bequest of Henry Clay Frick, long demonized among generations of Pittsburghers as the man who ordered hired Pinkertons to attack striking laborers at the Carnegie Steel Company. Historians estimate that the bloodshed at the Homestead Strike effectively suppressed the labor movement in the U.S. for more than a generation.

Eventually, both Carnegie and Frick retired to mansions in New York City, but Pittsburgh is where they started and their legacies are evident throughout the area. Unfortunately, the two men did not remain on good terms. In fact, at the end of their lives, when the conciliatory Carnegie proposed a meeting, Frick's response was reported to be, "I'll see you in hell, where we are both most certainly going."

When Leo and I first moved into our home, Frick's aged daughter still lived at Clayton, a moldering mansion two blocks away. She died soon after, leaving an endowment for the place to be restored, and now tour buses regularly puff up Reynolds Street to show visitors how life was lived by the well-to-do in the late 19th century. At Clayton, the Homestead Strike is referred to as "the Homestead riots," and visitors to the gift shop can buy a glowing biography of Frick, written by his daughter. History has been so carefully edited at Clayton that even the tobacco stains have been removed from the room where Frick smoked cigars and played poker with George Westinghouse, Andrew Mellon and other captains of industry.

I'm the granddaughter of a Swedish immigrant who worked at the Homestead steel mill. He arrived long after the strike, but everyone who worked or lived in the area reviled the very name of Henry Clay Frick for many decades. Now, more than a century later, Frick is far more famous for his art collection — and even locally, for his house — than for his corporate ruthlessness.

On my walks, I would sometimes wonder if anyone trying to get to Carnegie Hall gave a thought to the immigrants whose suffering made its construction possible? Thus is exploitation transmuted into gold in America. Or, in my case, into higher real estate values as neighboring Clayton became a cultural attraction, complete with café, art museum and antique car collection.

But in truth, my feelings about my house were more sentimental than financial. I felt connected to nature by virtue of the park, awakened in the morning by birdsong and sometimes, on very quiet nights, lulled to sleep by the call of owls. And the house also connected me to the dream of family that Leo and I had shared when we bought the house, shortly before our daughter was born.

Together and individually, Leo and I fell into the deep love trance that overcomes all new parents. We never tired of gazing upon Amanda when she was awake and when she slept; when she nursed and when she burped; when she smiled and when she scowled. She was a beautiful baby, with fine brown hair and slate blue eyes, and we lavished her with devoted attention.

Those first months, in spite of the demands of a newborn, were the best we would ever have with Amanda. Her development seemed perfectly normal at first, but by the time she was seven months old, Leo and I suspected something was wrong, and by her first birthday, we were sure. It took an agonizingly long time to pin down an accurate diagnosis. Her pediatrician noted that Amanda's head was no longer growing normally, and ordered neurological tests. The results showed that her development had slowed, but precisely what the cause was continued to baffle the experts we consulted for many months. Some of her symptoms indicated cerebral palsy, some autism, and others mental retardation. Finally, a specialist recognized that she was suffering from another "pervasive developmental disorder" called Rett Syndrome. That it was rare, and affected only females, was of no comfort to Leo or me. That it was genetic frightened us out of ever having another child.

Although her physical impairments were severe — for Amanda, just walking and moving about were ordeals of coordination — for us, her social deficits were far more painful. Although we could interest Amanda in interacting with us when she was a baby, she gradually lost interest in us, and in her environment. The clinical descriptions — "the progressive and persistent loss of mental and motor skills" — didn't begin to suggest the heartbreak of not being able to share a bedtime story with a child with severely impaired language development, or worse, having your own daughter regard you without interest or enthusiasm.

Rett Syndrome is not usually life threatening, but when she was three, Amanda suffered a severe seizure that sent her into a coma. She never woke up. At her funeral, Leo and I and our family and friends wept and hugged as we held one another's hands, mourning the child I felt we had lost not once, but twice.

The vivid dream that Leo had a few weeks later had galvanized my commitment to dream study. In his dream, Leo had gone into Amanda's room to check on her. When he came to the edge of her crib, Amanda opened her eyes and smiled. Then she reached up, put her arms around his neck and hugged him — something she had never been able to do. Then she had whispered, "I'm fine now."

Leo, who had suffered more stoically than I had, who didn't even know about how often grieving people are reunited with departed loved ones in dreams and who wouldn't have believed it if he had, was transformed by this dream. It had possessed a quality of super-reality, so clear that it seemed undeniably true. That Amanda had spoken words she could never have spoken, and embraced him as she was unable to in life, didn't weigh against the experience — instead they left him with an even stronger conviction that this had been a real visit. "It was more like a vision than a dream," he would say, as if a vision was a more convincing phenomenon than a dream.

I was more compelled by Leo's reaction than if I'd had the dream myself, and silently thanked Amanda, or the gods, or whatever power makes such things possible. For my part, I reacquainted myself with the 19th century transcendentalists — Emerson, Thoreau — who believed that each of us is part of an over-soul which manifests in many forms and lifetimes. I comforted myself with the notion, which gradually became a conviction, that Amanda had come into this life to experience its challenges, and had completed her objective in just a few years.

That night, in spite of the wine, I felt restless as I climbed into bed next to Leo. I realized I'd forgotten to tell him about my afternoon at the Morgan's and said, "Hey I meant to tell you..."

"Hmmph?" said Leo.

"Never mind. I'll tell you tomorrow."

"Um-hmmph."

Falling asleep is as easy for Leo as falling off a log, and then he sleeps like one. I, on the other hand, have to follow a distinct protocol.

Always, I have to read something. Sometime between Nancy Drew books and undergraduate texts, reading myself to sleep became a necessity rather than an option. My brain didn't seem to know how to shut down until lines of text transformed themselves into caravans moving across my field of vision and off the page.

I lay in bed with the new issue of the IASD journal in front of my face, but I wasn't reading it. I was thinking, about Leo and our history. When our marriage was breaking up, I would wonder whether caring for children would have changed the outcome. I'd seen how other marriages crashed, or bumped along, among my sisters. All of them had children — my nephews and nieces — whom I loved perhaps more dearly than I might have if Leo and I had children of our own to distract us.

If we'd needed to, would Leo and I have stayed together for the sake of the kids? Or would the stresses of raising a family have magnified our problems? It was impossible to say. I mused over my sisters' sons and daughters, who loved their Uncle Leo as much as they did me; one of the hardest aspects of divorcing had been the extended family's disappointment that we were breaking up. I realized that a number of people would be very glad if Leo moved back in with me, and decided not to consult with that camp until I had given the idea a lot more thought.

Chapter 15

I had been looking forward to meeting with the dream crew again, but when I arrived at the Latte Lenya coffee house, and turned into the back room where we always sit, I came to a complete stop. There at our customary table were Joe, and Trudy, and Maxine — and no Bonnie.

"C'mon in. Misery loves company," said Max, red-eyed and sniffling into a tissue.

I came to the table, took my customary seat and let out a long sigh.

"I should have seen this coming," I said to no one in particular. "What a hole she's left!"

Joe was staring hard into his espresso cup as Trudy rubbed Maxie between her shoulder blades.

"In grief counseling," Trudy offered, "we call this an 'aftershock.' A sudden and unexpected reminder that someone's gone. It's part of the process."

"Aftershock is a good name for it," said Joe, clearing his throat.

Trudy sat back and observed, "Social work jargon — sometimes it's actually meaningful!"

"I was *so* looking forward to seeing you all again. Really, I mean it," Max insisted in a mournful tone, and then smiled. "No matter how I'm behaving!"

This made me smile, and I nodded. "In this instance, *meeting* is such sweet sorrow, isn't it?"

"Or in my case, dreaming is," said Joe. "I want to read you one I had shortly before you and Bonnie went to the conference."

He adjusted his wire rimmed glasses and opened his journal. Joe typed his dreams in a word processor, then ran off hard copies that he kept in a three-ring binder. No two of the group members kept their records in just the same way, but all of us are interested in reviewing past dreams. We're often rewarded with unexpected links to events that later come to pass.

He cleared his throat again, trying to override the emotion in his voice. His first words wobbled with feeling, but then he read calmly and evenly.

"I discover that a crow has flown into the living room. I think it must have come down the chimney. I go to the window to open it, so the crow can fly out, but before I can turn the crank, a duck comes flying at the window and hits it. I see it lying on the ground and realize that its neck is broken." Joe looked up. "I woke up from this with a start. It had the feel of a nightmare."

Trudy said, "You dreamt of a bird with a broken neck just before Bonnie died of a broken neck?"

"Looks that way," said Joe.

"Whoa," said Max.

"Would you call that prodromal?" said Trudy.

"Do you mean precognitive?" asked Max. "Looks like it to me!"

"Hold on," I said. "First we ought to have this dream. Okay Joe?"

"Yes, please."

We asked Joe questions: Was it night or day in the dream? (Day.) What was the weather like? (Overcast and windy.) In the dream did he fear that the duck would break the window? (No, and anyway it wasn't that big.) Where was the crow while you were watching the duck? (I don't know.)

After we had as complete a picture of the dream as Joe could give us, we offered our feedback.

"If this were my dream," Max said wide-eyed, "I'd be scared, because my Grandma Bess, the one from Kentucky who knew all that mountain superstition — or folklore, maybe you'd call it — used to say that a bird in the house meant someone was going to die."

"That's funny," said Joe, "because after I wrote this down, I remembered how, in the movie *Resurrection*, the main character talks about how crows foretell a death."

Max shivered. "All the more reason to feel spooked!"

"Let me ask you two," I nodded to Trudy and Max, "has Bonnie been in any of your dreams since Hawaii?"

"Not yet," said Trudy. "Not that I remember."

Max said, "Me neither. Have you?"

I told them about my O.J. Simpson dream, and the synchronicity that followed it, of being asked for advice for an abused woman. Then I checked myself, careful not to reveal any names, recalling that both Trudy and Joe had met Karen.

"But I'm diverting us from Joe's dream," I interrupted myself. "And I should concentrate on the content before I start speculating on the context." Dropping a fist on the table like a gavel, I insisted, "Let's get down to business and have this dream."

Maxine volunteered, "If this were my dream, I'd feel helpless, because I couldn't let the crow out, or do anything about the — dead duck!" We all laughed at the surprise of this pun before Max added, "And, I think I'd feel guilty that my window was responsible for the duck's demise."

"Me too, I think," said Trudy. "If this were my dream, it would remind me of what happened when my neighbors put up a bird feeder. Birds came in droves to eat, but sometimes we'd hear a thud and find that a bird had flown into our picture window." She continued thoughtfully, "That was when we lived at our old house, so I guess if I had had this dream, I'd wonder what might be going on in my life now that reminds me of that situation."

"Committing involuntary bird-slaughter?" Max said, and all four of us broke up. It felt so good to laugh that we all took our time doing it. It was reassuring, healing even, to know that we could still have fun.

"No," Trudy protested when she could talk, "I mean, I'd look to see if the feelings I had then — not just about the bird dilemma, but about that time in my life — might match something going on in the present." She started giggling again and wiped at a tear. "That's all."

"Okay," I said, pulling myself together. "If this were my dream...well first, there are a lot of crows in the park near my house. They're big and noisy and kind of icky, so if one came into my house in real life, I'd be grossed out. However," I paused, because really, really imagining what you would make of a dream can be mind-bending work, "on a symbolic level, I have better feelings about crows. In Nordic mythology — and you know, Trudy and I are part Swede — crows are magical. The king of the gods travels with a crow on each shoulder, and they fly around and tell him what's going on all over the world. That's supposed to be the source of his great wisdom. So, maybe I'd play with that idea if a crow turned up in a dream, and especially in my house. Maybe some kind of wisdom is visiting me. Natural wisdom, maybe, because it comes from an animal."

Joe was nodding and jotting notes "Max, your grandmother's belief about the bird in the house makes me think of how birds are often symbols of the soul," he said.

"I was just telling someone about the Egyptians' idea of the ba, the bird-soul," I added. "Coincidentally."

Joe went on. "And Trudy, your remark touched on something that I hadn't really described when I wrote the dream down. I did feel — well, not responsible for the duck, really, but I felt — resentful, or offended. Because this seemed unnecessary, preventable."

"Did you feel you were to blame?" Trudy asked.

"No, not at all — it was like, whoever was in charge was to blame." He half-smiled. "Whoever that is."

"The air traffic controller of ducks?" Max blurted, and another spasm of laughter overtook us.

"This is serious!" Trudy protested helplessly.

"I know!" I agreed, and laughed some more.

Finally, Trudy got a grip on herself and said, "You know, it's because this is so significant that we're having this reaction."

"Okay, okay," Max agreed. "But it's got to come out somehow and you gotta admit that laughing is more fun that bawling."

"Joe, did you do anything to 'honor' this dream?" Trudy asked. One practice we all enjoy is thinking up ways to bring a strong dream into waking experience. It's our way of acknowledging the power of dreams.

"Well, of course I made a note of the synchronicity, and then I taped the clipping of Bonnie's obituary into my journal," Joe answered. "Frankly, although it really did feel like a 'big dream,' it wasn't one I wanted to dwell on."

"Certainly you wouldn't want to, say, order duck at a restaurant or something, would you?" said Max.

"Maxie, you are so bad!" Trudy pretended to slap Maxine's hand, but she was laughing again.

"Joe, would you say this was a prodromal dream?" I asked.

"What's that?" Max asked.

Joe explained, "That's a dream that foretells a physical injury or ailment. It goes back to Hippocrates and Aristotle, but there are plenty of modern accounts of dreams that foretold bone fractures, miscarriages, heart attacks, even the locations of tumors, before they occurred or were diagnosed."

"But Joe, you didn't dream of something wrong with your own body," Trudy observed.

"I have read of cases where, for example, a spouse dreams of a partner's as-yet-undiagnosed illness. But you're right — I'm not sure that's considered prodromal."

"So the idea is that the body knows what's going on with itself before the symptoms turn up?" Max asked.

"Well, that's what Hippocrates thought. To my mind, it's a fine line between prodromal and precognitive," I offered.

"A lot of people suggest that prodromal dreaming is caused by something that already exists but is hidden," Joe weighed in. "Therefore, there's a cause and effect explanation, unlike precognitive dreaming." Then he grinned devilishly under his beard and speculated. "But maybe the future also exists, but is hidden."

Max said, "Oh, you mean like that stuff you told us about? With the unfolding implications or something? That made my head spin!"

"I thought it was cool," said Trudy. "Boggling, but cool. Explain it again, would you?"

Joe obliged. "The physicist David Bohm proposed that there is an explicate order — the physical world we experience through our senses — and an implicate order. The first, although very obvious to us, is a kind of illusion, like a hologram. Underneath all this" — Joe gestured around the room — "lies a deeper order, enfolded within. He called that the implicate order."

"May the force be with you!" Max barked.

Joe raised an eyebrow and nodded. "Change that to 'May the source be with you' and you're pretty close. Bohm thought that the implicate and explicate were constantly interacting, the one unfolding itself into the other. And he applied the idea to precognitive dreams too. Take, for example, the guy who booked passage on the Titanic and then dreamed of being on a sinking ship and decided not to go. Bohm said that the dreamer hadn't 'seen the future' — he actually changed the future by not going on the trip and drowning. Bohm speculated that there was an anticipation of the future in the implicate order. It's like what the Hawaiian kahunas say about the future — that it's 'crystallizing.'"

"Good grief!" I suddenly sat up very straight. "I wonder if Bonnie dreamt anything about what happened to her?"

Everyone seemed to go still, taking a moment to wonder at such an idea. Then Max said with a note of sadness, "I guess we'll never know,"

Trudy was looking at me. "What about her journal?"

I began nodding emphatically, as if to convince them and myself. "I have it!"

"She gave it to you?" said Trudy.

"No, no — Frank and the kids — they asked me to be, like, the conservator. In case there's ever an archive, or some research..."

"Wow, that's heavy," said Joe. There was a long pause while we all considered the implications of reading Bonnie's last dreams.

"This could be <u>really</u> interesting," said Max

"And it might be really <u>sad</u>," said Trudy.

"I'd feel like — I'd be violating her privacy," I said. "I hadn't really considered reading her dream journals, just saving them. God, I'm going to have to think about this." Trudy, ever perceptive, picked up on my discomfort and obligingly changed the subject.

"You know, there was something in Joe's dream that none of us mentioned. What about the chimney?"

"Well," Max said, "a chimney is for smoke to get out of a house, but in the dream, it's the way something comes into the house. If this were my dream, I'd think that was wrong, like the wrong way, something out of kilter."

Trudy mused, "A chimney makes me think of the hearth, the heart of a home — the source of heat and light. Since in my dreams a house often represents me, the self, I'd think about those connections. So, Joe, what did you think of the chimney?"

"Well, after all this conversation, I think I see it as a dark place, hidden from sight, and therefore corresponding to — the implicate order!" He grinned at his own cleverness. "And out of this flew a symbol of the future, of a death, which was to become explicate."

"Definitely precognitive," Max said.

"Definitely," said Trudy.

Joe turned to me. "Did you have any thoughts about the chimney?"

I was holding my head in my hands, elbows on the table. I lowered my face and into my hands and then looked up again. "I'm having thoughts about Bonnie's dream journal. Maybe I <u>had</u> better have a look." I could hear the doubt in my voice.

After a thoughtful pause, Joe volunteered, "Well, I can tell you that if it were me, if you had my dream records in circumstances like these, I would want you to look."

"Y'know, so would I," said Max. "Because there might be something significant there, for her family, or for any of us who are missing her." She reached out a freckled hand and patted my arm. "Plus," she added, "I trust you."

"So do I," said Trudy. "I'm sure Bonnie felt the same way."

"So, you have our support," said Joe.

"Thanks," I said weakly. Then I blew out a long sigh and nodded. "Okay," I said. "I'll do it."

Chapter 16

I left the coffee house with a feeling of both vigilance and dread, which quieted when I pulled into my driveway and discovered that Leo was home. I walked into the kitchen and found him putting away groceries.

"You shopped! Leo, thank goodness. We were out of everything!"

"Yes, well, if one wants to eat, one must acquire foodstuffs." He said this without a hint of sarcasm. When we were married, during the bad times, his buying groceries was usually accompanied by wisecracks implying that I was falling down on the job.

"What does it mean when blue cheese has grown green mold?" he asked, peering inside a carton of crumbled gorgonzola.

"I'm developing a new antibiotic," I winked as I took the carton from him. "I'll just move this to the lab." I pressed the foot pedal on the waste can and dropped the carton into it.

"Look here…" Leo enthused as he extracted a package of something wrapped in white butcher paper from a grocery bag. "Guess what's coming for dinner?"

I read the printed label. "Tuna steaks. Leo, what a treat!" I love fish; Leo avoids it. "What's got into you?"

"Omega-3 fatty oils, after I grill these babies. And," he noted proudly, "they were on special."

"My god," I was thinking, "the guy went shopping, he's not complaining about it, he bought fish for dinner and now he's actually bothering about cholesterol?" I impulsively put an arm around his waist and squeezed. "Thank you!" I said, with the accent on "thank," not because I appreciated having seafood for dinner, but because I was touched that he was trying so hard.

"And, I have another surprise," Leo continued. "Frank is joining us for dinner. I called about a golf date and talked him into coming."

"Good for you!" I said. "How'd he sound?"

"Okay I guess. He seemed glad to hear from me."

I nodded, then turned on the water and started rinsing a head of romaine. "I hope his drinking is under control," I said under my breath. Leo didn't hear me.

Frank seemed subdued when he arrived, so that if he had been drinking, it wasn't obvious. My fears abated as he and Leo watched a golf tournament on TV, chatting quietly and eating peanuts while I puttered in the kitchen. I hesitated to set out wine glasses, but then decided that hospitality trumped anxiety.

It wasn't until we were enjoying Leo's excellent tuna steak teriyaki that I got a good look at Frank. He appeared sallow and drawn and I reached over and patted his hand.

"How's it going for you, Frank?"

He shrugged. "No worse, no better."

"You look tired. Haven't you been sleeping well?"

Leo said, "You of all people should be able to treat that!" I shot him a look.

Frank grimaced and drummed his fingers on the table. "It ought to be simple, then, huh? I wish!" His smile was not very convincing. Then he added, "There's just — a lot on my mind."

"How are the kids?" I asked.

"Oh, they're doing as well as could be expected," he said, and then snorted, "<u>Very</u> well, economically speaking." He set down his fork and pushed himself back in his seat. "It just burns me up."

"What's wrong?" said Leo.

"My goddam brother-in-law, Larry. He talked Bonnie into putting her money into a trust for the kids." He shook his head in disgust. "As if <u>I</u> wasn't to be trusted with it."

"Really?" said Leo. "Are we talking a lot of money? Enough to pay for college?"

"It was a lot more money than that," Frank glowered. "It's from her parents. Her father was a bond trader when that was really lucrative, and had an impressive portfolio when he died. Then her mother got it."

"So we're talking — a million?" said Leo, unable to stem his curiosity. I shot him another look, but he wasn't paying attention to my nonverbal cues.

"We're talking maybe twice that," Frank said. "I <u>suppose</u>," he added sarcastically. "Larry is the trustee, so I would have to <u>ask</u> to see the latest figures."

"And you didn't know about this until now?" Leo asked.

"Of course I knew about the money her mother left her. We had discussions about mutual funds and money market funds and index funds, all that stuff. But ah didn't know about this trust business, no," he said, his native drawl winning out over his northern diction.

"Do you have any idea why she would do this and not tell you?" I asked.

"No, ah don't!" Frank smacked the table with his hand, and Leo and I both jumped in our seats as the silverware rattled. I glanced at Frank's wine glass, fearing that he was losing to control of himself. But it was half full.

Leo was saying, "This has really upset you, hasn't it?"

"You're damn straight. It's infuriating."

"She must have had some reason to think this was best for the kids," I said in a voice that sounded calmer than I felt.

"Bull. This was all her brother's doing, trying to maintain control of the family money. He talked her into it, no doubt about it." Then he rested his elbows on the table and spoke with more composure. "You understand, it's not the money. It's the principle."

"Sure," said Leo. "I'd be pissed too."

I said nothing.

Heading back into the house after seeing Frank to his car, I closed the door and turned to Leo. "What do you think?

"You mean, his drinking? He seemed okay to me."

"But what about all that business about Bonnie's money?"

"Yeah, he's really sore about that."

"You know, Caitlin mentioned something about that to me, but I had no idea it was so much. I knew Bonnie's parents were well off, but we never talked about her finances." I paused, reluctant to revisit my earlier suspicions, but then said honestly, "Now I have to wonder whether in fact Bonnie <u>didn't</u> trust Frank."

Leo looked at me warily, "Are you going there again? Seems to me the guy had good reason to be upset. Doesn't mean he did in his wife."

I regarded Leo and wondered what he would score if he were tested for emotional intelligence. Below average, I suspected, at least this evening. "Don't forget that I did see him out with Janet."

"And you thought that was innocent, or so you said."

"You're right, that's what I said at the time. But Trudy didn't think so. And I'm wondering, what if there has been something going on with Frank and Janet? Maybe that's why Bonnie wanted to protect her money for her kids."

Leo was shaking his head, and waved his hand to brush off the idea. "You know Trudy. She's suspicious of everybody."

"No she's not! I mean, sometimes she's overly cautious..."

"Remember the peeping Tom?" Leo smirked. Trudy had called the police over what turned out to be a neighbor's cat.

"That could have happened to anybody!" I insisted.

"But it happened to Trudy," Leo replied with assurance.

I rolled my eyes and decided not to pursue this any further. I really didn't want to hear Leo hold forth on my sisters' shortcomings. Instead, I told him about my meeting with the dream crew, and the suggestion that I check Bonnie's dream journal.

"At first the idea felt like . . . trouble." I looked at Leo, and saw that he caught the word I used. I suspected he'd been tempted to use it himself a moment ago. "But then I thought maybe I should take a look, and so did the others," I continued. "What do you think?"

"Well, I guess I'd ask myself what Bonnie would do."

"Oh!" I felt surprised that this hadn't occurred to me already. I considered the idea as we carried plates and glasses to the kitchen. "Well, Bonnie would definitely look into this. She was dogged about dream research, and she would have seen this as an opportunity to learn something. And," I added, "Bonnie was fearless."

"Is that what's really bothering you? Fear?"

I thought about that. "Maybe."

"Of what?"

I tried to sort it out. "Well, maybe—no probably—there's fear of provoking more sadness. But deep down I think there's something more. In my gut. It's like — I shouldn't mess with it." I scraped a plate and set it down. "It's like — well you know, every culture has some kind of taboo about not disturbing the dead. I didn't realize it till just this second, but I think I feel..." I struggled to find the word.

"Creeped out?" Leo offered.

"A little. I guess the right word is, superstitious. Except that I'm not a superstitious person." Then I laughed. "Except apparently I am!"

"You know what I would do if I were you?" Leo had the serene look on his face that he got when he had solved something.

"What?'

"Sleep on it. Do one of those dream incubation things. Ask your dreams to help you." He said this as if this were the most obvious thing in the world.

"You are exactly right," I said, clapping him on the shoulder with sincere admiration. "Why didn't I think of that?!"

As bedtime approached, I began to wonder about how best to incubate my dream. I thought about it as I went upstairs, brushed my teeth and put on one of Leo's white cotton T-shirts. One of the assets of having him live here was a generous supply of what were, in my experience, the most comfortable sleepwear made. I turned the window fan on exhaust and created a breeze through the room. It was less muggy than it has been — we'd sleep comfortably tonight.

I settled into bed and opened my dream journal to a fresh page. Ordinarily, I would just write a few sentences about what I was incubating a dream for, but this time I thought about writing a note to Bonnie, asking for permission. I quickly nixed the idea — it brought on the creepy feeling. Instead, I decided to write a note to my dreams.

Dear Dreams

I need advice about how best to proceed. Please help me to decide about reading Bonnie's dream journal. I will remember my dreaming and write it down as soon as I awaken.

With thanks for any assistance you can provide,

Willa

Leo, back from his turn in the bathroom, began to climb into bed next to me. "All ready?" he said.

"As ready as I'm going to be. Do you think it's weird to think of sleep as a time to get things done?"

"Not for you," Leo said as he checked the alarm, plumped up his pillow and turned off his light. I leaned over and kissed him under his ear. With eyes already closed, he pursed his lips and sent a return kiss in my general direction. Thirty seconds later, he was snoring lightly.

I sat in bed, thinking about Bonnie, and the idea of writing a note to her. It wasn't just that the idea made me feel sad; it also seemed vaguely alarming. I thought about the famous Chief Seattle speech: "Be just and deal kindly with my people, for the dead are not powerless." But by the same token, funeral rituals around the world emphasize the separation between the dead and the living. In some cultures, there is a taboo against even speaking the name of the deceased, and personal belongings are destroyed to keep the dead from being tempted to sustain an attachment to earthly realms. In many parts of the world, the dead are thought to linger around familiar places for some time.

I only knew about these things because of my study of death and dying; my own American upbringing had included no beliefs about the dead at all. Yet, I recalled that as a child, in my heart I'd felt a sense of taboo when, after my grandmother died, I felt strange when I went to her home. I was in third grade and had very little preparation for this — good WASP families didn't dwell on unpleasant things, and especially not with children, even curious ones. But soon after the funeral, when I walked to the doorway of my grandmother's bedroom, I could smell her familiar scents and felt certain that my grandmother was not gone at all. She seemed as near as I was to her room, but I would not step into it. I didn't know why.

I turned off my light and settled down into bed, thinking that at age eight, I wasn't quite old enough yet to understand the finality of death. So what was it that I felt that day at the threshold of my grandmother's room? An innate need to separate from the dead? Perhaps, I thought drowsily, we're all born with this, like the fear of falling.

Then, remembering that I needed to reinforce my incubation request, I mentally repeated to myself, "I will remember my dreams and write them down. I'm asking for help from my dreams. I need guidance about reading Bonnie's dream journal." The mantra wasn't lulling me into sleep as it ordinarily would, however, so I propped myself up on one elbow and reached for my journal again. I turned on my special night-time pen, the one that sheds a dim blue light in the dark, and added a line to my note. "P.S. Nothing scary, please. Thanks." Then I rolled over and quickly fell asleep.

I sit across from my grandmother. We're at a small table by the window in her bedroom, playing cards. I say, "Give me all your eights." Gran, smiling radiantly and with great affection, says, "Go fish." I reach across the table and pick up a card. When I look at it, it seems to have a picture of a goldfish on it, but when I look at it more closely, I see that it's the Sleeping Goddess. "You win!" says my grandmother.

Then I'm walking on a beach in what looks like Hawaii. A woman's walking ahead of me in a yellow T-shirt, and I realize it's Bonnie. I try to speed up but Bonnie stays the same distance ahead of me. I decide to place my feet in the impressions that Bonnie's feet make in the sand. I do speed up then, but before I could reach her, I woke up.

As always when a dream occurs, I needed a moment or two to be able to do physical things — remember to reach for my pen, and then, find words for what I had just experienced and remember how to write them. Ordinarily, when dreams occurred in the middle of the night like this one did, I was too stuporous to interpret it. But I did write at the bottom of the page of this account, before I dropped back to sleep, "Following in her footsteps?"

The next thing I knew, the phone was ringing on my bedside table. I shot up and grabbed the receiver before it could ring again. It was very early in the morning.

"Hello?" I said, keeping my voice low for Leo's sake. I sounded groggy, which of course I was.

"I knew you wouldn't be up yet. I'm sorry."

"Trudy?" I said. "What's up?"

"It's Dad. The club just called. He's having some sort of spell or something, and they called paramedics."

"When? Was he drunk?"

"Apparently this just happened. He got up to use the bathroom in his room and couldn't stand," she said. "He managed to call the front desk." Then her voice relaxed. "Anyway, I don't think the club would call an ambulance because a club member got drunk, do you?"

I had to laugh at that. "No, I don't think so."

"They called because they want to know which hospital to take him to. So I'm calling you. "

"Wow, give me a minute."

Our father lives in Palm Beach, Florida from September through June, but likes to spend his summers back in Pittsburgh. He stays at the Fort Pitt Club in the cultural district, a venerable gray stone building peopled by the wealthy and powerful of the city. It features high ceilings, elegant furnishings and floors that creak under the footsteps of its many staff members as they scurry across vast expanses of carpeting. A grand ballroom with shimmering chandeliers and full-length satin draperies serves as the dining room where I and my sisters were herded to dinner more often than we cared to remember. That we had to get dressed up for these forays, and behave ourselves for an inordinate amount of time, was reason enough to hate the place when we were little. But for both Trudy and me as teenagers, the fact that the club had whole areas that were off limits to women drove us wild with indignation.

Our father dealt with our outrage over such sexist policies with a sexist defense — we were, by virtue of our gender, high strung. When, after a lawsuit, women were finally allowed not only to walk through the building freely but to actually join the place, our father behaved as though that had been the just and proper thing to do. By then, he had become a modern guy, having left our mother for wife number two, or maybe it was three, both near our ages and no prizes, despite their trophy status.

Now he was single again — since wife number three had discovered she was in love with her yoga instructor — and now he often called our mother and asked her out to dinner at the club. Usually, Trudy and I were invited as well, like one big happy family. For both of us the phrase "the club" was code for boring pretensions, family turbulence and our exasperating father, who has always loved the place.

"Wait, wait, I need to think, " I said. "What did you tell them?"

"That I'd call back in a minute or two."

"Does he still have a doctor here?"

"I don't know!"

"Would Mom?"

There was a pause as we both pondered a question we usually prefer to avoid — how close were our parents these days?

"Y'know what?" said Trudy. "That's who we ought to call."

"You're right. You want to do it or should I?"

"I'll do it. I'm at least out of bed."

"And you're peeing, aren't you?" I recognized the sound.

"Hey, I'm in a hurry. I'll call you back as soon as I speak with Mom. Bye."

I was already in the kitchen brewing coffee five minutes later when Trudy called back. "Mom said East End Hospital, because that's where her doctor is, and he knows Dad. I called the club back, and the paramedics were already there. I told them to tell Dad that we'd meet him at the hospital. Mom said she'd come too."

"I should pick you up. You're on my way."

"Great, then we'll only have one car to park."

"Do you have any idea what's going on, Trudy?"

"I dunno — doesn't sound like he's in pain, so maybe not a heart attack."

"That was always the fear."

"And what we expected." We shared a sisterly silence, remembering all the heart attacks that had struck our parents' circle. For a generation or more, fear of heart attacks stalked our father and his friends as TB and influenza had stalked their parents before them.

"I wonder," said Trudy, "could it be a stroke?"

"Maybe. What are the symptoms?"

"Well, they can be vague, like weakness in an arm, or of course paralysis if it's a bad stroke. And remember old Mr. Collins up the street? He couldn't talk."

"Oh lord, I hope he's not that bad off!"

"Let's get over there." The anxiety was audible in Trudy's voice.

"I'll pick you up in fifteen minutes," I said, trying to sound confident.

"And Mom said, 'Better bring a book.'"

"Because she thinks this might take a long time?"

"She says she and her friends spend all their time escorting each other to their doctors. It's what they do."

"Okay, I'll pick you up in fifteen minutes <u>and</u> I'll bring you a slim volume of verse."

"Very funny." We hung up without bothering to say goodbye.

I hurried back into the bedroom and tried to dress quietly. What does one wear to the emergency room? I pulled on khakis and a knit top and strapped on my sandals. Make-up: did I need it? Make-up is an option I use if there might be an advantage. I and my family were about to be subjected to the rules and protocols of a huge and impersonal institution, dependent on the personnel there for help. Might a resident or intern give me a little more information, a little more time, if I looked better? It can't hurt, I thought as I quickly brushed color on my cheeks and swiped my lips with gloss. Then Leo stirred enough to ask what was going on, and I had to fill him in. Groggily, he offered to get up and come along. I assured him I didn't think that was necessary and that he ought to get his rest, but he sat up and put his feet on the floor. "I can make coffee then," he said.

"Actually, you can drink it because it's already made." I heard myself affecting a light tone of voice, and realized that his concern was bothering me. This isn't a big deal, I wanted to say. Or at least, we don't <u>know</u> that it's a big deal. "But you should do yourself a favor and wait for the alarm to go off." I said this as if inducing a hypnotic trance, sounding so easy and relaxed that he acquiesced by sinking back into bed as I slipped out of the room and trotted down the steps.

I had car keys in hand and was almost out the door when I remembered to take something to read. What was it I was going to work on? Oh yes — Bonnie's journal. I quickly opened the cardboard storage box in my office and picked up the notebook that lay on the top. I flipped the pages and saw that the last third of them were blank; this must have been the most recent one. I slipped it into my bag.

"Okay," I said under my breath, narrating my movements. "I have the keys, I have my bag, I have something to read." Then I opened the door onto a sparkling, dew drenched morning.

Chapter 17

East End Hospital had been gradually engulfing its neighborhood for the past thirty years, and now even the high rise lot that was supposed to alleviate neighborhood parking problems was overcrowded. I dropped Trudy off at what had once been the main entrance of the hospital and proceeded to the newer and more distant garage that had just opened to accommodate a new building for doctors' offices. To enter the lot, I had to pass through a gauntlet of construction vehicles and orange funnels. When I finally succeeded in finding a parking place, I got lost trying to make my way from the elevator to the office building to the hospital proper. Finally, I found Trudy in the waiting area of the emergency room, already looking like a fixture.

"So what's the deal?" I said as I sat down next to her.

"Well, they need to do tests, of course. But they said we can see him for a minute before he goes for an MRI."

"Are they saying anything?"

"They said their initial assessment is that he's had a stroke, and they're treating it already. But it will take time before they know the extent of the damage or how well the medications are working."

"So, we wait?"

"We wait."

It seemed ludicrous that we had rushed here to be told to wait, but emergencies are always this way, urgent and nerve wracking. All the energy generated by a crisis can only fester in idleness while you sit interminably in a room with strangers with as much to worry about as you have, watching mindless television shows. I scanned the area and saw that the only other occupant of the waiting room was dozing in front of a commercial for a car dealership. I groaned inwardly. I would far prefer to suck the poison out of a snakebite or dive into turgid waters to perform a rescue than to sit here in this blank room, waiting for Someone to tell us Something.

"Hey, want a cappuccino?" I asked Trudy. "I passed a coffee bar on the way here, in the new building."

"I'd love one, but make it a double. Want me to get it?"

"Hell no," I told her, "I want to walk."

There was a very long line at the coffee bar, but I preferred standing in it because at least there would be some reward for my patience. When I got back to the waiting area, Mother had arrived, and I felt calmer at once. My mother has always made me feel grounded. Peg Nilsson was one of that stalwart generation that had endured the Depression as a child, married after the Second World War and brought up a big brood in the suburbs. Raised on a farm, she seemed at ease with all things natural — weather, animals, birth, death — all part of a grand design that was never questioned, just accepted.

She'd been considered a bookworm when she was a child and aspired to become a doctor, but was discouraged by convention and circumstance. Her coming of age was a time when the whole nation was celebrating the return of its soldiers and sending women back to their homes. She was in nursing school when she met Stanley Nilsson, a patient recovering from surgery to repair a shrapnel wound that had not been adequately treated overseas. She claimed to have fallen in love at first sight, and happily quit school, which had proved to be more scrubbing than science, to marry him.

She always said that motherhood agreed with her, and none of her children would object, all five of us the beneficiaries of her even temper and intelligence. That wifehood had been less than rewarding was something she didn't dwell on. She'd gone through a low period for several years after Dad left her, but gradually had come to feel more free than she ever had before in her life.

"Mummy, you look so nice!" I said, giving her a hug. Mother always did look nice, but I thought she'd gone to extra trouble this morning. She was wearing a blouse with bright blue and yellow flowers over casual white pants, yellow button earrings and a matching string of yellow beads. "So cheery."

"Well, I thought your father might need to be brightened up." That she could be thoughtful and generous toward the man who had brought so much pain into her life was typical of her, but I've always found it puzzling. Once when I had asked her why she wasn't angrier, she'd simply shrugged, "Well, I loved the guy." It was certainly true that we all benefited from her not becoming thoroughly bitter, but I had given up trying to understand how she had avoided it.

"And I see you brought a book. What is this tome?" I leaned down to read the title, "*From Dawn to Decadence: 500 Years of Western Cultural Life*. Mother, couldn't you have brought a smaller book?"

"This is really very good," she replied.

"And the unabridged dictionary wouldn't fit in her bag," Trudy quipped.

Our mother's reading habits were family legend. She was addicted to print, and reading was her primary hobby, outlet and coping mechanism. If you wanted her attention when you were little, you had to wedge your face between hers and the newspaper, or wait for her to close the book on her lap, or hide her reading glasses. When she cooked, she always read at the kitchen table between tasks, and many a scorched vegetable and overdone chop was the result. Compensation for the cuisine came at bedtime when she read us stories, sometimes even after we were old enough to read to ourselves, because we loved listening to her. Part of growing up included overhearing familiar old stories being read to younger sisters, the adventures of Madeline or Curious George providing background music to homework assignments.

A nurse came to the entrance of the waiting room and said, "Oh, you're all here then? Good, you can come see him now." We followed her through double doors to the treatment area, where examining tables were spaced at intervals along the walls, some with curtains drawn. She opened one of them and nodded us in.

"Mr. Nilsson, here's your family."

As soon as our father saw us there, he fixed us with a somber look and said deliberately, "I am *non compos mentis*."

Taken aback, I said, "Dad, if you can use '*non compos mentis*' in a sentence, I don't think you can be."

Trudy and I kissed him on the cheek and made room for Mother by the bed. "Peg," he said, and she took his hand in hers.

He looked pale, but otherwise not unwell. I realized that it had been a long time since I'd seen him in bed. He looked vulnerable lying on his back in a hospital gown. He was longer than the bed and his feet protruded over the end. It had been a private joke among his daughters that in his old age, Dad was starting to resemble Max von Sydow, and we'd wondered if perhaps all Swedes look alike at an advanced age. Today, Dad looked like Max von Sydow playing a proud but bewildered man. He had an IV in one arm, and he looked down at it curiously. "Can't get my arm to work," he complained, as if he'd discovered a defective auto part.

Trudy said, "They're going to run some tests, Dad, so they can find out what's going on." She said this slowly and distinctly, as if he might not be able to make out what she meant.

"They think I had a stroke," he said mildly, but then his expression changed, his face grew red, and suddenly, he was crying. I had never seen my father cry, and I didn't know what to do. He had been such a formidable presence that this was an astonishing display. I was torn between wanting to console him and wanting to look away, to pretend for his sake that I wasn't seeing this. I glanced at Trudy, who looked as shocked as I felt, and her eyes were welling with tears. It was Mom who managed the moment while her daughters stood frozen.

"Well, Stan, you've had yourself a pretty tough morning so far," she said matter-of-factly, still holding his hand. "Just try and relax until we find out what the tests tell us."

I backed out of the curtained bed space and caught the nurse going by. "Excuse me, but my father is crying in there," I whispered hoarsely. "Is he being treated for pain?"

The nurse, short and fiftyish, with thin lips, glasses and a short blonde perm, looked as if she'd seen it all. Now, if only she would be willing to share it with the me. She smiled wanly. "This happens a lot with strokes. Emotional lability. People's moods can shift suddenly and unexpectedly. They often cry easily, even over things that aren't sad."

"So you don't think he's in pain?"

"He hasn't reported any. There are a lot of symptoms that can go along with a stroke, but pain usually isn't one of them. I think we might have a pamphlet around here somewhere that explains strokes. I'll see if I can find one for you." She proceeded on her brisk way, but I was grateful for the promise of information. I ducked back inside the curtain. Dad had closed his eyes and seemed to have fallen asleep.

We left him to rest. Trudy took Mom to the cafeteria for some breakfast while I stayed behind to monitor any updates. Finding myself alone, and not at all interested in *The Price is Right*, I pulled my bag onto my lap and looked inside. There was Bonnie's notebook.

"Oh, Bonnie," I thought to myself, "did I even decide whether I should read this?" I recalled then that I'd asked for guidance, and that I'd dreamt something and written it down, but what was it? I struggled to remember.

It really bugs me when this happens. I know that the brain chemicals responsible for memory are at low levels while dreaming is going on, but that doesn't relieve my frustration when I want to remember a dream. Bonnie once pointed out that from an evolutionary standpoint, a creature who could recall dreams as well as waking life would be at a distinct disadvantage. What if you dreamed that you could fly by jumping off a cliff and acted on that the next day?

I tried to remember what I'd written down in the middle of the night, but couldn't. I squeezed my eyes shut. No luck, but when I opened them, my eyes fell on a computer monitor with a screensaver featuring swimming fish. That was it, playing fish! Then I remembered the winning card with the sleeping goddess and took a deep breath. This was as close to a green light as I could have wished for, or stood. I knew it would be all right to read Bonnie's journal, to follow in her footsteps.

I opened the large spiral notebook. Dividers with pockets broke the pages into three sections. The first entry was dated last February and the ensuing entries made their way to June. I flipped to the back. The last entry appeared to be quite long, several pages of Bonnie's longhand in blue ink. I backed up to the beginning of the entry, which was dated two days before we all left for Hawaii. The dream account was surprisingly short:

"Driving up a hill, a mountain road with twists and turns. Stephanie Morgan is in the back seat — I'm taking her to the vet. There is a large fowl, like a duck, sitting in her lap, that is sick or injured. It seems I may never get to the top. Then suddenly, it's like a roller coaster and the car plunges down a steep incline, totally out of control. I woke up before we crashed."

I blinked, trying to follow all the connections my mind was feverishly making. Here was a duck, of all things, injured like the one in Joe's dream. And here also was a plummeting vehicle, reminiscent of the terrible fall that broke Bonnie's neck.

Underneath this brief account, Bonnie had written "PUNS: sitting duck?" And under that she'd written CUES, her shorthand for the daytime events that might trigger a dream. This section went on for over two pages. I read:

"As soon as I woke up, I knew this was about the Morgan dilemma. I am very concerned but without proof, or direct testimony from Stephanie, I cannot proceed. In the current legal atmosphere, an official record seems risky — and even deleted files can be used against you these days. I've stopped writing about this on computers at work or home, I'm so paranoid. I also feel that I am being cowardly in not addressing this head-on, but I run the risk of ruining my practice if I'm not careful. There are several good reasons for me to hesitate.

1. Gloria Dunlap enough said. She's probably uninsurable."

I stopped to wonder what this might have had to do with Bonnie. Gloria Dunlap was a psychotherapist who had been sued by the parents of one of her patients, a teenage girl who was being treated for depression. Over the course of treatment, the girl began to relate sexually abusive events that took place at home with her father. Following the proper legal procedure, Dunlap reported the abuse. The girl's father, protesting his innocence, was arrested. Soon after, the patient announced that her mother had abused her as well. The girl was removed from the home, and the mother was arrested.

Eventually, the girl also claimed that she'd been ritually raped and tortured by a neighborhood band of devil worshippers, and had secretly given birth to children who were then murdered. The case made headlines over several years, as arrests led to lawsuits and abuse claims escalated from implausible to impossible. There was no evidence of the injuries the girl reported, and many witnesses who saw the girl in school every day during the months she claimed to be pregnant. At the trial, Gloria Dunlap testified that it was her job to believe her client, not to doubt the truth of her experiences. The jury found with the parents.

So, Bonnie was afraid of reporting someone falsely? Did this mean that Stephanie had said something that suggested abuse to her? I was riveted now. I continued reading Bonnie's backhand scrawl.

"2. Rich, influential father who would spare no expense to protect himself, another O.J. Simpson (without the fame)."

I sat back, stunned at that O.J. reference. Another synchronicity with my dream of Bonnie on the phone. What did it mean? An example of clairvoyance? Had I been picking up on something at a distance — Bonnie's dream notes? Or had I been alerted somehow to Bonnie's unfinished business, what was obviously much on her mind when she died?

"3. I'm not sure. That's the root problem. Without more evidence, I don't dare proceed. It is awful to suspect that a man has abused, and may have caused the death of, his older daughter and is now starting in on the younger one, as Stephanie's dreams suggest. But being wrong about this would bring a horrendous outcome. The sensible thing is to consult with a clinical ethicist who can hear me out, and then a lawyer. I won't tell Frank any of this until I can do that, because anything having to do with liability will alarm him and increase the tension. I can't do much until we get back from Hawaii, so I will continue to sit tight for now. In my head, I know it's wise to proceed carefully, but in my heart, I feel very anxious to act."

I stared at the page. "Ho-ly shit," I said under my breath. My mind wanted to run away from the implications. There was too much here to think about.

"I found this for you." My eyes met with a white pamphlet in front of my face. I looked up to see the blonde nurse, and tried to gather my thoughts.

"Oh, yes!" I took the booklet and read the cover, "About Strokes," by the American Heart Association.

"This will help to get you started. I could only find the one, though. Can you share this with your family?"

"Sure, yes, of course." I was slow to realize that the nurse had gone to some trouble for me and I added appreciatively, "Thank you so much for this."

"After he's done with the MRI, your father will be taken to intensive care. They can keep a close eye on him there."

"Oh," I said, "is he worse?"

"No, but a stroke is an ongoing event. A stroke patient is monitored very closely during the first hours."

"Oh," I said again, nodding this time with real understanding.

"Do you know where ICU is?"

My mind was so distracted that for a moment, I didn't understand "I see you." Oh yes, Intensive Care Unit. And where was ICU? I shook my head mutely.

"Well, you turn right when you leave here and keep going until you get to a bank of elevators. Don't take those. Keeping going until you come to more elevators. Go up to five and follow the signs. There's a nice waiting area up there."

"Come on down!" the emcee shouted from the television, accompanied by ringing bells and tooting horns. I began to stand and then realized I should wait for Mom and Trudy to return. I sat back in my chair. There was just too much to think about all at once, I realized. My mind felt like its operating system had come to a stop, and I wished I could somehow reboot. I smiled weakly at the nurse.

"I'll wait for my family and take them up too," I said, and then remembered to say, "Thanks again."

"Good luck," said the nurse with an encouraging nod, and moved on her busy way.

I looked down. Holding Bonnie's journal with my left hand and the stroke pamphlet in my right, I understood only that this was overload, pure and simple.

Chapter 18

The day took on an endless quality as it progressed. We found our way to the intensive care waiting room and did what everyone else there was doing: sat around trying to control our anxiety. This was an entirely different atmosphere than the emergency waiting room. People waiting here were in for the long haul. Clutches of family members shrank and grew as some were permitted to visit the bedside of a loved one and then returned. One young woman had a pillow and blanket with her and alternatively dozed and wept. Snatches of conversation between visitors — "...about organ donation..."; "...on life support..."; "...living will" — increased my sense of urgency. When it was my turn to see Dad, I felt far more grave than I had before.

Like the emergency room, the ICU was a large space with a number of beds, but many more machines, and more personnel. "You can visit for a few minutes, but he's resting now," said the ICU attendant who allowed people in and out. It struck me as odd that a stranger could dictate whether or not I could see my own father. But today, everything was beginning to strike me as odd. I stood by the bed watching the pale man sleep, holding the hand that didn't have anything sticking into or out of it, and silently returned to the waiting room when my time was up.

By mid-afternoon, we had spoken with the attending neurologist. He had at first addressed Mom, but she deferred to us. "These are the next of kin," she said, as if to pass on some sort of magical family scepter. Trudy and I listened as attentively as we could to the report on our father's condition.

"He's had a stroke, which is basically bleeding in the brain. It can continue for some time. We think we've arrested the bleeding but will keep a close eye on him in ICU for at least twenty-four hours. The injury is on the left side of the brain, and this has paralyzed the right half of his body. This is called 'hemiplegia.' With physical therapy, he can learn how to use his right side again. He will also have speech and swallowing difficulties. These can be treated too, but it will be a long time, as much as a year, before we have a clear picture of how far his recovery will go."

Trudy looked ashen, and Mother's expression was solemn. I pulled an envelope out of my purse and started writing on the back of it. "I'm never going to remember all this if I don't take notes," I murmured to no one in particular. "Is 'hemiplegia' spelled the way it sounds?"

After the doctor left, Mother announced, "We'd better call everyone now." Her other three daughters live in three distant places — California, New York and Texas — and all needed to be informed of what had been transpiring. We made our way to a bank of pay phones outside the waiting room, and each of us placed a call. We ended up leaving messages for all three of my sisters.

"I wasn't sure what to say," Trudy said, nervously patting her chest. "I didn't want to be overly alarming. What did you say, Willa?"

"I just said that Dad was at East End Hospital and left your cell number."

"I just said to call me A.S.A.P. What did you say, Mom?"

"I said that your father's had a spell and we're having him checked at the hospital."

Before we could sit back down in the waiting room, Trudy's cell phone rang.

"No cell phones allowed in here," said the girl with the pillow. Her eyes had been closed but she opened them now. "You have to go to the cafeteria or outside. Too many monitors around here."

The rest of the afternoon was filled with trips to Dad's bedside and rounds of conversation as my sisters called in. These are the times that try the souls of large families, I thought. Just getting information to everyone was exhausting, but it was also comforting to hear the concern in their voices, and the love.

By the end of the day, Dad's condition was stable and Marcia, Glad and Mary were planning with one another whether and when to fly in to see him. It was dinnertime when I found myself back in my car with Trudy, and suddenly remembered Bonnie's journal.

"Trudy! My god, I haven't told you!" I involuntarily hit the brakes as I stopped for my thought.

"What!?" cried Trudy, bracing herself on the dashboard.

"Oh god, sorry! Hold on, I'm going to pull over. I can't handle rush hour and this too."

I turned the car into a parking lot for a mini-mall, featuring a laundromat, a drug store and a "Wine and Spirits" shop, Pennsylvania's euphemism for "State Owned Liquor Monopoly Outlet." I eased the car into a space but left the engine running. It was the hottest part of a hot day.

"Okay," I said, "remember about Bonnie's journal? How I was going to read it?"

"Yes," Trudy nodded, but then shook her head in disbelief, looking like a pitcher who was rejecting a catcher's signal. "Was it only yesterday that we were at the coffee shop? It seems like three months ago!"

"I know it. Anyway, I brought it with me today, and I was reading it in the waiting room when you took Mom down for breakfast." I reached behind my seat for my bag and the journal. "You won't believe this."

I kept one hand on the notebook in my lap, testifying. "Trudy, the last dream Bonnie wrote down was about driving this young client, Stephanie Morgan, to a vet. The girl had an injured duck on her lap!"

Trudy blinked and remembering, said slowly, "Joe's dream had a duck that got hurt."

"That's what I thought of! But that's not all." I recounted meeting Karen Morgan through a mutual friend, and then encountering her again, with Stephanie, at Bonnie's funeral. "And now I'm acting as a kind of dream tutor for this child. I've been to their house in Mount Clair, and I know that Stephanie did have an older sister who died — drowned in the family swimming pool."

"Maggie Morgan?" Trudy asked. "I remember when that happened. She was one of our students."

It hadn't occurred to me that Trudy might know the Morgan family from her work as a counselor at Mount Clair High School. "I didn't know her personally," Trudy continued, "but I remember speaking with a couple of her friends." She sighed. "Death hits teenagers so hard, especially when it's someone their own age. Even though it happened during summer vacation, kids were having trouble when they came back to school in the fall and were reminded that she was gone."

My heart was pounding. I wanted to blurt out the rest of the story, but felt almost fearful. Why? It couldn't be a violation of anyone's privacy if I shared the speculations of our dead friend. Especially not if they were true.

"Trudy, that's not all. Bonnie wrote a whole lot more than that dream. She went on for pages about suspicions she had about the father, Cliff Morgan. She was pretty sure that he had sexually abused the older daughter, and she thought he was starting in on the younger one, Stephanie."

"Are you kidding?" Trudy's eyes were wide with shock. "Did Bonnie report it?"

"No, because she didn't have direct evidence, only the dreams that the younger sister was bringing into therapy. But she speculates that the father may have been responsible for the death of the older sister."

"May I see that?" asked Trudy incredulously, and I handed her the notebook. Trudy scanned the pages while I looked over her shoulder.

"She writes that she was going to consult a lawyer after she got back from Hawaii, and she mentions Gloria Dunlap," I told her.

"The analyst who got sued?"

"And screwed."

"Oh my, poor Bonnie," Trudy said as she finished reading. "And if it's true, poor Stephanie!"

"I know. It's mind blowing just to think about this. And you know, I've met Cliff Morgan," I added. "At first he seemed really nice, and then really uptight. I think he may have a drinking problem, and I'm pretty sure he's knocked his wife around." I held my fingers to my lips, thinking. "Although none of that proves he's a sexual abuser, does it?"

"It doesn't prove it, but men with this kind of history often have alcohol or chemical abuse problems. I'll tell you one thing though." Trudy reached over and put a firm hand on my forearm. "You do not want to mess with Mount Clair parents. Some of them are rich enough that they would and could stop at nothing to ruin someone who made trouble for them." She sighed. "No wonder Bonnie was worried."

"And now maybe we should be."

Trudy looked at me and shivered. She rubbed her arms and reached to turn down the air conditioning. "There's no indication here that the father knew that Bonnie suspected him, is there?"

"Not that I can tell. It sounds like she was being very careful not to reveal anything until she knew where she stood legally," I said.

"Yikes," said Trudy. "What should we do about this?"

My answer was a slow head shake. As the engine rumbled and the air conditioning hummed in my old car, we sat for another long moment without speaking. My thoughts were piling up on one another. I couldn't shake the impression that Bonnie's death had been beneficial to a number of people, including Cliff Morgan, if Bonnie was right about him. Caitlin and Andy were now the heirs of a sizable legacy, although there was no question that they would rather have their mother than her money. But then there was Frank, who'd had reason to believe he would benefit financially whenever Bonnie died. And Frank also may have benefited by becoming, suddenly, a free man. Once again, the memory flashed before me of seeing Frank turn over Bonnie's body and start CPR. I blinked away the scene, unable to abide it.

Trudy inhaled deeply and announced, "This is just too much." She held out her hands, palms up. "Look at you, look at us. We're both exhausted from an emotional, draining day. Dad's had a stroke and is paralyzed. Life is never going to be the same." She suddenly stopped talking and bit her bottom lip as a tear rushed down each cheek. I patted her on the back, blotting my own tear on the sleeve of my shirt.

"You always look so pitiful when you cry," I said.

"At least my nose doesn't turn red and glow, like yours," Trudy sniffled. She reached into her bag and extracted a packet of tissues. "Want one?"

We both blew our noses and stared out at the parking lot.

"Y'know what?" Trudy said finally. "I'm going to pour myself a big glass of wine when I get home. Care to join me?"

"I need to get back to the house and fill Leo in. I spoke to him early this afternoon and he's still waiting for an update." And, I realized, I longed to wrap myself in the comfort of Leo's arms. I put the car in reverse and turned to look out the back window but then applied the brake and looked at Trudy. "I'm supposed to have another tutoring session with Stephanie this week," I told her, and the idea made me very nervous. "I guess I'd better educate myself about — what might be going on with her."

"I'll tell you what I know," Trudy offered. "But it's still a pretty shady area of study. Incest got a lot of attention back in the 1980s — it was like a taboo against discussing it had been broken, remember?"

I nodded, listening as I negotiated the parking lot and pulled into traffic.

Trudy continued, "But then there was that wave of sexual abuse cases at preschools that ended up more like witch hunts. And then things began to get really out of hand. Remember when people were freaking out about Satanism? There were parent meetings about rock groups and cults, and books about ritual sexual abuse and even murder. There was this hysteria around sexual abuse. Lots of women were going into therapy and becoming convinced that they'd been violated. There were a lot of outraged patients, and then outraged parents of patients."

"Like the Gloria Dunlap case," I said.

"Right, and then we began hearing about 'false memory syndrome,' and how people's accounts of things that happened in the past aren't necessarily to be believed. So there's been something of a stand-off. Incest is like this stepchild of school counseling. There are rules about what you have to do if a student reports something — notify authorities — but people tend to avoid the subject." Trudy sighed. "Which has been the case through time immemorial. Which is how adults get away with it."

"Trudy," I said thoughtfully, "would it be possible for you to check to see if Maggie Morgan ever sought counseling while she was alive?"

"That's a good question," Trudy said. "It would depend. I'm not sure what happens to kids' files when they die. Do you know if she was in the gifted program, or had any kind of learning disability?"

"I have no idea. Why do you ask?"

"Because those records are kept for a relatively long time. They're under lock and key in the pupil services office, and only school psychologists and parents can get access to them."

"Could you see them?"

"Oh sure."

"What's the significance of the gifted program, or a learning disability?" I asked.

"Well, that's part of special ed, which means lots of records are kept, including psychologicals. If she was a regular student, there wouldn't be as much in her file — if there still is a file."

"What if she was a regular student and confided a problem to someone on the counseling staff?"

"If she'd confided that her father was sexually abusing her, he'd have been reported to authorities. That's the law. The counselor would have written up a report and placed a copy in a locked file in pupil services."

"What if Maggie had gone in and talked about something less serious, some other problem at home — like her father's drinking?"

Trudy thought for a moment. "It's hard to say for sure. We have to be very careful what we place in students' files, because parents can ask to see them at any time. So, it would depend. But you know what?" Trudy's tone of voice was changing from speculative to resolved. "I am definitely going to check this out. How old is Stephanie?"

"Twelve, going into seventh grade."

"Then she won't get to the high school for two more years. Do you know which school she goes to now?"

"Not yet, but I'll sure find out."

"Good. I'll just see what I can do about this."

"I just hope there's a way to cope with whatever you learn," I said as we came to a stop in front of Trudy's house.

"Wait, hold on a sec," said Trudy. "I've got some material about this. A guide published for kids, but it'll help you too. Hold on and I'll bring it out to you." She was opening the car door when she turned around and said, "Unless you'd like to reconsider that glass of wine?"

"Hmmm," I said, "now that you mention it, I believe I will join you."

I parked the car and was soon sitting at Trudy's kitchen table, nursing a glass of white wine as Boomer insistently nudged my elbow, desperately seeking another round of ear-fondling. But I was becoming absorbed in a slim book called, "How to Stop Incest and Sexual Abuse." The cover featured a full color photograph of a young girl, her back to the camera, with a tall male beside her, his arm around her shoulder. It would have looked romantic if the words across the cover weren't so shocking.

"We get these free from publishers from time to time, like teachers get textbooks," Trudy was explaining. "I've hung onto it because I think it's a good source for kids, although I've never had a student who needed me to bring it to her, or him — as far as I know."

"Maybe if you put it on a shelf in your office, a troubled kid might open up," I suggested.

"Actually, we have to be a little bit careful about that too. The parent issue again — we try to make sure our offices are as bland as possible so that they don't feel threatened by what they see when they come in. But I know there's a copy of this in the library, so kids can get to this information if they seek it out."

I scanned the index and read out loud: "Child sexual offense, depression, grief, legal system, pedophile, perpetrators, secrets." I looked up and said, "You know, what little I learned formally about incest was in abnormal psych courses, but this book makes sexual abuse seem commonplace."

"Well, when you consider all the variations — including minor girls who become sexually active with older guys, or the coaches and priests who prey on young boys, and even older siblings exploiting younger ones, not to mention all the stepfathers out there who take liberties...."

"Ye gods, Trudy!"

"Well, that's my point! It is commonplace, more than we want to know, unfortunately. It's even in the Bible, a lot, actually."

I nodded, thinking about that. "It's in Greek mythology too, now that you mention it. Zeus was always jumping those poor girls."

"As were Apollo and Hades and all the rest of them."

"How was it that the subject of nonconsensual sex was never mentioned when we discussed mythology in school, I wonder?" I felt a little smile curling the ends of my mouth. Trudy snorted, almost bringing wine through her nose, then raised her hand in mock earnestness. "Miss Thomas, how come gods get to nail any girl they want?"

"And don't even take them out to dinner!" We both giggled for another minute and then Trudy said, "When you think about it, mythology just reflects reality. The strong exploit the weak. Men have had complete dominance over women until — well — I guess in most of the world, they still do."

"Remember the goddesses at the Garden of Eden? I bet none of them forced themselves on kids," I mused. "In fact, ever since that conversation we had at the store, I've wondered what it was like when sex was sacred. Maybe people were too reverent to force themselves on anyone."

"Do you believe there ever was such a time?"

"I guess that's the same as asking if there were really matriarchies before recorded history. We can only guess from other evidence, like those goddess figures." Then I told Trudy about the Sleeping Goddess in my dream. That, we agreed, was very impressive. Matriarchies or no, I decided to buy another Sleeping Goddess and place her by my bed, when I felt brave enough to welcome her considerable mojo.

Trudy and I sipped in silence for another minute before returning to the problem at hand: what was going on at the Morgan house, and what could we do about it? Trudy took up the book again and turned to the table of contents. "Here," she said, finding the page she was searching for and handing it to me. I read out loud: "Sexual Assault: Legal Degrees. Sexual contact with anyone under thirteen, a class B felony. If the victim is older than thirteen but younger than sixteen, it's a class C felony." I scanned the page without finding more. "Doesn't incest carry additional penalties? That doesn't seem right," I muttered. "There ought to be a firing squad."

"A lot of people do feel that way, but parents can't provide for their families if we have them shot," she said, laying a hand on my shoulder. "Usually perpetrators are at least removed from the home. But social workers and counselors and even district attorneys have to remember that these are families. Fathers and mothers have to provide for their children and we have to weigh that against the crime."

"Look here — 'failure to act' can get you in trouble. 'Anyone who has knowledge of illegal sexual activities involving children' and doesn't report it is committing a class C felony. Say," I wondered, "can the abuser be charged with both? Doing it AND not reporting it?"

"I doubt it."

I put my finger in the book to save the place. "I wonder if Bonnie knew about this," I said.

"Well, clinicians and counselors know that it's illegal <u>not</u> to report sexual abuse to authorities. But, you should have knowledge, not just suspicions."

"What constitutes knowledge? Witnessing it?"

"That's almost never the case. Abusers are very careful to make sure they're not observed, and they're very clever at playing on children's feelings of loyalty, fear or guilt so that they won't divulge what's going on."

"The rats."

"Does it help to know that a lot of abusers were themselves abused?"

I shrugged. "So perpetrators have been victims?"

"Very often."

I mulled this over briefly and then said, "They're still rats. And they're going to pass this on to another generation, like a stealth virus."

"Well, we who work with students and families hope that our modern ministrations will prevent this from going on and on the way it has in the past."

"But what's the remedy? I mean, if we can't shoot the perps."

"We encourage kids to talk. That's what this book tells youngsters to do — tell somebody. That's the main way we find out what's going on. Finally, the kid speaks up. The power of the abuser is broken when the secret is revealed."

"We're back to power again."

"Ain't <u>that</u> the truth."

"And then what — the family goes off to therapy and all is well?" I snorted. "How can someone heal after this?"

Trudy shook her head. "It's a pure mess, for sure. Think about what people go through! There's prosecution for the abusers and all the trauma <u>that</u> brings to a family, and very often the other parent — the mother usually — is a basket case, and if there are other kids, they're angry or terrified, and may also have been abused. And the poor victims — well, they feel horribly guilty for causing all this. So, yeah, everyone in the family does need a lot of help. It's a tragedy. But people do put their lives back together. And the victims are freed from sexual exploitation ."

I rested my forehead in my hand. "God, this is such a burden. If Bonnie was right in her suspicions, then I, we, <u>have</u> to do something. If Bonnie was wrong, well...."

Trudy finished my thought. "It would be terribly destructive if an accusation were lodged against an innocent man. And don't forget how powerful these people might be. Their money can buy them the best legal advice. They undoubtedly know influential people. It wouldn't be pretty."

I sighed and sat up straight, the way Mother taught us to, and said, "Then what we have to do is find out the truth. Because I'm not afraid of the consequences of a true accusation, only a false one."

Chapter 19

When I finally pulled into my driveway, I was surprised that Leo's car was not there yet. I walked into the kitchen and thought about taking something out of the freezer for dinner, but didn't feel up to making a decision. Instead, I walked into the living room, turned on a news channel, lay down on the sofa with my feet up and promptly fell asleep. The next thing I knew the TV was off, someone was making noise in the kitchen and it was almost dark out. The cicadas outside were winding down for the night, but the crickets were still busy.

I roused myself from the sofa and shuffled into the kitchen, where Leo was emptying the dishwasher I'd run the night before.

"Hey," I said sleepily.

"Hey!" he said, and came over to give me a hug. "You were really zonked out when I got home."

"I've had a big day."

We held the hug for a long moment, and he rocked me gently from side to side. I'm enough shorter than Leo that I can rest my head on his chest. "Hmmm," I said, "this feels good," and we rocked some more.

"So," I finally said, pulling back, "are you starved?"

"I'm sure getting there, are you?"

"I will be when my stomach wakes up. I didn't do anything about dinner," I was scratching my head, remembering, "and you weren't home yet and I couldn't think what to defrost. Where were you?"

"At the hospital."

"You went to see Dad?"

"Sure did."

I was surprised, and unexpectedly pleased, that he'd bothered. After our divorce, Leo had vanished from the extended family, but since we'd been seeing one another again, Leo had not minded, as he once had, being included in family events. I handled his reappearance gingerly, not wanting to encourage those who liked Leo to become hopeful, or those who were wary of him to be worried. My father was a member of both camps.

In fact, my father disliked on principle every boy who ever expressed interest in his daughters, and every prospective son-in-law had been treated to a cold reception.

However, as time went by, and grandchildren were born, and he himself proved to be feckless in marriage, he seemed to find it easier to abide his daughters' husbands, at least the ones who could enjoy a round of golf and a long stop at the nineteenth hole afterward. In this respect, Leo did measure up.

"What did you think? How was he when you saw him? And hey — I thought only family was allowed in intensive care, how did you get to see him?"

"Actually," he said sheepishly, "I told them I was his son-in-law. I left off the 'ex,' and nobody said anything."

"And did he know you?"

"Oh yes! In fact, he seemed really glad to see me. He gave me something like a big, tight handshake, with his left hand though. His right side seems pretty impaired."

"It is. Let me give you the full story, and let's eat."

Not until the whole day at the hospital had been recounted and two strip steaks consumed did I return in my thoughts to Bonnie's journal, and her suspicions. I wondered for a moment if I had the energy to tell Leo this whole long story too. I was tired, and tired of feeling worried, and was longing to crawl into bed and lose the day to blissful unconsciousness.

"Sleep knits up the raveled sleeve of care," I said out loud.

"Are you showing off your Shakespeare or is that an invitation to go to bed with me?" Leo said.

I laughed sarcastically, but was glad of his interest anyway. "I'm actually debating whether to fill you in on yet another crisis."

"You mean with your dad?"

"No, no, this is something completely different. It's about Bonnie."

"You're not going to start in on the paranoid business about Frank again are you?"

"No," I said coolly, "I'm not, and even if I did, I wouldn't talk to you about it." I stifled my irritation then and added, "Not tonight."

"What then?" said Leo. I took a deep breath and thought that I might as well get this out. It could help to go over it before I went to bed, in the hope that sleeping on it would help me to arrive at a strategy.

After I finished telling him everything I knew about Bonnie's notes, the Morgan family and the treatment of sexual abuse, Leo's face was set with what looked like anger.

"Willa," he said seriously, "this sounds like trouble."

I blanched at the word. "Well, clearly, Bonnie was worried about professional consequences, and so am I."

"No, I don't mean just professionally risky. I mean dangerous."

"You mean physically?"

He nodded and said, "I mean, all ways." He wasn't just angry, I realized, he was anxious.

"What makes you say that?"

"Listen to what you're saying. A teenager's death may have been caused by her own father, a man who owns a lucrative business that provides 'industrial security.' You know what that means?"

"Charlotte says he arranges for agents to travel with corporate executives, serve as escorts, that sort of thing. Like the Secret Service for private citizens, I guess. Or Pinkertons, maybe."

"And what sort of men do you suppose go into that line of work?"

I scanned my brain for ideas. "I dunno — ex-army guys?"

"Probably, and other sorts of people who are expert at weapons, and martial arts — men who've served in special forces, who have been trained in covert operations. Not to mention ex-cops, and the kinds of people who find jobs in the back pages of 'Soldier of Fortune' magazine."

He was implying that I was too dim to have seen the obvious, but it seemed quite a reach to me. I said frostily, "And your point is…"

"I wouldn't want to make trouble for a man who has his reputation and freedom at stake and a small private army at his disposal."

"Leo, really. You think an Army veteran who escorts the CEO of Alcoa to South Africa is going to come after a college teacher? Like a hit man? Now who's being paranoid?"

"I'm just saying that you should watch out for yourself."

"I can't believe that you're saying this! I should back off because of your wild imagination? I think you're just being — gutless!" I blurted.

"Gutless?" Leo sounded astonished. "Willa, it's not gutless to suggest that you need to look at the big picture here. Being impulsive may come naturally to you, but this isn't really your business, is it?"

Impulsive — the word stung, as he knew it would. It's the word I use on myself in moments of self-blame. I had been impulsive with Rob and impulsive when I contacted the police with my dream about him, and I was still suffering for it. I had always been more emotional than Leo, and just this minute, I hated him for it.

"What's a child like Stephanie supposed to do, if she's being exploited and violated and has nowhere to turn?" I demanded indignantly.

"Surely you're not suggesting that I don't care about such things."

"I'm suggesting that — " I could feel my face flushing with outrage, and it was an effort to hold my voice steady — "this kid is helpless if someone doesn't try to intercede. What if one of the kids in our family were in a horrible situation like this? We'd be on this like white on rice. Would you be telling me to back off if this were" — and I lost the battle with my fierce emotions as I choked out the name — "Amanda?!"

There it was, the undiscovered nub that was driving my need to do battle with this threat, to not let it rest for a night, to fight it out with Leo if not the perpetrator. It hadn't reached my conscious awareness until now that Amanda would have been a contemporary of the Morgan sisters, about the same age as Maggie Morgan, and that they were both dead. I hadn't detected the match-up in my mind until that moment, and I immediately saw that I had gone too far.

"God, I'm sorry!" I said to Leo's retreating back, but he didn't turn around, and didn't stop before he walked out of the house, started his car, and drove away. I sank into a kitchen chair and held my head in my hands. It took a long minute for me to realize just how profoundly I'd offended Leo, by comparing our daughter to an incest victim. I groaned out loud, and tried to guess how many minutes it would take for him to get to his apartment so I could call him and apologize. I decided not to waste any time and called his number to leave a message.

"Leo, I didn't mean what I said, I didn't even know what I was saying, and all I can do is ask you to forgive me. I am really, really sorry. Please call me back when you get this message."

I paced the floor for a few minutes, thinking what I had meant by "gutless," which had started the ball rolling. I resented the suggestion that I ought to avoid helping Stephanie because of the remote possibility that my own safety might be jeopardized. I decided that my conclusion was perfectly valid, but I'd come at it wrong, and wished I could say so to Leo.

I scraped and rinsed the dinner dishes, and still the phone didn't ring. I reached for the phone, dialed the number again and Leo picked it up on the second ring.

"Leo, I'm really, really sorry!" I said in a rush.

"I know, I just listened to your message." He didn't sound angry. In fact, he sounded cool.

"What I said was just — well it was a revelation for me to realize that in the back of my mind, there's a connection between Amanda and this girl."

"I understand," he said, and sounded like he really did.

"This is a pretty hot button, I'm afraid," I said honestly. "I sure didn't mean to take my anger out on you. Are you going to be able to forgive me?"

"I imagine I will." He said this almost sorrowfully, as if there were no justice in the world. "But it might take me a day or two. A little distance might be helpful to you too."

"You mean because I'm emotionally strung out and crazy?"

I could hear him smiling when he said, "Well, I wouldn't put it quite like that." After a pause, he added, "And I didn't make life any easier for you tonight, did I?"

I heard him take a deep breath before he spoke again. "I want to tell you that on the way home, I realized what was provoking me about this Cliff Morgan guy, and his industrial security business. It was something I saw a long time ago on 'Sixty Minutes,' or one of those other shows. It was about how easy it is to have someone murdered in this country. And the killers are often these ex-military types, men who have training in killing and they do read the classifieds in 'Soldier of Fortune.' It was so chilling that it made crime movies seem warm and fuzzy."

I was silent for a moment, and felt myself shiver. "You're giving me the creeps," I said.

"I think I'm overreacting," he said. I almost exclaimed, "I agree!" but held my tongue this time.

Leo continued, his voice a little hoarse with the effort of getting out something emotional. "This was one of the problems when we were married, you know. I kept feeling responsible for you, for making you happy, and when there were problems I couldn't fix... well, you saw what happened."

"You ... got depressed, clammed up and pulled away," I said. We had had this conversation before, but insight alone never seems sufficient to prevent old habits from reasserting themselves.

"Right," he said tersely. "So I need to get a grip. But let me ask you one thing — are you planning to do anything about this situation with the girl right away?"

"Frankly, I don't know what to do," I told him. "I guess the first thing is to find out what Trudy can dig up about the sister. And maybe, call Vicki Golombiewski and see if she can tell me what my legal vulnerability is. And of course, there will be my sessions with Stephanie."

Leo sighed at the other end of the phone. "Would you like some advice?"

"Okay." We each sounded wary of irritating the other.

"Take it easy on this. No matter how protective you feel about this girl, or outraged on her behalf, you really have to proceed carefully."

"That's good advice," I said evenly.

"If you can take it."

"I mean to," I said, and I did. "Of course I will."

"*Very* carefully," he repeated. Leo seldom knew when to quit.

"I hear you."

"And take your time."

"All *right*, Leo."

"I won't say any more."

"Good."

"Goodnight then. Sleep tight, Willa."

"Sweet dreams, Leo."

Despite my exhaustion, I felt too agitated to go up to bed right away. I poured a half glass of wine, sank into the living room couch and switched on the television. There I came upon a show about psychics who solve crimes, which struck me as a fine synchronicity. I wondered about making a trip up to Lily Dale, where someone might be able to give me Bonnie's perspective on all this. Would she know, now, what was really going on at the Morgan house? The idea of actually communicating with her filled me with a sense of hope. I imagined how pleasant it would be to drive up to Lily Dale on a fine sunny day, due north through groves of trees and golden farmland until Lake Erie began to glint on the horizon.

And that's all I remember until I woke up a half hour later, turned everything off, checked the doors, and dragged my sorry ass to bed.

The tricky part of being a dream journalist is that every wakening involves the same slow recognition — that there is such a thing as being awake and that you are going there; that there is such a thing as dreaming, and that you have been doing it; that dreaming is something that you want to pay attention to while awake; and that the scenario that has just been transpiring must be captured quickly, even as it vanishes from sight and mind.

My problem the next morning was a thunderstorm. The noise startled me away from whatever it was that I had been doing, the experiences I'd been having for the last seven hours, and thus I returned to waking life with no trace of dreaming at all.

I stretched and lay in bed, listening to the rain pelt the porch roof outside my bedroom. Soon enough, I'd be rushing off to teach classes, and this divine luxury of lingering in bed would be restricted to weekends. Just for now, though, I might roll over and catch another forty winks, listening to the rain splash on the sycamore leaves and run through the gutters.

Which I might have succeeded in doing if the events of the day before hadn't suddenly crashed into consciousness. Oh yes — Dad's had a stroke! And I had a fight with Leo! And oh god, what'll I do about this Stephanie business? I threw a pillow over my face, but the gesture wasn't sufficient to block out reality. So I just lay there for a few minutes more, thinking through what I had to do, and how and when I would do it. Check on Dad, get over to the hospital to see him. Find out which sisters are flying in, and when. Work on class preps. Check calendar — when was the next session with Stephanie? Read book on sexual abuse. Call Trudy, call Vicki.

And — should I call Leo? I sucked in my breath as if I'd pressed on a new bruise. Ever since we started seeing each other again, we'd been very diplomatic with one another, considerate and careful. Last night was a major departure from that status quo, and may well be foreshadowing more trouble ahead. "Bet he's having second thoughts about moving back in with me," I thought as I swung my legs out of bed. As I planted my feet on the floor, I wished the idea didn't bother me.

Chapter 20

When I brought in the morning paper, its protective plastic bag was dripping with rainwater. Although I tried to remove it carefully, the front pages were gray with wet spots, so I flipped to the inside and pulled out the magazine section. Protected from the elements by the other three sections, all its pages were dry, as good a place as any to start the day. Here were your comics, your advice column, your reviews, and your columnists, including the ubiquitous Jane Flynn, recorder of society balls and other fundraising events. I don't usually read this column, but I like to scan the pictures, to see if I recognize anyone. Most of my current circle includes teachers, dreamers and psychologists, people rarely featured on the boards of the opera or the museum, but once in a while I'll spot someone I've gone to school with, or was a friend of my parents, or an acquaintance from my neighborhood. Today, I recognized the smiling faces of Cliff and Karen Morgan alongside another couple.

"Poolside Fund Raiser" ran the header by the picture and I saw that I was looking into the Morgan back yard, where a tent had been erected near the pool and a dance floor and musicians could be seen in the background. "Hosting a summer picnic to benefit the athletic fund for the Ferris School, where their daughter Stephanie will enter seventh grade, are Clifford and Karen Morgan, left. Cliff joins the board this year and with him are school head Suzanne Campbell and board chair, Gerald Mitchell. Guests included...." The rest of the article was nothing more than a list of names, as all such items were. These features seemed mainly an opportunity for prominent people, or people hoping to become prominent, to see their names in print.

"Well, whaddya know," I murmured to myself. Now I knew where Stephanie went to school — the same private school I had gone to, back when it was still all girls. I drummed my fingers on the kitchen table and sipped my coffee. "There goes our chance to find out anything about Stephanie through public school records," I thought ruefully. "Smart move, Cliff," I said out loud, and then I checked myself and added, "If you have something to hide." But I immediately reverted to my suspicions again. "Good idea to join the board too," I said between gritted teeth. I couldn't imagine what would happen at the Ferris School if a student confided to a staff member that her father was messing with her, especially if that father was a member of the board of trustees.

My phone rang then, and I wasn't surprised to hear Trudy asking, "Have you seen today's paper?"

"Yes I have."

"Is that the couple in question?"

"Yes it is."

"Despoiling the sanctity of our alma mater?"

"Looks that way."

"Gross."

Neither I nor Trudy had bothered much with our old school as adults. Once in a while, we might show up for a reunion, but one needed to keep a low profile. The alumnae development people were constantly trawling for volunteers and contributors, and a city resident had to lie low to prevent yet another friendly phone call.

It wasn't that we hadn't enjoyed an excellent education at the Ferris School — in fact, we'd been so prepped for college that most of our freshman year courses were superfluous. And we had loved a number of our teachers, engaging older women who were dedicated, bright and sometimes even brilliant, but born too soon to enjoy the wider opportunities that the women's movement would bring. Their confined circumstances were their students' gain.

But, once we were out in the wider world, we had seen that Ferris was essentially an incubator for the well-to-do, and as our politics swung well left of our father's, regretted the inescapable conclusion that our dear alma mater had far less to do with merit than with money. When Ferris went co-ed some years later, it lost the one thing that had redeemed it in our minds — an environment in which every role, from basketball star to student council president, from newspaper editor to National Merit Scholar, was undertaken by girls. That, we both had realized soon after being released into the real world, had been an extraordinary opportunity.

"Well, we're not going to get anywhere on this Stephanie business through the Mount Clair school district," I said resignedly.

"But I can still check for Maggie Morgan's records. In fact, I wanted to tell you that I could go in today. It's a teacher in-service day, so all the staff is there, even though school doesn't start for another week and a half."

"Are you expected to be there?" I wondered.

"No, but it's not unusual for counseling staff to come by," Trudy said. "Why do you ask?"

Why did I ask? I sighed and rolled my eyes, torn between caution and urgency. "Oh, well, y'know, I just wouldn't want anybody to think anything strange was going on. I mean, if you go rooting around for the file on a dead student."

"You're thinking that might be a problem?" Trudy sounded like she wasn't following.

I was flashing on Leo's lecture the night before, wondering how seriously to take his suspicions. They seemed pretty far fetched in the warm and damp light of day. "Let me ask you something," I said. "Can you just go retrieve this file by yourself, or would you have to sign something?"

"Well," Trudy said consideringly, "in the regular student records, I can just go in and pull a file. But those are the ones where there isn't much detail. The extra ones, for the special ed and gifted kids, are in a separate place and I do have to sign for those. But that's where I think we'll find the most information."

"I think you ought to go slow on this, Trudy."

"Really? Why?" She sounded both surprised and disappointed.

"Well, because...because I told Leo about this last night and he got all paranoid and then I blew up and we had this huge fight and then we sort of made up and then I promised him that...I'd go slow."

"I see," said Trudy, and she was trying to. "And?"

"He thinks Cliff Morgan might be, um, dangerous to mess with."

"I told you that!" Trudy protested. As a next-to-youngest, Trudy had often been overlooked and she was always quick to resent it when it seemed to be happening again.

"But, Leo doesn't mean like lawsuits-and-financial-ruin dangerous, he means *dangerous* dangerous."

"Really? How dramatic!" Trudy took a moment to absorb this and then asked, "Did he say why?"

"Because of something he saw on *Sixty Minutes*," I said, and it sounded so ludicrous that we both began to giggle. When Trudy asked, "Something Morley Safer said, was it?" we laughed out loud.

Finally, I tried to explain Leo's fears more sensibly. "It's because of what Cliff Morgan does — did I mention any of this to you?"

"Nope."

"He has his own company, providing security personnel who escort executives when they travel, that sort of thing."

"And Leo thinks this is dangerous?"

"He thinks Cliff Morgan might have people around him who can be. Plus, Leo'd seen a feature on *Sixty Minutes* once about how easy it is to have someone murdered in this country."

Trudy sighed deeply, a sound that telegraphed frustration rather than fear. "You know what I think?"

"What?"

"I think Leo loves you, and he's really protective because of it."

"Thank you, counselor," I said. "It's always helpful to hear another point of view." I still hadn't told anyone about Leo's pitch to move back in with me, and now did not seem the time.

"You're welcome. Now, what do you want me to do?"

In the end, Trudy agreed to check only the files she could get to without signing anything, and I agreed to take the first shift of hospital visiting while she did it. For a dark moment after we hung up, I wondered if this was about to become a regular feature of our lives, comparing notes daily on who would visit Dad, and when. But I pushed the likelihood out of my mind; it was simply too much to dwell on now.

Upon arriving at the hospital, I learned that my father was being moved from intensive care to a room on the neurology floor. It seemed good news that he was out of danger, but when I found him on a gurney in a hallway, waiting to be transferred into his bed, he was scowling.

"The maids..." he said angrily, his speech slow and slurred. He had grasped the side rail with his left hand and raised his head off the pillow, for emphasis.

"They're cleaning up your room?" I prompted, and peeked in the door. It was an empty semi-private, both beds made up and ready for occupancy.

Dad lay back and waved his hand in a gesture of impatience. "They're slow." He said the last word so distinctly that I took it as an attempt at irony, another good sign.

"Have you been waiting long?" I asked.

"All day!" he said indignantly. I looked at my watch. It was a little after ten.

"Let me see what I can do about this, Dad," I said. "I'll check at the nurse's station." I roamed the hallways until I found the desk. A young African-American nurse in a white uniform and a navy blue cardigan was talking on the phone and taking notes. I stepped back and waited politely until she was finished. The nurse looked up appreciatively and said, "May I help you?"

"I'm here to see my father, Stanley Nilsson, and he's wondering when he'll be put in his room."

The nurse turned, pulled up a clipboard and scanned the top sheet. "He's not in his room yet?"

"He's outside his room, in the hall."

Another nurse came behind the desk and looked over the shoulder of the desk nurse, who pointed at the chart with a questioning look. "Oh, yeah. We're getting to him." This was a middle-age woman, short and plump, with light blue eyes and a strong jaw. She looked directly across the desk at me and said, "He calls us maids."

I felt my face drain of color. "He does?" was all I could say. Stan Nilsson was as much or more of a chauvinist than any man his age, but this was outrageous.

"That's awful," I said, and it was, but not really out of character for the man. I thought of saying, "Imagine being his daughter," but I didn't. Then I wondered whether this was a product of the stroke — did he think he was still at the club? I considered telling these two women that he customarily stayed at a private club where he was catered to by maids and wait staff, but thought better of it. I did say, with feeling, "I think he may be confused." The older nurse snorted just a little before shrugging her acceptance of this explanation and proceeded down the hall to my father.

As he was being settled into the bed near the window, I was again acutely aware of the fine line one must walk when one is dealing with an institution. The nurse raised the rails on either side of the bed and adjusted the back at a low angle. After placing the call button so it was near his left hand, she rolled the bedside table alongside him and placed a urinal on it. "You know what this is for?" she asked. My father looked over at the plastic jug with an expression of disdain, less for the urinal than for being asked a question he found stupid, I suspected. He nodded without comment.

"I want you to call us when you need to use it," she instructed, and handed him the call button. "Press here," she said. "Let me see you do it."

He obliged her silently, and I prayed that he wouldn't express his annoyance. The nurse promptly turned off the resulting signal and made her way toward the door.

"Whatever you do, don't try to get out of bed. Whenever you need something, push that button." And she was out the door before Stanley Nilsson could talk down to her again.

"Dad," I said, leaning on the rail by his head, "the nurses who are helping you here are professionals. You should call them nurses."

My father lifted his left hand again, dismissing them all — maids, nurses, daughters, women — with a wave. Apparently, he'd also waved away the discussion, because then he suddenly reported, "I had a dream."

Was he saying this because he was remembering that dreams were my specialty? His attitude toward this in the past had ranged from disdain to amusement, but never approval. Certainly he had never told me a dream before. But here he was now, forging ahead, in strained, choppy phrases.

"President Nixon … was in a crib," he said. "He … couldn't get out." His facial expression had turned to anguish over the predicament of the president, and I instantly understood its meaning. Witnessing his favorite commander-in-chief lying helplessly in a bed with bars was an allegory of his own powerlessness. And in another moment, I understood that telling me this dream was not a non sequitur after all. I saw the connection between his belittling the nurses and his need to maintain a sense of dominance. It was his old trick of asserting superior status by taking everyone else down a peg.

Unfortunately, he was now in a situation in which he actually was helpless and dependent. I wondered how long it would take him to figure this out.

"Dad," I said, "you need to be nice to the people who take care of you. If you want them to do a good job."

"They get paid," he said sourly.

I sighed. Who was it who'd said, "The rich can afford to give offense wherever they go"? I remember reading it at Ferris — was it Jane Austen? *Pride and Prejudice*, probably. And then I flashed on another high school memory. Who was it who had written 'noblesse oblige' on the board? Ah yes, it was Martha O'Neill, the horrible Latin teacher who replaced the beloved Miss Dumont after her fatal heart attack.

"Does anyone here know what this means?" Miss O'Neill had asked, pointing to her perfect cursive with a piece of chalk. She wore a handkerchief on her belt and seemed to purse her lips when she spoke. No one raised a hand. "It is French of course, but comes from the Latin. *Noblesse oblige* means that the nobility are obliged to behave especially honorably. Those of you who go to school here are sent by families who consider themselves nobility. Therefore, I expect the highest standards of deportment from you all."

Even the dullest scholars in the room had recognized this as a shot across the bow. Her meaning could not have been clearer if she had written, "The students at the Ferris School are by definition spoiled brats, but try to surprise me." Not surprisingly, no one tried. But the lecture and the insult lingered in my mind, a moment of revelation in my coming of age. Some people were prejudiced against families who were well off. In fact, lots of people were. I gradually came to understand that the decorous WASP traditions of formality and restraint were tools for getting along in a world where people naturally hate you.

Stanley Nilsson knew the rules of conduct, yet here he was completely screwing up his chances of building rapport with the people who would be caring for him. Perhaps it was simply beyond his ken to grasp that he was dependent; or perhaps, he needed to keep his hand in, to assert his power until he could exercise it again. Whatever the reason, he was making life hard on himself and either didn't realize it or didn't care.

Not that this was new. My father had never paid much attention to the feelings of others; the emotional understanding that my sisters and I developed was entirely due to our mother. It was true that as he made his way from immigrant's son to founder of a large accounting firm, his manners were gentlemanly, but this was because it suited his business objectives. Unfortunately, the more successful he became, the more he seemed to feel entitled to behave like an arrogant bully.

I looked down at my father, who had closed his eyes and was breathing evenly. His lids looked like parchment paper, and I watched as the movie started, which is how I like to think of REM. I hoped he was having healing dreams, and sighed. My father was helpless and that was sad; that was the bottom line. I was trying to accommodate the unusual sensation of feeling pity toward him when my mother walked in.

I jumped up, put my finger to my lips and crossed the room. I took Mother's arm and walked her into the corridor.

"Mom, I'm glad you came! Maybe you'll be able to talk to Dad."

"What's the matter?"

"Well, he's being obnoxious to the staff. He's referring to the nurses as maids."

"In front of them?" Her tone was incredulous.

"Oh yes," I said, rolling my eyes in exasperation.

"Well, then," she said, "I'm glad I brought these." I saw then that she was carrying a large box of chocolates under her book.

"For the staff?"

"It never hurts to give people a reason to look in on you."

"God Mom, that's brilliant."

"Not really. Remember, I was married to your father for a long time," she said with a wry smile.

I regarded her gratefully. She didn't have to participate in the grind of coming to the hospital — this was not her husband — but here she was anyway, making the load lighter for her daughters and, undoubtedly, for the old bastard sleeping inside the room.

"Willa, you look tired," my mother was saying. "I'll stay awhile and you can go."

"I do have a lot on my mind," I admitted, "and on my desk!"

"Then scoot," she said, giving me a peck on the cheek and a pat on the behind. I hiked my purse onto my shoulder and gave my mother's arm a squeeze. "Thank you so much!" I said, and set off down the corridor, then turned and called, "Tell Dad I'll see him tomorrow." Mom waved and I turned back to head for the elevator, plunging back into my own life again and its other crises.

Chapter 21

The first thing I did when I got back to my desk was to log onto my computer and click to my e-mail account. That was the fastest way for me to reach my old friend, Victoria Golombiewski. Calling the law firm meant hitting the receptionist wall, but with e-mail, I knew that Vicki would read my message personally and respond as soon as she was able.

But first, I had to wait for over a hundred messages to download, the back-up resulting from my absence the day before. Many went to the spam folder, and I ignored the rest while I typed a message that I hoped would convey my sense of urgency without alarming my friend.

"Have a problem for which I need counsel," I typed, and then stopped. "Counsel" connoted formal legal problems and I wanted to avoid anything that smacked of jeopardy. Vicki was already mildly paranoid, as most diligent lawyers are. Like doctors, lawyers know just how much can go wrong, and how badly. And having already steered me into protecting myself during the legal crisis of becoming a suspect in a murder, Vicki shouldn't be frightened unnecessarily. I deleted what I'd written and started again.

"Yo! Heeding your expert advice, am now contacting you BEFORE I do something semi-rash. Call me when you have a minute, sooner is better. Love, W."

I peered at what I'd written and decided the tone was right — good natured and not dire. I clicked on "send" and then proceeded to read through my e-mail. In spite of my filter, I deleted a number of offers to have my penis enlarged or to profit from a confidential, urgent business relationship with someone in Africa. But I was surprised to find a note from Earl Newman, and clicked to read his message.

"Dear Willa, It was good to see you the other day, in spite of the sad circumstances. I spoke to Frank Conrad about the disposition of Bonnie's dream journals, and I got the impression that he was planning to place them in your care. I just want to let you know that we here at the longitudinal study project would be very happy if you chose to share them with us. Toward a better understanding of dreams, Earl."

I hit reply and typed fast. "Earl, Bonnie treasured dreaming for qualities that you ridicule and for which you skewered her publicly. She may be beyond caring, but I am not. Trust that I will never share her personal dream diaries with you or contribute them to any research led by you. Don't even think about asking again, Willa." I stopped myself, realizing that this was one of those times that I ought to think before acting. But on the other hand, I was pissed. I hit "send."

Then I proceeded to the rest of my e-mail, deleting come-ons for work-at-home schemes, lower mortgage payments and opportunities to gamble online. I wondered if somehow the senders knew that my income had dropped. Just as marketers know that I shop online, could they also have deduced that I need money? I shook my head, rejecting the idea as paranoid, but then thought, for the first time since my father's hospitalization, of what it would mean financially if he died.

I had no idea how much money he had, but it was a lot more than I did, that was certain. Three ex-wives had been taken care of, however, so his assets must have been diminished somewhat. And then there was the little matter of his inclination to claim he would disinherit whichever daughter was displeasing him at any given time. Over the years, I and most of my sisters had each, at one time or another, managed to be threatened with this, a fact of life that we each learned to blow off. Usually, Dad's diatribes occurred after drinks and dinner, and we hoped and assumed that the threats were forgotten in the morning-after fog. But in fact, none of us knew whether he called his lawyer after the time one of us became engaged to a Latino, or when another insisted the Republicans had sold out the country. It had become an issue of some nervous bemusement among us just what would come to pass when the old man finally expired. If he hadn't written me out, I could be worth many times my current meager assets when he died.

Discussing Dad's affairs had not even occurred to us in all the anxiety of yesterday's emergency. Where was his will, I wondered? His stock portfolio? Who had power of attorney? Was there a living will? Was all this in Florida and if so, where in Florida? I began to scribble notes to myself, things to talk to sisters about, when the phone rang.

"What <u>now</u>?" Vicki's voice feigned foreboding. "You are nothing but trouble, you know that?"

I laughed, "Hey, I tried to make it sound casual! You're just overly sensitized."

"And who wouldn't be, after what I went through with you! My lands!" This exclamation was a mutual joke, a line from our class play in the fourth grade.

"We have known each other <u>way</u> too long!" I groaned.

"But hasn't it been fun, what with finding you a criminal lawyer and all? Now tell me, what's on your mind?" She sounded downright chipper.

I took a breath and looked at the ceiling, trying to organize my thoughts. "Okay, what if you suspected that someone may have committed a crime?"

"What if I suspected a crime, or you did? I'm an officer of the court, and have responsibilities that don't necessarily pertain to you."

"I, what if I, an average citizen, suspect that a crime may have been committed."

"Would you like to tell me the nature of the crime?"

"Child abuse," I said, and then tried refine it. "Sexual abuse. Incest actually."

Vicki didn't betray any emotional reaction, but when she spoke again, her voice was serious and even, the way it is when she's wearing her lawyer hat.

"I trust this is no one close to you or your family."

"God no!" I said. "It's someone I've just met recently. A twelve-year-old."

"If sexual abuse is something you suspect may be happening, you should report it to authorities so that it can be investigated."

"Even if I don't have any proof?" I noticed that I was twisting the phone cord as I spoke.

"Can you give me more specific details?" Vicki asked.

"Yes, but can this just be between the two of us?"

"If you're asking about attorney client confidentiality, maybe you'd better come into the office."

I thought about that for a moment and replied, "This is as much a moral dilemma I'm having as a legal one. More, really. Do you have time to hear me out?"

"I'm all ears."

And so I recounted, as briefly as I could, my work with Stephanie, my discovery of Bonnie's suspicions and my current quandary.

"So, let me get this straight. You fear this child is being victimized but have nothing to go on but Bonnie's remarks. And Bonnie's suspicions are based only on the girl's dreams?"

"That's right." This time I heard Vicki exhale her own perplexity.

"You haven't learned anything from the girl herself?"

"No, I've only had one session with her. The next one is ..." I extracted my date book from the rubble on my desk, "...tomorrow."

There was a long pause on the phone and then Vicki said, "Hold on, I'm trying to find something." I heard her put the phone down and return a few seconds later.

"Okay, I can give you this much. There's an anonymous hotline for anyone to report child abuse. So one thing you could do is make a call. I've got the number here."

"Then by all means, give it to me. Is this the county's child and youth agency?"

"The hotline is run by the state, but they refer you to local services," Vicki said.

"And if I made this anonymous call, what would happen as a result?"

"Authorities would investigate. That's the law."

I tried to imagine what that would be like, picturing a couple of underpaid and overworked caseworkers ringing the doorbell of the Morgan home. What would happen next? They would say why they had come, and probably question the father, and maybe the daughter. And then what?

"Remember that this is a very well-to-do man with a lot to lose. Don't you think the first thing he's going to do is call a lawyer?" I asked.

"Yes, that's probably exactly what he'll do."

"And realistically — unless the girl incriminates the father right off the bat — that lawyer will bring pressure, legal and possibly even political pressure, on the agency and its caseworkers, right?"

"She or he might, yes," Vicki said.

"Then they would probably back off, am I right?"

"In the absence of testimony or evidence? I'm afraid so."

"Sooo," I said, "I don't want to try the anonymous call ploy unless and until I think the girl may be able to speak up."

"If you believe the guy is guilty, you may want to call anyway. At least you will have done something."

"And that would certainly make me feel better. It's awful to worry that a child is being harmed, but not even know if it's true. And that's the bottom line — I don't really know if the guy is guilty."

There was a silence while we thought about the options. Then Vicki asked, "Have you tried speaking with the girl directly?"

"I only found out about this yesterday, so no."

"You should try to draw her out, see if she has anything to say that gives you a better sense of what she may or may not be going through. And what about the mother?"

Yeah, what about the mother? I hadn't even tried to fit her into the picture yet. I flashed on Karen driving her silver BMW, consulting her golden Rolex. "She appears to be a Mount Clair suburban type, you know, buff and fashionable. I don't know much more than that, except that her husband has a drinking problem and has physically abused her at least once."

"Ho boy."

"I know," I was nodding. "What a mess." I thought about Stephanie, her tone with her mother, her muttered "Drinky-poos" and what a smart kid she was. "You know, you're right, I might get a lot farther along here by spending more time with Stephanie, getting to know her better."

"She might be able to confide in you," Vicki offered.

"But the truth is that she didn't confide in Bonnie, who was her therapist. All Bonnie had to go on were the girl's dreams."

"Well, you can try. That's all you can do."

"Except call that hotline."

"I wouldn't use that that until I knew more. Unless the girl speaks up, unless you have something more than suspicion to go on, you don't have a case."

"You see what I mean about a moral dilemma," I said.

"I certainly do. I hope you will keep me posted on this. I'll help if I can."

"I knew you would. Thanks."

"I'm off to a meeting in a few minutes, so let's talk later."

"Oh yes" — I suddenly realized I hadn't told her anything about Dad — "I have much else to tell you," I said in a rush. "Dad's in the hospital, but I'll give you the details later."

"Well, I won't worry about him — he's a tough old bird!"

I shook my head with a smile and said, "You said it. Later, kiddo. And thanks. Again."

After I spent the next hour or two working at my desk, preparing for the courses I would soon begin teaching, the phone rang and I picked up to hear Trudy sounding distracted.

"Have you talked to Mom yet?"

"Not since this morning."

"Well, Mary's flying in tomorrow from Austin. I told Mom that I could go pick her up but I just realized that I have a periodontist's appointment. Mom said she could pick her up, but I'd rather she not drive all the way out there."

"Ditto," I said. Mother was no worse than the average elderly driver, but no better either. She generally avoided high speed forays like the Parkway to the airport, to everyone's relief. "What time does the flight get in?"

"American Airlines at 4:05."

"That's doable." I could head for the airport after my session with Stephanie. Mary was our youngest and least reverent sister. Being with her would be a welcome antidote to the week's distress.

"Good," said Trudy, "and now, about those files on Maggie Morgan."

"Oh yes — were you able to learn anything?"

"Only that a dead student's file seems to disappear from the records room. I even asked around, just one or two people, to see what the practice is when a student dies, but nobody knew for sure. But there was no file for Maggie Morgan in either the regular records section or the special ed files."

"So you <u>did</u> sign in for the special ed file?" My voice was tinged with alarm, but Trudy sounded breezy.

"There was a form that I had to sign, but since there was nothing there, I just took it back with me. The secretary didn't think anything about it."

"So, there's no record of your interest?"

"Not on paper."

"Well, good." I said. "But is there any other record?"

"Not really, but I did have a conversation with my fellow counselor, Loretta. You know, the friend who told me about the Garden of Eden? It turns out she had some dealings with Maggie Morgan, and she found some notes about it in her files."

"When was this?" I asked.

"It was the spring semester before she died, so two and a half years ago. A friend of Maggie's came in because she was worried about her. Maggie was taking pills of some kind, confided in the friend about having dizzy spells, and the friend got scared and came to Loretta."

"And what did she do?"

"Well, she spoke to Maggie, who claimed she was on medication for allergies."

"And did it stop there?"

"No, because when Loretta asked to see the prescription, it was for Adderall. And it was made out to her mother."

"What's Adderall?"

"It's marketed as therapy for Attention Deficit Disorder, but it also works as a diet pill. Basically, it's an amphetamine. The kid broke down and said her mother takes this stuff regularly, and she thought she could take some and lose weight before the spring dance."

"I can attest that the mother is super svelte," I said.

"Let's hear it for speed," said Trudy.

"So then what did Loretta do?"

"Well, the protocol is to call the parents, but Loretta made it a point to call the father at work instead of the mother."

"Because it looks like Mom has a problem?"

"Well, maybe Mom has an attention deficit disorder, but I doubt it, don't you?"

"So Loretta called Cliff Morgan," I said, following the trail, "and how did he respond?"

"She said he was great. He seemed very concerned, offered to come in, by himself. He had a serious talk with Loretta and then they had Maggie come in. Loretta thought he was a model father, listened to the daughter, told her she looked fine just the way she was, asked her what she thought was best."

I flashed on seeing Cliff Morgan greet Stephanie when he came home that day, looking fatherly and affectionate. "What was the outcome?" I asked.

"Loretta never knew for sure, but in her office that day, Maggie swore off the diet pills. After that Loretta never heard another thing about it, from Maggie or her friend."

I struggled to take all this in. "So this guy might be a regular loving father who's had a terrible loss, and this whole prospect of sexual abuse could be false."

"I guess Bonnie's suspicions could have been wrong," Trudy agreed. "Then again, a father who had a sexual interest in his daughter might also behave the way he did, to prevent a school counselor from prying any further." She exhaled with frustration. "When do you see Stephanie again?"

"Tomorrow afternoon."

"Have you thought about how you might be able to address this with her?"

"I was hoping to know more before I tried. It's all so damn — murky!" I groaned.

"Truly. And you're still just getting to know her."

I listened to Trudy's breathing for a minute. We were both thinking.

"Rapport, that's what you need," she said.

"I agree."

"She may be able to speak if she feels she can trust you."

"So that'll be my goal tomorrow. Just making her feel comfortable with me."

"Yes, and don't expect this to happen overnight," Trudy cautioned. "Making kids feel like it's safe to talk to me is one of the harder parts of my job, and it sounds like this kid may have a lot of reasons to distrust adults."

I felt my shoulders tightening and rubbed the back of my neck. "I appreciate the advice, and I may need more of it."

"Any time."

After hanging up, I tried a neck roll and felt the twinges of muscles reacting to two days of stress. I stretched my arms over my head and heard faint cracking noises in my spine and felt a pinpoint of pain in my shoulder. I knew the best remedy was exercise and decided I would have to take time for it, whether I could afford to or not. Then I smiled at the thought of swimming. Not only would it cool me off, for the afternoon had grown muggy, but it would also calm me down. I shut down my computer, wary of more thunderstorms on the way, then searched for my bag and noted that everything was there — goggles, cap, swimsuit. I went upstairs for a set of clean clothes, packed them into the tote and headed for the health club.

I had only recently been swimming regularly, and that was thanks to Leo's Christmas gift of a year's membership at a nearby gym that featured a pool. I had loved to swim as a child, and to body surf whenever I got to the seashore, but swimming for exercise was something I approached gingerly. Since my knees could no longer withstand jogging, I had to try something. My first attempt featured fifteen minutes in the hot tub followed by five in the swimming pool, gasping after six laps. Little by little over the past eight months, I kept at it, forcing myself to keep going an extra minute or two every week. Gradually, my strength grew and I found that swimming offered payoffs beyond endurance, flexibility and maintaining a medium-sized figure. I now thought of it as "taking the waters" in its most promising sense, of healing ablutions. Over time, I came to feel that my motion and breathing created a kind of liquid meditation. Being underwater reminded me of dreaming, seeing a world invisible to those above the surface, and coming up for air reminded me of being awake to the daytime world, with its noise and its light. Splashing in and out of the depths gave me a feeling of expansion, as if able to experience both waking and dreaming at once. Fifteen minutes into a workout, I've entered a trance in which I'm at one with the water and the air and the universe.

I warmed up in the whirlpool, slipped into an empty lane of the pool and settled into my rhythm of stroking and breathing. This seemed to be the truth of encroaching age: use it or lose it. Then the picture of my father came into my mind, lying in bed, half paralyzed. Would the man who taught me to swim ever swim again? Would he ever be able to use his right side? After physical therapy, could he return to Florida? I reached the end of the pool and kicked off, thinking how wonderful it was to have a body that works. How would my father come to terms with having one that didn't?

I swam and wondered about him and his whole generation. Would historians looking back on the last half of the twentieth century say, as I had come to believe, "Well, all these guys went off to the Second World War and most who returned suffered from post traumatic stress disorder. But no one knew what that was or how to treat it in those days, so mostly, men worked hard and drank a lot and were difficult to live with." The story at my house — irritable and sometimes scary father, calm if weary mother, a house full of kids — had been repeated in homes all over our neighborhood, all over the country. It had taken me years to realize this wasn't necessarily a given of family life, that something had happened to this generation to make them the way they were. Just as the Vietnam War and the draft that came with it — a message to the young that said, "Don't question our policies, just get in line and sacrifice yourself" — turned their offspring into protesters and peaceniks.

I reached a wall and flipped onto my back. My strokes reached behind my line of sight as I wondered what life would have been like if my father had had a son. Each of his daughters had, in some way or another, tried to compensate for the fact that she wasn't a boy. For me it was academic, acquiring the most advanced degree I could. However, my father had not expressed much pride in my Ph.D., except for joshing that now I was a "doctor of Thinkology." This line from the *Wizard of Oz* was delivered with affection, but it was also sarcastic. My father was never one to credit intellectuals, even if one of his daughters had officially joined their ranks.

Trudy won his approval as the family athlete; Marcia followed in his footsteps and became a CPA. Glad had started out majoring in social work, which our father found more foolhardy than virtuous, but redeemed herself by marrying a successful Silicon Valley entrepreneur and producing triplets, all boys. And then there was Mary, who hoped to immortalize the Nilsson name by becoming a best selling writer. She had style, good training and could have drunk Hemingway under the table, but the sales of her first novel had been disappointingly small. She was fortunate to be married to a dentist who was happy to be the provider while she toiled at her writing and raised their two kids.

Each of us had attended the best college we could get into, but we all felt ourselves a disappointment to the old man. All of us had to deal with the peculiarly feminine challenges of trying to do it all —

raise a family, sustain a marriage and succeed at a profession. None of us had managed to do it all, at least not all at once, and thus none provided what a son would have — the gung-ho trajectory of the hardworking careerist, which is to say, the mirror of the father. Now it's very possible, indeed likely, that a real son might have been a disappointment too, but in his absence, we daughters had only a perfect phantom with which to compare ourselves.

I swam smiling to myself that I really was behaving like a doctor of thinkology today. The repetitive movements and steady respiration seemed to heighten my concentration. And what I wanted to focus on was meeting with Stephanie tomorrow. How to encourage a twelve-year-old to open up? Perhaps I would ask about her nightmares and see if she volunteered any dream content. Or ask about her sessions with Bonnie, perhaps? Although that might open up a vein of sadness, for both of us.

Doing the breast stroke, alternately plunging beneath and over the surface of the water, I tried to think about what it was like to be twelve. You're right on the cusp then, your body maturing much faster than your mind can encompass. It's a liminal time, I realized, and Stephanie was betwixt and between childhood and adolescence. Suddenly, I remembered a Christmas when I was that age and feeling very torn about the newest Barbie dolls that my younger sisters received. I knew I shouldn't want to play with them, was even ashamed of my attraction to them, but the child part of me had not died away just because I was getting periods and breasts.

And that was when I came up with what seemed like a terrific idea — I would approach Stephanie not as a preteen on her uncertain way to adolescence, but as the mature and accomplished child she already was. I gave an extra little kick of enthusiasm at having arrived at this promising approach, and plotted the next day's session.

Chapter 22

When I arrived at the Morgan house this time, it was with a sense of wariness. Now that I knew that something very wrong might be happening in this house, I eyed its verdant lawn and manicured shrubbery with disdain bordering on contempt. Was making things look perfect this couple's way of exonerating themselves from responsibility for their children's well being? Cliff Morgan must come home to this every night and feel reassured that all is right with the world, no matter what he does when he's had his drinks. The home now seemed like a magician's trick, a way to misdirect the attention of the community. Here's this fine place, paid for by this successful man. Here is their daughter going to her fine school. This must be a model family; couldn't be any trouble here.

Although it was early in the afternoon and I doubted that Cliff would return home before I left, I was careful to park my car on the street instead of the driveway. Gritting my teeth over his previous rudeness, I slammed my door too hard and realized that my rage was showing.

"Willa," I muttered to myself, "get a grip for godssake." I paused in the sunlight and took a deep breath. "Remain calm," I told myself. "You can't do this child any good if you act like a hothead."

I lugged my book bag from the back seat and headed for the front door, which opened before I reached it.

"Hi!" Karen said, throwing open the door. Today she was wearing a perfect ensemble of tailored beige Bermuda shorts, a pink placket shirt and a green visor that read, "The Masters."

"I'm glad you're on time. I have to get going to a golf lesson. I hoped you wouldn't mind if I go out while you work with Stephanie."

Mind? I was delighted. "Sure, that's no problem," I said. I followed Karen into the entry as she called up the stairs. "Stephanie, Dr. Nilsson is here." Stephanie appeared almost instantly, and smiled at me as she trotted down the steps. It was an expression that Karen didn't see as she gathered up her purse and headed toward the garage.

"Stephanie, would you be sure to get Dr. Nilsson an iced tea, or whatever?" She didn't wait for an answer. "I have to run. Have a good session you two." She was halfway through the door when she turned back and said. "Oh, and there's an envelope for you on the kitchen table. Bye now!" The heavy metal door closed with a thud.

Stephanie and I looked at each other as the garage door rattled open and the car's engine revved. Stephanie asked, "Can you play golf?"

I shook my head. "Never even tried," I said.

"Me neither. It seems kinda — dumb."

"A lot of people love it though."

Stephanie nodded and led the way into the kitchen. "There's lots of stuff to drink," she said. "Iced tea, and there's Diet Pepsi." She opened the refrigerator door.

"Diet Pepsi sounds great, thanks."

"Or how about a martini?" Stephanie turned around with a sly grin on her face. Her brown eyes were framed by dark lashes that grew straight out of her eyelids, and her expression made me feel like I was talking to a smiling camel.

I cocked my head and smiled back. "Naw, I think Pepsi," I said, hopeful that such joking constituted rapport building between us. "How about you?"

"I'm making chocolate milk. You want some?"

I shook my head. "Pepsi's fine."

As Stephanie poured the drinks, I decided to start right in on my theme for the day.

"You know, I've been thinking about something having to do with dreams, and I wondered what you thought," I began.

"Me? Why?" Stephanie extracted a bottle of Hershey's Chocolate Syrup and squeezed a goodly amount into her glass of milk.

"Because I'm a little rusty on my children's stories. But I've been trying to think of all the ones that feature dreaming. The first one I thought about was *The Wizard of Oz*."

The squeeze bottle emitted a noisy, almost-empty blurt as Stephanie's face lit up with recognition. "Oh, you mean because it turns out the whole story was a dream." Then she corrected herself, "The whole color story, I mean."

"Yes, exactly."

"Or a nightmare," Stephanie continued. She produced a long handled spoon and stirred her milk as it turned more and more brown. "Actually, I feel kind of sorry for Dorothy when she wakes up. I mean, you feel glad that she finally got home, but everything is black and white again. And her house is all wrecked up and maybe that mean witch is going to come for Toto again." She opened a drawer and pulled out two straws. I accepted mine and sipped my Pepsi with a half smile.

"Do you think real life was like a nightmare for Dorothy?"

"When the lady takes her dog away? Sure!" She took a sip of her milk and added, "Her aunt and uncle didn't do anything about it."

"That's kind of scary isn't it?" I mused. "When grown-ups don't do the right thing, or can't."

Stephanie shrugged, looked up at the ceiling and said, "*Alice in Wonderland*."

I nodded, slowly because of this sudden turn. "Yes, right, that's all a dream too isn't it?"

"I have the video. A lot of stuff in that is scary too."

"But not before she falls asleep, right?"

Stephanie thought about that. "Nope, I don't think so. I hardly watched it," she said in a confessional tone, "because I never liked it very much. Mom buys all the Disney movies because she likes them."

"How about *Sleeping Beauty*?"

"I *love* that one," she said enthusiastically. "But there's nothing about dreams in it, really. Just about sleeping."

I nodded, "You're right."

"You know what else I like? *Snow White*." Stephanie placed a hand to her chest and sang in a falsetto voice, "I'm wishing...." and then began to giggle. I had never seen her laugh before, and grinned at the sight of it.

"Snow White falls asleep on the Seven Dwarfs' beds," I recalled, "but I don't think she dreams anything, does she?"

"Well, no," Stephanie agreed. "But you know what? She sleeps a lot! After she eats the poisoned apple and she drops dead? She's really just asleep, right?"

"Right."

"But everybody thinks she's dead and the dwarfs chase the witch and she dies and then everybody's crying around Snow White's coffin."

I nodded and listened.

"And then the prince comes, and makes her wake up. But you know what? The witch told her if she'd eat the apple, her fondest wish would come true. And that's what she wished for."

Remembering the Disney movie's triumphant finale as the prince gathers up his revived sweetheart, I nodded my head in amazement. "I never realized that before!"

Stephanie nodded. "Snow White probably thought that old lady with the apple was her fairy godmother! She wished for the prince to come and take her to his castle."

"And the next thing she knew, that's exactly what happened!"

"Yep!" Stephanie sucked the last of her milk through her straw and then noisily tried to vacuum up the syrup left at the bottom of the glass. "Sorry," she said breathlessly, looking like she wasn't.

I was marveling at what a remarkable insight this kid had come up with. Snow White slept through the bad stuff and woke for the good — how about that? This idea I'd had, to meet Stephanie on her own ground, was proving fruitful in ways I hadn't expected.

"*Peter Pan*, maybe." Stephanie was moving on. "They don't actually *say* that everything has been a dream, but they sorta make you think so, at the end."

"You're right," I agreed. "I think they do."

"Oh wait, I know a good one! Hold on, I'll be right back!"

Stephanie trotted up the steps and reappeared within the minute with two books.

"Do you know the Babar books?"

I regarded the bright yellow cover of a picture book featuring an elephant with a crown. "The King of the Elephants? I used to."

"Well, first he's the 'little' elephant and then later he gets to be king." She opened the book and began leafing through its pages. "He has a big dream in this one. He gets to be king but then all this bad stuff happens." She found what she was looking for and opened it for me to see. Babar was sleeping in his royal bed, dreaming with a furrowed brow.

"He hears this voice in his sleep," said Stephanie, and then she read dramatically, *"It is I, Misfortune, come to pay you a visit."* She turned to the next, two-paged spread. On the lower left, monstrous looking figures with names like "Despair," "Ignorance" and "Fear" were being chased away by angelic elephants swooping in from the upper right, labeled "Hope," "Patience," and "Courage."

"Wow," I said admiringly. "This really is some dream. I remember this now that I see it again."

"And when he wakes up, everything turns out to be okay," said Stephanie.

I nodded and turned the last pages. "Yeah, I remember." I looked up and said, "And what's this other book?"

Stephanie was holding it against her chest, her arms wrapped around it. "This is my <u>favorite</u> story." She turned it around so that the cover faced me and held it out.

"The Twelve Dancing Princesses," I read. "I know this story too — in fact, it was one of <u>my</u> favorites."

Stephanie's eyes widened. "Really?"

I reached for the large hardback picture book and opened it. This was a newer version than the one I had as a child, and the illustrations were rich and delicate. "Wow," I said, "these pictures are beautiful. Is that why you love it?"

"Partly," said Stephanie, "but I love the story too."

"Let me see if I can remember," I said. "The king cannot understand how his twelve daughters wear out their shoes every night, right?"

"Right, because every night they lock the door to their chamber and sneak down a secret staircase, and twelve princes meet them."

"And they go over a river to a forest with jewels or something?" I tried to remember.

"They go through a forest of silver, and then a forest of gold, and then a forest of diamonds." Stephanie recounted patiently, and leafed to the pages that showed the beautiful scenes. I sighed, "Oooo" in appreciation, and then said, "This <u>is</u> a lot like a wonderful dream, isn't it?"

Stephanie kept turning pages. "And then they would dance all night and wear out their shoes."

"Every night," I said again, realizing what the appeal of this story had been when I was young and then wondering whether to share it with Stephanie. I decided I could, with some judicious editing.

"You know, I remember why I liked this myself. I had four sisters, and it was fun to imagine that we had a secret passageway to a beautiful land where we could do what we wanted, and dance all night." I didn't say, "Where we could get away from our father's tyranny and enjoy being free," but that was my memory. Sometimes, when the household was at its most oppressive, I had looked forward to going to bed and being released into dreaming for the night. I had always imagined that the twelve princesses were in similar need of escape. A passage to a beautiful realm stocked with gems, a castle, and underground boyfriends sounded like a garden of girlish delights to me. And I now had enough Jung under my belt to know that whenever characters set off into the underground, it suggests venturing into the unconscious. Maybe the name of the story should be, "The Twelve Dreaming Princesses."

"My sister Maggie liked this too," Stephanie was saying. "She used to read this to me a lot. We used to play princesses." Stephanie's voice was low and confidential.

"And did you sneak out and go dancing with princes?" I asked with a grin, matching Stephanie's muted tone.

"No, but we did go swimming."

"At night?" I asked.

Stephanie nodded, and in an excited near whisper added, "Skinny dipping!"

"Skinny dipping!" I repeated, and for the next moment I was speechless, trying to frame an appropriate response. Here was Stephanie opening up to me and I didn't want to blow it, but I felt as if someone had tripped an alarm in my head.

Stephanie was continuing. "We started doing it when Mom and Dad were out and Maggie was babysitting me."

"I wonder," I said, casting about for a neutral thing to say, "did you feel safe, swimming by yourselves?"

"Sure," said Stephanie. "Maggie and I were always allowed to swim alone, as long as we were together — you know, the buddy system." Stephanie's voice sounded as if she felt defensive, and I tried to correct for coming on like an authority figure.

"I remember skinny dipping when I was about your age. It was fun." I flashed on visiting a friend at a lake in upstate New York, of creeping down to the dock at night, slipping into the water and then removing our suits. "We had to be really quiet, because that's the only way we could do it without somebody catching us — or seeing us."

"That's what we did too," Stephanie said, "so no neighbors would hear." The mood had changed into one of mutual conspiracy. "Then one night, Dad came home before we knew it and you know what he did?"

"What?"

"He turned on the underwater lights."

"What did you do?"

"We screamed, so he turned them back off."

"Was he mad?"

"He laughed like he thought it was funny, but then he sent me to my room."

"And Maggie too?"

"I guess." Stephanie shrugged. "I went to sleep."

I sat wondering whether to try and probe further. Stephanie, looking down at the counter with no real object in her gaze then volunteered, "She was in more trouble than I was." She sounded serious, and sorry.

"Because... she was older, supposed to be in charge?" casting about to keep the conversation going.

Stephanie shrugged again, "I guess," she said. "Plus, you know, when the king is mad..."

"What happens when the king is mad?"

"Well, it's just like in *Alice in Wonderland* with the Queen." Stephanie made a slashing gesture across her neck. "Off with their heads!" She raised her head to meet my gaze, and we looked each other in the eyes across the polished granite counter top.

"Sounds like the king can have a pretty bad temper."

Stephanie nodded. "Oh yeah. I wrote a poem about it once. 'When my dad gets mad it's very sad.' And my third grade teacher called my mom about it."

"And then what happened?"

"Mom told me not to write about that again. She said that our family business is private and I shouldn't talk about it." She lowered her head and looked up me. "She told me about kids who get taken away from their families if people think something bad is happening at home."

I paused and then asked, "And how did that make you feel?"

"Scared," she said. "I had more nightmares after that, the kind I can't remember, the terrors."

"What are those like?"

"I can't remember anything about them. All I know is, Mom or Dad or Maggie would be shaking me awake and telling me I'd been screaming. They'd be saying I woke up the whole house."

"Yes, that's what happens with night terrors, all right. Do you remember having nightmares that you could remember?"

"Sometimes. If I was scared, Maggie would let me get in bed with her. A couple of times, she got into bed with me."

"And that would make you feel better?"

Stephanie nodded and added, "No matter what I was scared of." Her lower lip quivered and when she blinked, a single tear escaped, ran down her cheek and plopped onto the counter. I reached out and stroked the top of her head. "You must miss her very much." Stephanie sucked in her lips and nodded again.

"I do," she said, wiping her face with her hand. "I dream about her sometimes. It's like she's here with me. She tells me what to do, like she used to."

"She tells you what to do? What about?"

"Like what to do when the king comes. She always told me, if the king comes at night, just be asleep. No matter what. She said staying asleep is like when the princesses lock their chamber door at night. Then the king can't get them."

I wanted nothing more then than to hold my head in my hands and try to absorb what I was hearing, to make sure that what I was surmising was really true. I needed to figure out how to respond and what to do next, but this door of opportunity had opened and I didn't have time to pause at the threshold.

"Does that work?" I asked, and I felt my heart beating harder. "To stay asleep no matter what?"

Stephanie's voice had faded to a near-whisper. "I'd rather lock the door."

Chapter 23

The drive to the airport was long but I didn't mind making it, because I needed to think. How much could I say I knew for sure and how much was speculation? I felt certain now that at the very least, Maggie had been subjected to some kind of inappropriate behavior on the part of her father involving nighttime visits to her room, and that Stephanie knew something about this. At the most, both Maggie and Stephanie were incest victims. How much could I claim with absolute confidence, or at least enough confidence to sic the law onto Cliff Morgan?

And was the legal remedy the best one? What outcome would be the best under these circumstances? I remembered what Trudy had said about families healing, picking up the pieces and moving on. So, therapy, and lots of it, for the victim, and certainly some kind of treatment for the parents?

But how in the world do people live with such egregious behavior? How does an abusive father go down to breakfast after messing with his daughter? I shook my head and glanced at the speedometer — I was going way over the speed limit. I eased off the gas and tried to make myself calm down, moving into the slow lane to enforce some moderation.

An SUV cut me off so that I had to I hit the brake and I honked at it, loud and long. Does four-wheel drive make people think they can defy the laws of physics? I saw the driver as the car sped onto the exit ramp to the mall. It wasn't some crazy teenager, but a grown woman. Was she that anxious to shop, or was there some reasonable justification for such conduct?

Which brought me back to the Morgan family, because I had to ask myself, where's the mother in all this? She looked as if she had it together — that flawless body, the salon coiffure, the manicured hands — but maybe they were just the personal version of the interior decorating and the landscaping. In truth, Karen was the abused wife of a problem drinker, and she was an amphetamine user to boot. Then I was struck by the thought that making things appear to be perfect might be the only way that Karen could feel in control in an uncontrollable situation.

Is it possible that a woman could know her husband was sexually abusing their daughters and not do anything about it? I answered my own question with a shake of my head. I couldn't imagine a mother that cold. And Karen was attentive to her daughter's needs, in fact had taken her to the sleep clinic and hired me to be her tutor. So I had to conclude that Karen didn't know. And telling Stephanie not to talk about their home life not only kept things under wraps, it reinforced the great WASP way, the stiff upper lip, the reliance on decorum that dictates invisible protocols from the golf course to the board room. Leo says that WASP doesn't really stand for "White Anglo-Saxon Protestant," but "We Are So Polite."

I realized that I had more options than I thought. Notifying child welfare authorities, with the attendant likelihood that skillful and expensive lawyers would get Cliff Morgan off the hook, was only one of several. Another was to do nothing until I could learn more from Stephanie, but I felt that the girl had told as much as she was capable of imparting. Repression is a healthy reaction, allowing victims to get on with their days, and Stephanie's was reinforced not only by the rule that she must not talk about trouble at home, but because her real experiences were confounded with nightmares and dreams, and with the fairy tales and fantasy play that she had shared with Maggie.

My third option, and the one that now seemed the most promising, was to sit down with Karen and have a heart to heart talk. This would take some planning — you couldn't just drop a bomb on a person and expect them to be able to do something. No, I would prepare for this meeting, would be ready with the resources that Karen could access for families dealing with substance abuse, domestic violence and yes, incest. I'd make a list of all the resources that offer support and counseling. I would have names and phone numbers ready. I would not only give Karen the bad news but help her to make her way through her pain and alarm.

By the time I was coming to the airport ramp I was feeling better. Learning the awful truth had made me queasy, but now my stomach seemed to have settled down. It was true that there was a serious and sickening problem, but I felt hopeful that I had come upon the means to try and solve it. I passed through the entrance to the airport, one of the biggest and best in the country, demarcated by massive granite slabs topped by circular emblems, a design that always reminds me of the monuments erected by the Third Reich in honor of itself. So much for the bad guys, I thought. The good guys can intervene and win the day, I reassured myself, and looked forward happily to seeing my sister again and enjoying the comfort of family.

Mary was already standing on the curb outside the baggage claim when I crept by, expecting to make at least a few more passes. I nosed in, popped the trunk and leapt out to give her a hug.

"Can you believe it? My flight was actually twenty minutes early!"

"You look great!" I effused, and meant it. Mary, the tallest sister at 5'8", was wearing jeans and cowboy boots and looked like a true Texan, lean and long.

"It's because I haven't been with my kids in…" Mary looked at her watch "…six hours. I got to finish an entire crossword puzzle on the plane and I had a snack and a drink all to myself. I feel like I've been to a spa!" She heaved her suitcase into the trunk and bounded into the passenger seat. "I'm a free woman!" she yelped, then turned, placed a hand on my arm with an exaggerated solemnity and said, "Okay, now how's Dad?"

I navigated the ramps leading from the airport while I updated her on what we knew so far and how long it might take before we had a clear picture of Dad's recovery.

"But, okay, so, HOW is he?" Mary wanted to know.

"Oh, you mean, how IS he? He's his old self. He was calling the nurses 'maids' yesterday, acting as if he had checked into a five star hotel instead of a hospital. Mom's been coming in to see him every day and I think he behaves better when she's around."

"Isn't that funny? He certainly never cared how he behaved around her when they were married," Mary snorted.

"I think that's the reason, actually. She doesn't have to visit him or concern herself with him at all and he knows it."

"And what's in this for Mom, do you think?"

"Truthfully? I think she's doing it for us. Trudy and I can't be in the hospital every day for hours, and she's really helping to fill the gap." I looked over at Mary. "And thank god you're here now!"

"You know, I wonder — don't you think she still feels loyal toward him? In spite of the fact that he was a rat to her."

"I think she does," I nodded. "Actually, Mom and Dad have kind of re-bonded since Dad's last divorce. I don't think it's romantic or anything, but they share deep roots."

"Yeah, well, five kids, that's deep. Now that I have two, I can't imagine what an ordeal it must have been to raise five. Maybe that's what drove him to seek other companionship." Mary was rummaging through her purse as she spoke and pulled out a plastic tube, a tampon case. "But where are those young trophy wives now?" she continued. "They couldn't cut the mustard!" Mary's husky laugh turned into a coughing spasm as she opened my ashtray and pushed in the cigarette lighter.

"Hey, I thought you just quit smoking!" I protested.

"Oh, I did!" Mary assured me, as she extracted a thin white cigarette from the bottom of a tampon tube. "Seventeen days ago. This is my therapy." She pulled out the lighter and pressed it to end of the cigarette, inhaling deeply.

"A joint!" I cried. "You brought that on the airplane? Are you crazy?"

"I've done it before," she said casually, after she'd opened her window and exhaled onto the Parkway. "This is how I managed to quit smoking. As long as I avoid tobacco all day, I slip out to the garage after dinner and have me a little mellow time. It's really working."

"Well, I wouldn't share that with the Surgeon General if I were you," I said, turning off the air conditioning and opening all the windows of the car. The high speed wind made me have to yell. "Why not a patch for godssake?"

"Been there, tried that," Mary yelled in reply, "but I can't use the stuff because it makes me dream really crazy. I feel like I'm not getting any rest."

I knew about this side effect of nicotine replacement therapy, but protested, "And you find that marijuana is preferable?"

"Well, yeah! Not only does it take the edge off the cravings, but it also makes me a much calmer mother at bedtime. And of course," she fixed me with a devilish grin, "there's the sexual enhancement. Jake's not complaining, I can tell you, not about the sex and not about my being a bitch on wheels, like the other times I tried to quit."

"Well, sounds like you've found the ideal therapy for the tobacco addicted, except that it's illegal. Don't they like, put people to death in Texas for this sort of thing?"

"Not in Austin! It's the capital of Mellow."

I shook my head in a gesture of resignation. "You know, I was planning on driving you right to the hospital."

"Why do you think I'm smoking this now, instead of after dinner? Want some?"

"Don't be ridiculous, I'm driving!" I heard the disapproval in my voice.

I looked to my right to see that Mary was carefully extinguishing her joint and returning it to its hiding place. Then she looked over at me with a wide smile. I put the windows back up and turned the air conditioning back on. Smoking dope was certainly no great crime in my youth, so why was I reacting judgmentally now? I smiled back at my sister. "Maybe later though."

Mary nodded agreeably. "Sure, whatever. Hey, you got anything to eat in here?"

I didn't remember my plan to call Karen Morgan until after dinner. Taking Mary to the hospital turned out to be an occasion for very mixed feelings. When Dad set eyes on his youngest, he once again turned tearful, which sent Mary into an emotional tailspin. I explained about aphasia and the stroke victim's inclination to weep over anything emotional, even happy events, as I comforted Mary in the hall. Seeing our father half paralyzed was a sobering sight, but Mary's mildly stoned condition seemed to make it easier for her to collect herself and attempt a cheerful visit.

Mary had asked to stay with me instead of at Mother's, because Mom still smoked and Mary didn't think she could handle the exposure. We called Trudy and tried to coax her to join us with the promise of Chinese takeout, but her periodontal work had laid her low. Eventually, Mary and I relaxed and caught up with each other over Moo Shu Pork and a bottle of wine. Updating her on my employment prospects made me remember my resolution to speak to Karen, and I excused myself to make the phone call.

I'd had just enough to drink to feel friendly and sound it on the phone. Could we meet for coffee sometime, I asked Karen, working not to betray the seriousness of my mission. I sounded casual as I pretended to examine many dates on my calendar. Oh, here's something lucky — would tomorrow be convenient? Karen seemed hesitant at first but then allowed that she did have time late in the morning. As it happened, I told her, that would work perfectly for me. In truth it would, because I could spend the early morning gathering the information I planned to present to Karen.

Chapter 24

That night, I wrote down a dream:

I have another baby, a girl. Leo's with me for the delivery. I'm in this facility that's supposed to be a hospital but is also like a cafeteria, with a lot of people around. Mom is there, Mary, Bonnie, and other friends. I look at the baby with that fascinated gaze of looking at newborns and note to everyone that she has brown eyes. Mom says that Amanda had brown eyes and I remind her that they were blue. I put the baby away, in this cellophane sleeve they've given me, and put her in a drawer. But then I wonder if that's really good for her — I take her back out and hold her, looking into her eyes. She looks back at me and smiles.

This wasn't the first dream I'd ever had of delightful babies who look upon the world with a preternatural wisdom and understanding. They seem to be triggered by a new idea or project, a "new baby" I'm thinking of taking on, and when that's been the case, I take my "baby dreams" as a nod from the universe, or perhaps my own deep self, that here is a promising path to follow.

But I didn't associate the dream with my plan to speak with Karen until after I'd risen and gone to my office to begin collecting the information I wanted to give her. It didn't take me very long to realize what a daunting task this was going to be and wonder whether I ought to back out of my plan. Then I sat at my desk and studied what I'd scrawled in the dark. I wasn't sure what to make of the cellophane bag, but I felt undeniably positive about taking care of a brown-eyed girl child. However arduous this meeting with Karen might be, I felt reassured that I was doing the right thing for Stephanie.

Our appointment this time was at Luigi's, a coffeehouse in Highland Park that's an equal distance from my neighborhood and Mount Clair. It's more subdued than the funky Latte Lenya, with several tables tucked in the back where I thought we could talk relatively privately. I arrived first and secured the most remote of these tables, glad to see only two other patrons at that hour. Luigi's served light gourmet fare and sported the appointments to accompany it — a casement full of desserts, baskets of exotic teas and chalkboards announcing the soup and salad of the day. I was hoping the lunch crowd wouldn't start showing up until we were done talking.

Then Karen walked in and I felt my stomach lurch with nervousness as she scanned the room and found me. I raised a hand in what would have been a wave if I hadn't felt suddenly terrified. How could I say what I had to say to this woman? But then again, how could I not?

"What are you having?" Karen said as she set down her bag on the extra chair. Although she looked as perfectly coifed and dressed as ever, I noticed that up close, she looked painfully thin, her bare arms so devoid of fat that they looked like rope.

"I think tea," I answered. "They have all kinds." Karen scanned a menu as I mentally prepared myself. I didn't want to start talking seriously until we were served and settled in and so I carefully made small talk until we had each been brought a small pot of tea, mint for Karen and chamomile for me. I was hoping it would help me to remain calm. Only after the server had walked away did I begin.

"Karen, I want to talk to you about something that concerns Stephanie. Something that's very personal, but also very important."

"About her nightmares? She's been better since she started seeing you, I want you to know."

"I'm glad to hear that," I said.

"She made a lot of progress with Dr. Taylor, but then….well, it was hard on Stephanie to have another loss."

"Tell me, when did she start to see Dr. Taylor?" I realized I wasn't sure.

"Well, it was during the year after Maggie died. Stephanie had a lot of sleep problems after that. We'd been told that kids outgrow night terrors, but not this one." She rolled her eyes in exasperation. "Of course, I understand a lot more about bereavement now than I did then. I think that had a lot to do with it." Her mouth settled into a grim smile, and I reminded myself that this woman had lost a child. I wanted to tread very gently.

"And how did you find out about the sleep clinic?"

Karen looked up from the corners of her eyes, as if there were a display of recent history just above and to the right of her head. "Originally," she recalled, "I got a call from her school about Stephanie. Her grades were falling and she seemed to be — well, her one teacher thought she was depressed." Karen's eyelids fluttered in what seemed to be a rejection of the teacher's assessment. "I thought her problem was this sleep disorder, something she'd grow out of. But you know, when the school calls you because a child has a problem, they expect you to do something. So I called her pediatrician and he referred us to the sleep clinic."

"Was the school satisfied with that?" I inquired.

"Since it was a pediatrician's referral, yes. And I was glad to get her to someone who was an expert in the field, and not have some school employee counsel her." She shifted in her seat, moving closer in and lowering her voice. "Schools and school personnel can be, well, nosy. And I didn't want her sleep problems to be included in her school records. What good would that do?"

I nodded, wondering how many families would close ranks over the records of a ten-year-old. "And it sounds as if Stephanie made good progress with Dr. Taylor."

"Yes she did," Karen agreed. "I told Cliff that if I had known how much better we'd all sleep, I'd have done this a lot sooner!" She smiled and shrugged. "The medication she was prescribed helped her to stay asleep, and seemed to prevent her from lapsing into whatever it was that made the night terrors happen."

I took a deep breath and decided to latch onto Bonnie for assistance. "I happened to learn that Dr. Taylor had some other concerns about Stephanie, concerns that I share." My throat was suddenly very dry and I took another sip of tea. "That's why I wanted to speak with you today." I pushed the file folder I'd brought across the table. "This is for you," I said.

Karen looked at me questioningly and started to open the file. I laid my hand on it and stopped her.

"Before you read this, I want to tell you why I brought it."

"Okay," said Karen patiently. I folded my hands together and rested them on the table as I spoke.

"I happened to come into possession of some personal notes that Dr. Taylor wrote shortly before she died, including material about

Stephanie, and difficulties she may have been experiencing at home, with her father."

"Difficulties." It was spoken as a statement, not a question, and Karen tilted her head in a gesture that suggested that she was listening, or perhaps preparing for something.

"I'm sorry to have to be the one to tell you this, but I now agree with Dr. Taylor." I swallowed hard and asked, "Have you ever suspected your husband of behaving inappropriately with, well, either of his daughters?"

"Inappropriately?" This was a question.

"I mean, sexually." There it was, out on the table with the teacups.

Karen frowned and blinked, as if trying to grasp something complex and strange. Then she cocked her head to one side and narrowed her eyes. "Are you telling me that you think that Cliff has...." She frowned and shook her head for lack of a word to speak, and held her palms out as if she might catch one falling into her hands. She gave up, pushed her chair back from the table and shook her head again, then leaned forward and looked hard at me. "That Stephanie has been," she resumed, looking pale, "molested? By her father?" Her voice crept up so that the last words fell high and incredulous.

I was trying hard to follow Karen's progress through her grasp of this and nodded slowly, trying to be both gentle and honest. "I do believe that, and so did Dr. Taylor. And I didn't want to give you such bad news without making sure you would have support. That's what's in the folder. There is a lot of help out there for families with a problem like this."

Karen was wagging her head slowly, eyes wide. I reminded myself that I had thought about allowing for this, the likelihood that Karen might simply be unable to absorb this news. I tried to slow down for her.

"I'm sorry to give you such a shock. This must be very difficult. That's why I want you to know that I'm here to help."

Karen sat still for a long moment, then reached for the folder and opened it. She scanned the first page, a collection of resources with phone numbers and contact names. Then she read out loud, "Pittsburgh Action Against Rape?" and snorted. "I don't <u>think</u> so." She rolled her eyes and smirked.

"It's a great organization, a grass roots group that's become a national model for organizations that help victims of sexual abuse."

"Well, isn't that special?" Karen snapped, closing the file and tossing it back onto the table. "And I just call these people up and say, 'Hello, someone who barely knows my daughter told me to call you, so you can ruin our lives!'?" Karen's face had gone from pale white to flush. "This is absurd."

I sat with elbows on the table and fingers to my lips as Karen angrily pawed through her bag and retrieved her wallet. She extracted a twenty, slapped it onto the table and rose to leave.

"Hold on," I said. "Please, give me another minute here." Karen was breathing hard and had her eye on the door. "For your daughter's sake."

Karen slung her purse onto her shoulder, but sat back down in her chair. She positioned herself at a distance from the table, ready to spring for the exit at the first opportunity.

"This is not an easy thing for me to tell you, believe me. I wouldn't be doing it if I didn't believe that you are a loving mother. There are other ways to help kids in these straits, ways that involve child services and the justice system. But that's more traumatic than what I'm trying to do here." I did not dare to meet Karen's eyes while I spoke and continued to look down at my cup instead.

"I know that your husband has a drinking problem and I know that you've been hurt as a result." I heard Karen's intake of breath but still refrained from looking at her. "It is very common for victims of domestic abuse to minimize what's happened to them and it becomes second nature to deny the pain and unhappiness, to overlook the 'elephant in the living room,' as the recovery programs like to call it."

"Now," I continued, "it can be argued that your circumstances are none of my business, but you have asked me to work with Stephanie." Finally, I looked up. Karen was sitting with her arms crossed tight across her chest, her face fixed in a scowl. "And you've paid me very well. This is the least I can do for her, and for your family."

Karen said nothing. Fearing I'd failed, I plunged ahead in desperation. "Listen, I know what it's like to lose a daughter." Karen's face registered surprise and I nodded. "Our daughter died when she was three, and I watched that grief eat away at her father. And I also know what it's like to have a husband lose control of his drinking."

"I'm...sorry," Karen shrugged, and then added, "I didn't know about your daughter." She looked down at her lap and brushed away some lint, then looked up again. "Or your husband, for that matter. I'm — not used to talking like this." Her eyes darted around the ceiling of the room, as if she might find a window open up there and somehow fly out of it. Finally, she pulled closer to the table and spoke quietly. "Alcohol was sometimes a problem before Maggie died, but it's gotten worse," she said quietly, as if betraying a state secret.

I nodded, realizing that my task with the mother was turning out to be the same as the task with her daughter — building rapport.

"Alcohol does numb the pain, for awhile," I said. "I mean, there's a reason behind the 'Irish wake.' But in my case at least, Leo — my ex-husband — was withdrawing into himself, for years." Making "I" statements, talking about oneself instead of the other person, is a tried and true conflict management technique and I thought it was buying me time. I pressed on. "If I have a regret now, it's that I didn't see the big picture. If I had to do it over again..." I paused, not sure how much further to go.

"What?" said Karen. "What could you do?"

"Well, maybe I should have tried an intervention," I offered. "Gotten his family and friends involved in confronting him about his problem. But hindsight is 20-20. At the time, all I knew was that I was miserable and he was out to lunch."

Karen nodded, meeting my eyes, and I saw that she was more able to entertain my troubles than her own.

"So you see, I'm coming to you not just as a worried professional, but as a woman who's been through losing a child and watching a husband who's dying inside." I leaned in to fasten my eyes on Karen's. "I know what I've had to say to you is distressing, but I really believe I can help."

Karen was resting her cheek in her hand, looking pensive and troubled, and I felt I had made it through the wall of denial.

"I've highlighted two names there." I nodded toward the file. "One's the medical director and the other is the clinical coordinator of the Center for Traumatic Stress in Children and Adolescents. They are very skillful and experienced. They can perform an assessment, provide treatment and help your daughter..." I took a breath and added "...your family, toward recovery. Please, call them."

"Perform an assessment," said Karen with a vague nod, staring down the folder. I nodded. "Perform an assessment," she said again quietly.

"Yes, that's the way to get started," I reassured her.

"Have you spoken with them? Are they expecting to hear from me?" Karen asked.

"No, but I will if you'd like me to."

Karen took the file and said, "No, that's okay, I'll call and make an appointment."

"You can say I referred you if you want."

"Yes, I will," she said, then slid her chair back and rose. "I have a lot to think about."

I stood up too. "Please call me if there's anything more I can do. Any time." I reached for Karen's arm and gave it a squeeze. "I'm sorry to have been the bearer of bad news," I said.

Karen shook her head. "You have no idea," she said, and turned for the door.

I stayed at the table and finished my pot of chamomile, willing myself to relax. This terrible task had been completed but I couldn't entirely quench my queasiness. As much as I'd tried to make it sound like incest was a common family problem, trying to minimize it to help Karen feel empowered to grapple with it, the fact was that it was simply appalling. The fact that incest really is more common than most people realize was part of what made it so.

I squared my shoulders and resolved to get on with my day. I looked in my purse for the phone number of my father's room and found a pay phone by the rest room. I had dropped Mary off at the hospital earlier and didn't know whether she would want me to pick her up now or later. Mother answered the phone.

"Hi Mom," I said. "How's it going over there?"

"Oh, it's you, Dear. Good!" said my mother. "We need to talk to you. Something's come up."

I heard my father's voice in the background, sounding both agitated and unintelligible.

"All right, Stan," my mother said. "Willa, I'm putting Mary on. She'll explain what's been happening."

After a moment's pause, I heard Mary's voice, sounding cautious.

"Hi," she said.

"What's up?"

"Houston, we have a problem."

"Is Dad okay?"

"He's not any worse physically, but he's hopping mad." She lowered her voice, "I hesitate to use the word 'apoplectic.'" My initial apprehension receded as I realized that Mary sounded more amused than worried.

"What happened?" I asked. "Did those maids forget to leave a mint on the pillow?"

"Worse than that. Dad has me calling his lawyer." My father hated lawyers more than a bear market, more than the Democrats, more even than the IRS. He knows that sometimes he has to use them, but he bitterly resents that fact of life.

"Uh-oh, this must be bad," I said. "What happened?"

"Well, just after I got here, we had a visit from a hospital social worker who asked about Dad's advance directives, whether he has a living will." It was hard to believe that none of us discussed this during all our hours in waiting rooms, but we hadn't. That's probably why they're called "advance" directives, I thought. Families are nowhere near able to consider someone's ultimate wishes for treatment when they're in the midst of an emergency.

"Does he? I have no idea," I said.

"He does, he says, in Florida. And it turns out that the hospital has to have a hard copy in order to follow them, so Dad's trying to tell me what to do, but he's getting more and more cranked up, so I'm having more and more trouble understanding him. Finally, I get that he wants me to call Florida and have this document faxed up here. There's a copy, with his will, at his lawyer's office. So I find the number and call this office in Florida, but I couldn't reach the lawyer because he's out of town, which just made Dad more angry. But I left a message with a secretary and she or a paralegal was going to find the stuff and fax it up here. So then Mom got here and he calmed down some, but then we tell the hospital we're sending for these documents and ask for their fax number and they say, wait a minute, this document may not be valid in Pennsylvania, we'll have to check with our legal department."

"Oh my," I said. "Poor Dad. And now he's just..."

"Apoplectic, like I said."

"Poor Mary!"

"Wait, hold on a sec." I waited, overhearing a conversation I couldn't quite make out, with Mary, my mother and another woman.

"And can you give me that address?" Mary was saying. "Great, let me get you a piece of paper so you can write that down for us."

After another pause, Mary spoke quickly. "There's an aide here who says we can download advance directives from the Internet. She's giving me the address. Hold on."

"And this will fly in Pennsylvania?" Mary was asking. "They have every state? And you don't need a lawyer, just witnesses? Great, thanks." Then she spoke into the phone again. "Willa, if I give this website to you, can you run off the form and bring it in with you?" I could hear my father in the background, exhorting the women to action. I knew he was trying to be commanding, but what was coming out sounded far more like raving. I recognized that he was furious at being disabled, and the child in me shuddered even as I pitied him.

I wrote down the web address and promised to bring the forms as soon as I could get them. The last thing I heard before I hung up was my mother telling my father, "It's going to be all right, Stan. Willa's taking care of it."

Chapter 25

I returned to my house feeling like I'd already put in a twelve hour day. Nerves had prevented me from consuming breakfast, and now I felt ravenous. I opened my refrigerator and found a container of yogurt with an expiration date from three weeks earlier but promptly devoured it, secure in the knowledge that never, in my entire lifetime, have I known yogurt to go bad. Then, in spite of everything I should have been doing, I plopped down on the couch with the front section of the newspaper for a few moments of quiet reading and blessed solitude.

I made the mistake of reclining, and before you could say "story continued on A-4," I had drifted off. In fact, sleep seemed to highjack me, so that this wasn't so much a brief doze as a full bore, drool-on-the pillow nap. I woke myself up with my own snoring, or thought I did. Not sure for a moment where I was, I opened my eyes to see the newspaper resting on my face, the print too blurry to read. And then I heard a strange voice say, "Hello?"

I leapt up from the couch, flailing newspaper over my head and onto the floor, and half-screamed, "Omigod!" Standing not six feet from me, and my nap, was Earl Newman.

"What the — Earl, what are you doing ..." I sputtered, my hand to my chest. My heart felt like it was riding a pogo stick. "How did you get in here?"

Earl was putting his hands out as if signaling an audience to quell its applause. "I came to the front and rang the doorbell, but no one came to the door. I thought maybe your bell was out of order. I noticed a car parked in the driveway so I went around to the back, and there were keys in the lock..."

"And you just walked in?!"

"No, no, I knocked, and then I called in, and I heard what sounded like a groan and I thought I'd better check...."

"I was sleeping, goddammit!" I don't always snore, Leo tells me, but when I do, I can make a lot of noise. Earl probably did hear something, although "groan" sounded a little dramatic. I shrugged and sat down, still trying to catch my breath.

"I'm sorry to have disturbed you." He sounded more inconvenienced than sorry, but that's probably as sympathetic as Earl gets.

"Earl, you've not only disturbed me, you've probably taken several years off my life. What are you doing here?"

"Maybe this is a bad time."

I had to laugh. "Well Earl, this used to be a bad time, because I was asleep. But now I'm awake, and I'd love to know what has brought you here."

"May I sit down?"

"By all means!" I picked up the newspaper, rattled its pages back into place, and gestured for him to have a seat. He pulled up the knees of his khaki trousers as he sat down, exposing fine knit socks and loafers with tassels. On top, he wore the same kind of shirt he'd probably worn since kindergarten — blue oxford cloth, with a button down collar.

"I wanted to speak to you privately," he started.

I thought I knew exactly where this was going. "Earl, don't start in on Bonnie's journals. You're wasting your time."

"This isn't about the journals, or at least, not just about the journals."

I spotted the drool stain on the sofa pillow. I picked it up and drew it to my chest, thoughtfully. "Okay, then what else is this about?"

"Did Bonnie ever speak to you about how we knew each other, way back when?"

I scanned my memory bank and shook my head. "You mean, that you'd known each other in college? You had been a graduate assistant in one of her undergrad courses, something like that?"

He cleared his throat. "Something like that. Did she ever mention anything about — us?"

"You and Bonnie?" My tone of voice betrayed how preposterous that sounded to me. "No," I said flatly.

"Well, I had a thing for her."

"Really?"

"Yes, and we went out once, but she ..."

Dumped you, I thought, but didn't say.

"... was seeing somebody else. Actually, there were a couple of guys she was close to."

I was wracking my brain, trying to remember what Bonnie had told me about this acquaintanceship. All I could recall was that she hadn't liked him much then either. She'd called him an ironic snob, meaning he had no superiority to lord over others, only the presumption of superiority.

Earl's voice had dropped. "But I – well, I was smitten. I was pretty young — I'd started college at sixteen, and hadn't dated much. " He nodded his head slowly, his lower lip tucked in. "I was hurting there for awhile."

There was a long silence then, because I didn't know what to say. Why was he telling me this? Finally I ventured, "Well, no one could accuse you of favoritism when you published your criticisms of her work. Is that how you treat all your old flames?"

He smiled sorrowfully. "Well, that's really why I wanted to talk with you. I know that I was hard on her, harder than I should have been, and I really regret that." He leaned back, put his fingertips to his temple. "And I keep thinking that I'd like another chance."

Well, get in line, I thought. I too would love another chance to be with Bonnie, to talk to her, or just laugh with her.

"I know it doesn't make much sense logically," he went on. "But this was on my mind when I asked about her journals. Of course, I would like everyone to contribute their dream journals to our research, but there was more to it in this case. And I wanted you to know that."

In the end, I went WASP and asked Earl if he wanted something to drink. I gave him a glass of ice water and then we chatted amiably for a few minutes before he took his leave. I shook my head as he drove off. Maybe Earl really had needed to get this off his chest, but I was guessing that whether or not this was true, he'd like to gain my sympathy as a means to someday acquiring Bonnie's journals.

Then it struck me that he could have gone into my office while I was snoring and pilfered something. I rushed back there to take a look, and then had to laugh. That long wall in my office was still lined with boxes stacked on top of one another in teetering piles. It would have taken someone who didn't know where to look a good chunk of time to find what he wanted. If Earl had contrived to locate Bonnie's journals, he must have been sorely disappointed.

I checked the back door, retrieved my keys and made sure it was locked, feeling stupid and vulnerable. Leaving my keys in the lock is something I've done now and again when I'm distracted, and it always drives Leo crazy. But he wasn't here to chastise me now, which was a relief, but only briefly. Anxiety pricked my consciousness. How many days had it been since we decided to cool our heels for a while? Just a couple, but it seemed like a long time. Shouldn't I have heard from him by now? I went to the phone, lifted the receiver and heard the signal that a message was waiting. There was a voicemail message from Leo, sounding calm and friendly, the strain gone from his voice.

"Hi, it's me. Thought I'd check in, see how your dad is doing and ask if you wanna make up. I'm ready if you are. I'm working at home today."

I grinned to myself and called him back immediately.

"I'm calling about that make up offer? How long is that good for?"

"Little lady, we can oblige you whenever your schedule allows. Are you busy tonight?"

"Actually, Mary's in town and staying with me, so we wouldn't have much, you know, privacy."

"Oh, privacy!" Leo rolled the word out with great stress on the first syllable. "Well, m'am, if it's privacy you want, I suggest you visit our showroom. I'm sure we have something in stock that would satisfy your needs."

"You mean, today? Now?"

"Or, sooner would be nice."

I giggled and thought how much fun it would be to dally with Leo — after all, his apartment was actually on the way to the hospital — even as I was rejecting the idea.

"I would like that," I said, "but I have to get over to see Dad."

"Do you have to get there immediately?"

"Leo, do you think I'm the kind of girl who would just drop by for a quickie? In the middle of the day?"

"I <u>know</u> you are. C'mon." He sounded so ardent that I was longing to say yes.

"Yes," I said. I looked at my watch, trying to judge just how long a quickie would take. I would call Mary and tell her that I had to, um, run an errand, which was even sort of almost true. "I just have to print out something first, but I can be over there, well, shortly."

"I'll pole vault to the door when you get here!"

"I look forward to seeing that."

One of the great benefits of having known each other so long is that Leo and I really know how to make each other happy in the sack. We succeeded in making excellent use of our twenty minutes, but I hadn't allowed time for post-coital recovery. When I saw myself reflected in the mirror alongside the hospital elevator, I spied the telltale satisfaction on my face, so I traveled up to my father's floor practicing a scowl.

"Hey," I said as I peeked around the wide door. "How's it going today, Dad?" I didn't notice until I reached his bedside that his eyes were closed.

"I think he wore himself out being pissed off all morning," Mary spoke in a low voice from an armchair on the other side of the bed. "Did you bring the papers?"

"I did," I answered, and extracted them from my bag. "This 'Pennsylvania Declaration' is only two pages long, but there are instructions that go with it, and I ran those off too. But I haven't actually read any of this yet."

I perched on an arm of the chair. "Where's Mom?"

"Getting him some ice cream. He sent her off and then zonked out." We studied the form, and Mary read out loud:

"Being of sound mind, I willfully and voluntarily make this declaration to be followed if I become incompetent." Mary looked up.

"Is he?"

"Of sound mind?" I shrugged. "As much as he's ever been. He's paralyzed on one side and his speech is impaired, but otherwise, he's acting just like he always has — temperamental, bossy, self-centered."

"Boy, you can say that again," Mary agreed. We continued reading: "This declaration reflects my firm and settled commitment to refuse life sustaining treatment under the circumstances indicated below. I direct my attending physician to withhold or withdraw life-sustaining treatment that serves only to prolong the process of my dying, if I should be in a terminal condition or in a state of permanent unconsciousness."

Mother arrived with four little cartons of ice cream and plastic spoons. She saw that Dad was sleeping and spoke in a low voice. "I brought one for each of us," she said confidentially. "We've earned it." Having worked up an appetite, I consumed mine gratefully.

"Mom, have you done this too?" Mary asked, showing her the living will form.

"Yes, a long time ago. Trudy and Willa both have a copy, don't you Willa?"

I gulped. Somewhere, in a file marked "Family," I did have a copy of my mother's living will, but it was not something I ever wanted to peruse, or even think about. "Yeah, I do, somewhere." It was one thing to be sophisticated about death and dying as an instructor, but something else entirely to consider the death of your own dear mother.

"Well, check for me, will you? Because if you can't find it, I'll get you another. These things aren't any good if no one has a copy, especially in an emergency. I don't even want to tell you some of the stories I've heard."

"You mean, people being kept alive against their wishes?" Mary asked.

"And people receiving treatments they'd never have wanted, treatments that were painful and drawn out and kept them alive long enough to get bed sores. I knew one woman who took her mother, a sick, weak woman who was ready to die, to the hospital in the middle of the night. She was having a lot of discomfort and the daughter expected them to help ease her pain. They refused to call the mother's doctor, who knew and would have carried out her wishes to withhold invasive treatment, because it was so late at night. The daughter begged them to wait fifteen minutes while she ran home to get her mother's directives, but while she was gone they put her mother on a respirator. She suffered for three more weeks until she finally died." Mom pulled out her reading glasses and took the document from Mary. "I tell you girls, there's a war going on. The medical establishment wants to treat and it will treat unless you force it not to. You're too young to have heard some of the horror stories I have, but believe me, you have to watch out for yourself." She put on her glasses and added, "And for the people who have told you what they want if they can't speak for themselves."

She grew quiet as she read over the pages, then she walked to her purse, extracted a pen and began filling in the form. Mary and I regarded one another with curiosity, then rose to look over Mother's shoulder. She had filled in Dad's name and was checking boxes for

"I do not want cardiopulmonary resuscitation.

I do not want mechanical respiration.

I do not want tube feeding or any other artificial of invasive form of nutrition (food) or hydration (water.)

I do not want blood or blood products.

I do not want any form of surgery or invasive diagnostic tests.

I do not want kidney dialysis.

I do not want antibiotics."

"Mom," I said solemnly, "do we know what Dad wants?"

"Well, we'll go over this when he wakes up. But this is standard procedure. It seems incredible that you have to tell people, 'If I'm dying, don't prolong my agony,' but the sad fact is that you do."

Mom turned the page and asked us, "Shall I put you down as surrogates?"

"What does that mean?" said Mary.

Mother read, "I do want to designate another person as my surrogate to make medical treatment decisions for me if I should be incompetent and in a terminal condition or in a state of permanent unconsciousness."

I sucked in my breath. "Yikes, that's a heavy duty load."

"You may have to do this for me one day, and I want you to know that I really want you to do the right thing. Understand, these are my wishes, so you don't have to make any decisions. You're only being entrusted with carrying out mine." I nodded mutely, praying that I would never have to fulfill such a painful duty.

Mother continued, "Now, he can name a second, substitute surrogate." She looked at Mary. "I've listed Willa and Trudy in mine, because they live here in town. We should probably do the same here." Mary nodded, and Mom resumed writing.

"Wait," I said. "Mom, would you be willing to be the surrogate for Dad? I'm sure that he'd prefer that, really."

She looked up, cocked her head and considered the idea for a moment, "Yes, I can do that," she said matter-of-factly, and resumed writing. "And I'll put you down as the substitute."

"Yippee," I said weakly.

"But Mom, what are we going to do about this?' Mary was pointing to the next line of the document. "Declarant's signature," she read. "He can't sign his name with his right hand paralyzed."

Mother frowned for a moment and then brightened. "Then he can sign with his left hand. I can't imagine there's a law against that."

I produced the instructions from my bag and leafed through them. "It says here that you can direct another to sign this in the presence of two witnesses."

"So, even better, with the three of us here," Mom said. "And then," she read the last entries, "all we have to do is fill in the two witnesses. You each have to sign and print your addresses. That's all there is to it." She moved the document toward us and we signed. "Your father will be so relieved when he wakes up," she said. "All he has to decide is whether to use his left hand or have me sign for him." She shot us a mischievous look. "You know, I used to forge his signature, when he was out of town and checks had to be endorsed. I imagine I could still do an adequate job." She flexed the fingers of her right hand and smiled.

Mary yawned and stretched, then said, "I feel like I've been here for a week, at least."

"Well, you did a lot of heavy lifting this morning," I sympathized. "Dad sounded bonkers on the phone."

"Oh he was, believe me. I'm amazed at how quickly he can reduce me to helpless anger."

"But she was managing very well when I got here," Mother assured me. "Now Mary, you should run along. You've put in enough time for one day. Willa, why don't you take her home?"

I did not need more urging to leave the hospital and began rooting in my bag for my car keys. Then I nudged Mary. "Let's go, kiddo."

"Mom, please tell Dad I was here but didn't want to disturb him," I said. "How long will you be staying?"

"I'll wait for Trudy. She was going to stop in later this afternoon."

Mary said, "You're coming over for dinner with us, right? See if Trudy can come too. I haven't seen her yet!" She gave Mom a noisy kiss on the cheek, then turned and grabbed my hand. We exited the room like two schoolgirls escaping the principal's office.

Back in the car, Mary announced, "I would never have quit smoking if I'd known Dad was about to have a stroke! Right now, I would <u>kill</u> for a cigarette."

"You've had a really bad day," I sympathized. "Let's see if we can plan something pleasant for ourselves. You deserve a reward for courage in the line of fire. I bet you don't get much Middle Eastern food in Texas, do you?"

"Never!" said Mary.

No one knew why Pittsburgh had a plethora of Middle Eastern restaurants, but it did, and we had grown up on lemony salads and barbecued shish-ke-bob at Samreny's and Amel's. Halfway home, I pulled in front the Mediterranean Deli on Murray Avenue. I ushered Mary into the store, and let her pick what we would have for dinner: spinach pies, stuffed grape leaves, hummus, pita bread, feta cheese and for dessert, baklava, divine confection of honey and ground nuts. All we would have to do was put together a big salad.

But as we headed back to the car, Mary stopped and looked longingly across the street. "Look, there's a newsstand. I'm going to get a pack of cigarettes. Just to tide me over."

"No, no, no!" I cried, and grabbed her arm. "You've come this far, you don't want all the suffering you've already gone through to be for nothing, do you?" I opened the passenger door of the car and Mary allowed herself to be elbowed in.

"You just have to hang in there," I admonished when I got back into the car. "Visit the garage for some of your herbal therapy when we get home, if that will help you. Although I hope you're not in danger of becoming a pothead — are you?" I shot Mary a sidelong glance and raised an eyebrow, but Mary just snorted.

"You can't overdo that stuff and function like a grown-up, which is very much my job these days."

"Okay, just checking," I said. And Mary did visit the garage when we got home, and did seem to feel much better for having done so, although half the stuffed grape leaves were missing when dinner was finally placed on the table.

Chapter 26

When Trudy arrived at my house, she reported that Dad had snoozed through her visit as well. Since the three of us hadn't been together in months, I took the opportunity to update my sisters on my relationship with Leo.

"Before Mom gets here, tell me what you think. Leo wants to move in with me."

Mary's eyebrow shot up, but Trudy didn't seem at all surprised.

"Why don't you want Mom to know?" Mary asked.

"It's not that I don't want her to know, really. But she likes him so much, I don't think she'll be very impartial."

"Well, I like him too," said Trudy. "Now, anyway."

"And he was always like a kindly big brother to me," Mary said. "Of course, I didn't have to live with him," she added.

"The question is, Willa, what do you want?" Trudy said.

"I want to know what you think!" I insisted, reaching for a bottle of Sauvignon Blanc in the door of the refrigerator and filling three glasses. I brought them to the table with a plate of cheese and crackers.

"Okay," Trudy said, rolling her eyes heavenward. She swirled her wine a moment and spoke across the top of the glass: "I think that — it'd be nice," she said with a smile.

"Me too," Mary said definitely.

"Why?" I asked, suspicious of such a positive response.

"Because," said Trudy, stretching her arms out on the kitchen table in a gesture of declaration, "basically, you guys love each other. And, you have history."

"And I just want everybody to be working at a relationship so I can learn from them, which is what I've always done with my older siblings," Mary said with a sly smile. "So my approval is largely based on self interest."

We laughed, but knew this wasn't entirely facetious. Each of us had been influenced by the fact of our sisterhood; each one had been afforded a preview of life's challenges as we watched older siblings go off to grade school, be transformed by puberty, learn to drive, leave home. Our marriages, in all their wide variety, had proved to be just as instructive.

"So you should let Leo move in because it would be beneficial for Mary!" Trudy summarized, and I said, "Well, I'll certainly take that into consideration," and patted Mary on the hand.

"Honestly though, Willa," Trudy said seriously, "Where are you on this?"

"I'm tempted, but I'm also scared. Wouldn't you be?"

"I don't find Leo scary at all!" Mary piped up. "Exasperating sometimes maybe..."

Trudy gave Mary an elbow and tried to stay on point, ever the counselor. "What scares you, Willa?"

"Well, I've adjusted to living by myself," I said. "It's peaceful, if a little boring. So I'm pretty contented as I am. And right now, we have the best of both worlds. Did you ever see the interview with Katharine Hepburn, when she was asked about marriage? She said the ideal arrangement isn't living together, but to live nearby and visit often."

"That way, everybody gets to keep their toenail clippings to themselves," Mary said brightly. "It'd be a little bit harder to raise the kids, though. Like when they come into your bedroom at night with a fever and barf on you, you'd start to feel pretty bitter if their father was sleeping peacefully down the block."

"Thank you, Mary, for that vivid insight," said Trudy, "but let's not get derailed here." She fixed me with a no-nonsense stare. "You still haven't got to the part that scares you."

I took a deep breath and let it out again, screwing up the courage to confront my fears. "I'm scared that if we started living together again, he might backslide. I'd hate for things to go back to the way they were."

"Well, does anything appeal to you about having him back under your roof?" Mary wanted to know.

"Oh, sure. I like being with him. I like the way he smells. And he's sweet to me, nowadays." I paused and then said confidentially, "And there's the money."

"Money?" said Mary. "What money?"

"Oh, I didn't explain this — he wants to pay me rent. I'd be his landlady."

Mary's laugh came out like a honk. "Well, honey, this is no big deal then is it? You're just taking in a boarder is all!"

Trudy was smiling in spite of herself. "So, he knows your income has dropped and is proposing to kill two birds with one stone?"

"That's about the size of it," I said, still feeling perplexed.

Mary and Trudy exchanged knowing smiles as, for a silent moment, they reflected on my circumstances. Then the phone rang, and Mary took a call from Texas. As she set her husband straight on details of preschool car pool, I turned to Trudy and asked in a low voice, "Speaking of bed partners, how are things with Ted? How was the movie?"

Trudy blushed furiously. "I should probably be ashamed to tell you that the movie has been great. I still don't know how it ends though — we haven't been able to watch more than a few minutes at a time."

I grinned with conspiratorial success as Mary finished blowing kisses to her five-year-old and hung up. As if we'd never been interrupted, Mary plowed on.

"So, would you and Leo have a lease agreement? Could you get out of this after a year?"

Trudy said, "That's a good idea. Because it might not seem so overwhelming a decision if you felt it wasn't necessarily permanent."

I thought about that and nodded. "That's a good point. I'll think that over."

Mary said, "It's the best of both worlds — budget relief and term limits. Marriage should be so sensible!"

"I like Leo for proposing it, I have to admit that. I like that he wants to help you," said Trudy.

"And I admit that I like that he loves you," said Mary.

"Yeah, me too." I flushed, more from sentiment than the wine.

"That doesn't mean he'll be easy to live with," Trudy said.

"Who won't?" said Mother, who had let herself in the front door and was standing in the doorway to the kitchen.

"Mom!" we all cried in guilty unison.

"What's going on here?" she eyed us levelly.

"We're talking about men who are hard to live with," said Mary. "Speaking of which, how's Dad?"

"I have red or white wine, Mom, what'll it be?" I said.

"Come, take this chair, I'll get another," said Trudy. We are very practiced at distracting our mother, who, sharp as she is, is no match for two or more daughters at a time.

"Well, red I guess, if it's Merlot," Mom said. She eased into Trudy's chair and said to us all, "And your father woke up a few minutes before I left, but he said he was tired and wanted to go back to sleep."

"Do you think he's okay?" said Trudy.

"They kept taking his blood pressure while I was there, and there were no problems. I don't think we have to worry about him."

"And you didn't see how agitated he was earlier," Mary said to Trudy. "He threw a fit worthy of a man half his age."

"Over that living will business?' Trudy asked.

"Yes, and how did that work out Mom?" I asked. "Was he happy with that form?"

"Yes, it's been signed and is in his file," mother assured us. "So, he can rest easy now."

Dark falls noticeably earlier by August, and the shortening twilight foreshadows autumn. That night as we dined on the screened-in porch, we needed candles to light the table. I guess there must have been someone out there in the dark. I imagine he must have been parked across the street. He could probably hear us laughing as he sat and waited, wondering when he would be able to make his move. Eventually, Trudy and I came out of the house and walked to the first car parked in the driveway. We each hugged Mom, who then got into her car, backed out, and drove off. Then he must have watched Trudy's minivan back out and go on its way in the dark.

Anyway, that's what I think must have happened. All I know for sure is that I was standing at the sink rinsing dishes when suddenly somebody grabbed me from behind. There was an instant of total confusion, and then the pain set in. This was no surprise bear hug from Leo, no. What was this then? In another instant, my face was being pressed against the countertop. A strong, unbearably hot hand was pressing my neck down as my left arm was wrenched behind my back. A calm male voice spoke above me, vaguely accented: "You have something I need."

I couldn't speak for the pain, and he seemed to know that and relaxed his grip enough for me to talk.

"What do you want?" I said, and my voice sounded thick with compression and panic, not something I recognized as mine.

"You have some papers belonging to Dr. Bonita Taylor. I want them."

My mind was a blank. "Papers?" I said, and he wrenched harder, making me moan. It felt like my shoulder was being forced from its socket. I tried to look up, catch sight of the man who was holding me down, wanting to read his face for some clue to his purpose, but I was pinned fast. What papers?

"Don't pretend, it wouldn't be wise. You have some papers, and I want you to tell me where they are." He twisted my arm more and this time I screamed. Suddenly, I remembered Bonnie's dream journal.

"Okay," I gasped, "I know what you want. I'll tell you where they are, but let me go."

"I can't do that," he said. "You just tell me where to look and we'll go together. Just you and I." He pressed down on my neck, hard enough to restrict the passage of air.

"In my office," I said in what came out as a strangled whisper. I broke into a cold sweat and felt like I was about to pass out.

The next thing I heard was a shrieking cry. "What the fuck!" Suddenly, the sickening grip loosened, and I twisted my head in time to see Mary, back from a visit to the garage, execute an astonishing circular kick that caught the attacker squarely on the jaw with her cowboy boot.

The man reeled to the side and tried to stand up but lost his balance, pin-wheeling his arms as he fell backwards onto the hard floor, taking a kitchen chair with him on the way down. I lurched for the knives in their holder on the counter, grabbed a long one and tried to hold onto it with the pain throbbing in my arm. I turned just as Mary was delivering a solid, Texas-sized kick to the man's crotch. Still tangled in the chair, the man grunted and went pale, then turned his head to the side and vomited. He sank down full length onto the floor.

"I wouldn't try to get up if I were you," said Mary in a guttural voice, standing over him in a pose out of a martial arts movie. "Quick, Willa, do you have any duct tape?"

Duct tape? Of course I had duct tape, what a funny thing to ask! Then I caught on. "Oh, yes, or course!" I said, hurrying to the broom closet. And then Mary, in spite of her stoned state or because of it, managed to truss the man's ankles until they looked like a silver mummy's, and then to start on his wrists. The smell of vomit rose from the floor, but I stood over both of them with the knife, steadying it with both hands, ready to pounce if the man made a move toward Mary. But he lay very still and quiet.

"Now," Mary said breathlessly as she finished, "Time to call 911."

"What is the nature of your call?" said the dispatcher on the other end of the line, loud enough for both of us to hear.

Mary said, "My sister has been attacked by a man. We have him tied up, but hurry. We're in Point Breeze, at 702 Carnegie Place near Frick Park."

Mary listened and then asked, "Do we know the identity of the assailant?" I shook my head hard. Mary listened again, then asked, "Is there a weapon on the premises?"

Still vigilantly holding the knife over the man's supine body, I nodded.

"We can't tell if he was armed," Mary told the dispatcher. "My sister is holding a carving knife on him though. Yes, N-i-l-s-s-o-n. Yes, as soon as possible, please. Thank you." Mary gasped as she hung up. "I thought she was going to ask for our social security numbers, for godssakes."

"Mary, how did you do that?" I said wonderingly, stealing a glance in her direction. "How did you do that?"

"You mean, clobber him? I've been taking aerobic kick-boxing for a couple of years, did I tell you about that? It's really good exercise."

"I'll say."

"I've never done it wearing cowboy boots before," she said. "It's pretty lethal, isn't it?" She peered at the still man on the floor. "I wonder, is he Chinese or Japanese or Korean or what?" she said.

"I dunno," I said. The man hadn't moved. "Is he conscious?"

"Can't tell," said Mary. We both heard the siren as it began to approach us, probably from the Number 6 Police Station two miles away. I cautiously leaned over the man, knife at the ready. "He seems to be knocked out, but he's breathing, I can see that." As I stood there studying him, I realized that maybe he did look familiar after all. And I said to Mary, wonderingly, "I think I might have seen him before."

Suddenly, in one shocking motion, the man sprang into a sitting position, grabbed my knife with his bound hands and slashed it across his own jugular. I screamed and jumped away. "Oh my god!" Mary shrieked as blood sprayed in an arc onto the kitchen cabinets. The man smiled at us and sank back to the floor. We fled screaming from the mutilation and blood, out of the kitchen and out of the house, and stood on the front steps holding each other and sobbing with horror as the patrol car pulled up to the curb.

Chapter 27

Time stretched out, so that it seemed to take many minutes for the two uniformed police officers to emerge from their car and follow us into the house. It seemed to take hours for the medics to arrive and transport the injured man, who was somehow still alive, from the premises. And it took even longer than that for the officers to take a statement. I was by then bursting with my need to tell them what I realized must have happened, but the officers were not as interested in my speculations as they were in how the man on the floor of my kitchen came to be bound and slashed. It wasn't until we were interrupted by the arrival of the mobile crime unit, including a lab technician and two detectives in street clothes, that I realized that to someone just coming upon the scene, my assailant would appear to have been the victim.

Initially, I felt only frustration that such a misunderstanding could divert official attention from what was so clearly going on. How long was it going to take them to react to information about Bonnie's journal, with its indictment of Cliff Morgan, and of my talk with Karen less than twelve hours ago? Was Karen in danger? Was Stephanie? In my mind, I felt I was fixing a magnifying glass on a patch of dry grass, and the intensity of my focus was causing it to burst into flames. I couldn't understand why it was taking so long for law enforcement to smell the smoke. Surely, they should be dashing off to Mount Clair to apprehend the man who must be responsible for this assault.

But instead I was being asked to describe in detail how the evening had transpired, the dinner with my family, how much we had to drink, when my mother and sister left the house, and then my stance at the sink when the attack began, my position on the counter when I was pinned down, and my grip on the knife. I realized that this was simply procedure, a necessary protocol, and tried to keep my voice from betraying my mounting hysteria.

I sat with one detective, a tall, prematurely white-haired man with a lean frame and a pot belly, at the dining room table, holding my sore left arm against my side, while the other detective, a fit, balding black man, took Mary's statement in the living room. When I overheard the word "garage" I experienced a distinct shiver. Were they going to go out there and smell marijuana? How much trouble would we be in then?

"And you say you didn't know the assailant?" my detective was asking me. I tried to focus. "I didn't think so, but then I thought that maybe I have seen him before."

"And do you know where that would be?"

I slowly shook my head, stymied. How would I know this guy? From school, from the many Asian restaurants I frequent, from the neighborhood? I looked off into the middle distance and then looked back into the blue eyes of the detective, whose face was a study in professional detachment. "Omigod, I think it was in Hawaii," I said suddenly. I think..." I stopped again, following something that was reeling through my mind... "I think he was the man who was by my friend when she....oh God, I think he killed my friend!" I cried out as horror and fury hit me all at once. Then I burst into tears.

Mary abandoned her detective and rushed in to me. She put an arm around my shoulders and made me wince.

"Really," Mary said protectively, "can't you do this later? I think I should take her to the emergency room and see about this arm."

I shook my head, red-faced but sputtering through my tears. "No, I need to explain about this," I insisted, wiping my face with my hands. "Just get me some Kleenex."

"Well, we can follow up tomorrow," her detective was saying. "These initial statements are to get the details while they're still fresh. We always do a follow-up later." To me, he sounded too willing to retreat. I suspected that I was making this more complicated than he had reckoned. Either that, or he didn't like dealing with blubbering women.

"No, no, hear me out now, please," I said. "This is important." Mary ran off to the powder room and returned with a long strand of toilet paper.

"Thank you," I said, and blew. "Okay, now, let me tell you what happened earlier this summer, and how I think it relates to tonight."

And so I retraced the story of the trip to Hawaii, of our hike up Diamond Head, Bonnie's horrible fall, and the Asian man who was kneeling by her body. I described my discovery of Bonnie's suspicions of Cliff Morgan, and how my own work with Stephanie confirmed those suspicions. As I concluded my summary with the conversation I'd had with Karen just that day, Mary's eyes were wide with alarm.

"My god, do you think the guy who broke in here is some kind of hired killer? And you think he went after Bonnie?" She asked this of me, but then looked to the detectives for an answer.

I was nodding, thinking of Leo and how right he had been to be suspicious. "I definitely think that guy was strong enough to snap Bonnie's neck. And did I tell you what Cliff Morgan's business is? 'Vanguard Industrial Security.' He provides escorts and security for business travelers, that sort of thing."

The two detectives exchanged a look. "Do you know about him?" I asked.

"I've heard of him," said my detective. "A lot of people in our line of work also work security jobs."

The black detective nodded. "So there's some overlap, you might say."

Mary looked from one to the other. "So is this going to be a problem?" she said bluntly.

"You mean, investigating a man whose business is security?" asked the black detective.

"I mean, investigating a man who employs police officers."

The man shrugged and stuck out a lower lip. "Not likely."

I looked hard at the white-haired detective, whose mouth was set tight, perhaps in concentration, perhaps in suppression of whatever it was he was thinking and not saying. Finally, he spoke. "We have a lot of ground to cover." He looked at Mary. "Can you get her to the emergency room on your own? Is there someone you can call?"

"Leo," I said to Mary. "My ex-husband," I explained to the detectives.

"And boyfriend," said Mary.

"I'm sure he'll be willing to take me," I said, "but what about the house? Should someone stay here?" My eyes rolled toward the kitchen. "And how do I ever clean up that mess in there?"

"Well, I'm afraid you have to wait until our investigation is completed before anyone can even go in there. It shouldn't be too long, maybe by tomorrow afternoon. And then, there are cleaning services that specialize in crime scenes. We can give you a referral, but first you should check with your homeowner's insurance, see about your coverage for this sort for thing."

"Homeowner's insurance!" Mary said, marveling at the logic of it. "They never get into this on *Law and Order*."

"May I use the phone?" I asked.

"Not the one in the kitchen," said the black detective. "Here, use my cell."

I dialed and Leo answered on the third ring.

"I'm sorry, did I wake you up?"

"Well, yes, but I fell asleep in the living room watching the tube, so you're doing me a favor. Now I won't have to visit my chiropractor after spending the night on the couch." Then his voice went low and suggestive. "Did you want to come back for another visit to our showroom?"

I glanced up at the detectives and got right down to business. "I need you to come over here and take me to the emergency room."

"Oh no, what's happened?" He sounded stricken.

"I promise to tell you everything when you get here. But don't worry, I'm not at death's door or anything." Not now anyway, I added to myself. "And if you have any crow handy, you might bring that along. I've been working up an appetite."

Chapter 28

When Leo arrived to take me to the hospital, Mary suffered a sudden rush of panic. Never mind the hot bath and soft bed she'd thought she'd needed. "Don't leave me alone at the crime scene!" she wailed, and hopped in the car with us.

My second trip to the emergency room that week took less time but more endurance. My shoulder had been "slightly" dislocated, a problem that was corrected painfully but quickly. "It's a good thing you're a swimmer," the young doctor said. "You have more flexibility and strength in your shoulders than a lot of people." Then he said to Leo, "Hold onto her," and realigned the joint. I let out a yelp that Mary could hear in the waiting room.

The streets were dark and quiet as we drove home, and Mary and I both urged Leo to stay in the house with us. He agreed at once, but added that he needed to stop at his apartment on the way. It took him only minutes to fetch whatever it was he needed, but I was surprised, and then gratified, to see that he'd brought his gun with him. It lay in its holster in his half-zipped gym bag like a shaving kit. Leo came from a family where owning guns was normal. They lived in the country, and his father and his grandfather were avid hunters. Leo had tried hunting only once, and after crippling a rabbit, used his pistol only for target shooting. Nevertheless, its presence in our house had always made me nervous. Until now.

After we all retired and Leo and I had turned off the light, Mary appeared at the door of the bedroom and quietly tiptoed over to my side of the bed. "Sorry about this, but I don't feel too safe tonight," she said in a loud whisper. "I'm going to sleep on the floor here if that's okay."

I threw back the covers. "You come on in here with me," I said. "Desperate times call for desperate measures."

"But won't that crowd your shoulder?" Mary rasped.

"The painkillers have kicked in. I feel okay now. In fact, I feel great."

"Woo-hoo!" said Leo in a mildly salacious murmur. "Are my wildest dreams about to come true?"

"Shut up Leo!" Mary commanded hoarsely.

"Rats. Should I go sleep in the other room, then?" he offered.

"No!" we insisted in unison. "Just stay right where you are and kill anything that comes near us, okay?" I said. I settled myself and my sling between the two bodies and patted Leo on the hand. "We'll talk about your reward another time."

"I'm on the case," he mumbled, and soon began snoring.

I whispered to Mary, "Leo claims that snoring is an example of evolution. Man snores to frighten off predators. He says the proof of its effectiveness is that we have never been attacked by bears in our sleep."

"Well," Mary replied, "Let's hope he's right, and that it's true for predators that are human."

"Yes, let's," I said, and wearily closed my eyes.

I awoke to the smell of coffee and an Egg McMuffin, which Mary was waving under my nose.

"What is going on?" I growled, struggling to open an eye.

"You've been sleeping in," Mary said. "The kitchen is off-limits so Leo made a McDonalds run. I'd have let you keep sleeping but there are cops here again. They asked to speak with you."

I started to roll onto my side and let out a groan as I became conscious of my sore shoulder.

"I brought you your pain pill," Mary said, "but you can't take it on an empty stomach, so eat hearty."

"Good lord!" I moaned. "I can't eat this early."

"Food or pain, choose your poison," Mary replied brightly. "The sooner you take the pill the sooner you'll feel like moving."

"Okay, okay," I muttered. Mary helped me sit up, then I sipped coffee and nibbled until Mary let me have my pill.

"Have you talked to the police? Do they know anything about the guy?"

Mary shook her head. "I didn't ask questions, I just came up to get you."

Just then, Leo appeared in the doorway. "Willa, do you have Vicki Golembiewski's phone number up here?"

"No, it's on my desk. Why?"

"I think you'd better talk to her before you go downstairs."

"What's up?" My instinct was to respond calmly, to correct for Leo's inclination to think the worst, but my mouth went dry anyway.

"Well, they're probably going to ask for Bonnie's dream journal. I mean, that's what the guy came here for, right? Which makes sense, I guess, but do you have a copy anywhere? Shouldn't you have one before you turn it over to them?"

Mary and I looked from Leo to each other, searching each other's eyes for an answer. There wasn't one.

"I'll get Vicki's number from information and call her before I go downstairs," I said. "Hand me the phone."

Mary said, "Leo, could you quickly copy those pages on the scanner?"

"You mean, right now, without the police knowing?"

"I'll go down and talk to them in the living room and distract them. Willa, where's Bonnie's notebook?"

I was scribbling Vicki's phone number on the tablet I kept by my bed to write down dreams. I held the phone to my chest and told them, "It's in my office, on my desk. It's got a dark blue cover, and the pages where she wrote about this are her last entry. It's several pages long, both sides."

Leo cocked his head, thinking about this plan, and nodded his agreement as I dialed. He turned purposefully and headed to the steps with Mary close behind him.

"Victoria Golombiewski please," I was speaking into the phone. "Tell her it's Willa Nilsson and it's urgent." I was told that Vicki would be in court all morning. As I was imploring the receptionist to have her call me as soon as possible, I heard the call waiting tone and hurried to finish. "She has my number. Thank you."

"Hello?"

"Willa, it's Trudy."

"Oh Trudy, what a night I've had!"

"Did you already hear about Dad?"

"What about Dad?"

"He's had another stroke. He's in a coma."

"Oh no!"

"Mom just called me. She thinks we should get over there."

"Is she there?"

"No, but they called her because she's now his surrogate, remember? Apparently, they want her to decide what to do next. How much to do, I guess."

I discovered I'd been holding my breath. I let it out a long, sad sigh. "I'll come as soon as I can," I said. "With Mary. We have — some stuff going on here. It might be a little while."

"Well, Mom's on her way over there and I'll go ahead and meet her. I'll see you at the hospital."

"Yes," I said, feeling weak and distressed. "As soon as we can get out of here."

I managed to stand without undue pain, but dressing was a different matter. I found slacks with an elastic waistband and slip-on sandals, but there was no way to put on a top without straining my shoulder. I wanted to call down to Mary for help but feared interrupting her diversion. Leafing through hangers in the closet, I found a shirt that buttoned up the front and got in one arm at a time. I looked at the bedside clock and tried to guess how long my scanner would take to copy the pages. I called down the stairs, "I'll be down in a minute" as I headed for the bathroom to brush my teeth.

I was about to descend the steps when the phone rang. I returned to the bedroom to answer it.

"Dr. Nilsson! Willa," said a voice breathlessly. "It's Karen Morgan."

"Karen! Are you all right?"

"Yes, but I need your help." Her voice sounded strained, and I guessed that she had been crying. "You know about how to get into a women's shelter, don't you? Can you help me get there? That's supposed to be safe, isn't it?"

"Yes, it's designed to be the safest place a woman can go. Where are you calling from?"

"At a pay phone, at the mall on Freeport Road. But I need to get out of here. Can you meet me someplace?" Her voice dropped to a whimper. "I'm so scared."

"Where's Stephanie? Is she all right?"

"She's with me, she's waiting in the car. Where can we meet you?"

I was thinking as fast as I could. "Can you get to my house in Point Breeze? There are police here…"

"Police? Oh no!" She sounded nearly hysterical. "Cliff has a lot of friends in the police force. No police, please!"

"Okay, okay," I said, "how about at East End Hospital? I expect to be there soon. And it should be a safe, public place for you."

"Okay, that's good. Tell me where."

But I didn't know for sure where I'd be — the ICU waiting room again? Not if they were avoiding heroic measures. My father's room? I shook my head, unable to recall the number. I said, "Do you know where the entrance is on Centre Avenue? I'll wait for you there, in about one hour."

"Thank you! I'll be there! But…" Karen's voice sank to a whimper, "please don't tell anyone where I am or where I'm going. I just want to get to the shelter. Then we'll be safe." She hung up without another word.

"Officers, I'm sorry it has taken me so long to get down here," I said as I turned the corner into the living room. I was surprised to see two unfamiliar women but finished my thought. "It's hard to get dressed with a bad shoulder."

Mary said, "Willa, these officers are from the sex crime unit. They've been sent here because of what you reported last night."

"I'm really sorry to keep you waiting," I apologized, "but I have to tell my sister something." I turned to Mary. "We just got some bad news. Dad's had another stroke. Mom wants us to get to the hospital as soon as possible."

The older officer, a short woman with auburn hair and eyes that matched her blue uniform shirt, spoke up. "This sounds like an emergency, so I'll be brief. According to the statement you made last night, you have some written evidence that one Clifford Morgan has sexually abused his daughter…" she looked down at the clipboard in her arms, "…Stephanie."

Just then Leo stepped into the room, and gave me a slight nod. Mission accomplished, I hoped.

"Yes, that's right. There are notes written by my friend, Bonita Taylor, who was Stephanie's therapist and suspected the abuse."

"May we see these notes?"

"Certainly," I said. "Of course this is not really direct evidence, but I have spoken with Stephanie and I am now convinced that Dr. Taylor's suspicions were true." I continued, "I'd already checked to see if Dr. Taylor's clinical notes might have contained more about this, but the file on Stephanie disappeared, in a break-in, shortly after Dr. Taylor's death." I turned to Leo. "Would you go around to my office and get the blue spiral notebook that's on my desk?" Leo nodded and exited wordlessly.

"You should know that this notebook is actually a dream journal that Dr. Taylor kept. Her notes about Stephanie follow a dream she wrote down." Leo returned with the notebook and I opened it to the salient pages and handed it to them.

"We'd like to have this, if that's all right with you," said the redhead, leafing through the blank back pages.

"As long as you return it to me, yes."

"That we will do." The officers turned to make an exit, apparently having done what they came to do, but Mary interrupted them. "Say, do you have any news about the... assailant? Is he alive? Do they know who he is?"

"All I know," said the redhead, "is what I read in the report that I was given this morning, and that said that he left here alive." She shrugged. "Our job is to investigate sex crimes, and in this case, the perpetrator wasn't present at this crime scene." She reached in her pocket and pulled out a card. "But if you have any questions or have anything you'd like to add to these notes here, give me a call."

I hesitated. I wanted to confide in these women, to tell them that Karen and Stephanie were en route to a shelter and that I would be helping them, but I stopped myself. If Karen felt it wasn't safe to divulge her whereabouts, then I would not risk putting her and Stephanie in jeopardy. The police would learn their whereabouts soon enough.

Chapter 29

Mary drove to the hospital because I wasn't sure I could steer with my bad shoulder. Leo stayed at the house to make sure someone would be there when other investigators arrived.

Mary asked, "Did you tell Trudy what happened to you last night?"

"Didn't have a chance," I said. "And she has enough on her mind."

"You think we should spare the gory details until we know more about Dad?"

"Well, the business about being attacked is going to upset Mom no end. I'd just as soon put it off if we can."

"How are you going to explain that?" said Mary, keeping her eyes on the road while nodding toward my sling.

"We can say I hurt my shoulder," I mused, "and even that I had to go to the emergency room. But let's save the scary part until we know what's going on in there."

As we turned onto the hospital grounds, I said, "Would you mind dropping me at the main entrance before you park?"

"No problemo," said Mary. "I'll meet you up there." I didn't want to have to tell Mary about my plan to meet Karen, and realized there was no need. I got out of the car and Mary drove around the entrance to the underground parking garage.

I stood in the morning sunlight and watched for Karen's car, thinking through the logistics of getting her to the shelter. Usually, the first contact a worried woman would have with the shelter would be via their hotline. Operators were trained to screen these calls, assess the woman's situation and determine how soon they would be able to house her. In an emergency, they would find some place for a woman to stay, even if the shelter itself was full. But often a woman's first call to the shelter was exploratory, and the staff and the client would have time to set up a plan. Sometimes, a woman could arrive under her own steam, picking up her kids at school and driving directly to the old brick Victorian in Highland Park that could house as many as twenty at a time. Otherwise, it was easy enough to send a cab to pick her up. Occasionally, a woman needed to put a good bit of distance between herself and her abuser, and shelter volunteers had more than once picked up an out-of-state client at the Greyhound station, after "riding the dog" for a day or more.

The location of the shelter was closely guarded, but it was impossible to maintain total secrecy and so the shelter invested in gates and electronic monitoring. Offended husbands and boyfriends could be especially determined and creative. One man hid under a car parked across the street with a mirror, attempting to spot and intercept his wife when she left the building. Other men had persuaded female friends to call the hotline and to feign being in need of shelter, in order to learn its whereabouts. Sometimes, when the location was discovered, a client would have to be sent to a different shelter.

I did of course know where the shelter was — no more than fifteen minutes from where I now stood, as a matter of fact — but we would have to follow the protocol and let the staff know what was going on. I assumed Karen would have a cell phone, and if not, we could use a pay phone and get instructions on how to proceed.

The silvery BMW seemed to sparkle in the sunlight as it turned off Centre Avenue and made its way into the circular driveway. It came to a stop in front of me and the tinted passenger window went down.

"Karen, " I said gently, "how are you?"

Karen looked better than I expected. No visible cuts or bruises anyway, and presentably dressed, although clearly nervous. "Do you have your cell phone with you?" I asked.

"Yes," she nodded, gripping the steering wheel with both hands and looking like she might be about to drive the Grand Prix.

"Because we need to call the shelter first."

"Okay, sure. Get in," she said.

I climbed into the passenger seat and turned to greet Stephanie, but the child was not there.

"Where's Stephanie?" I caught the note of alarm in my voice and tried to correct for it. "Wasn't she with you?"

"She was, and I decided it was safer for her to be some place else. I'm afraid of being followed." I shot a glance out the back window of the car. Karen had pulled away from the curb and was turning out of the hospital driveway, but I saw no car that looked to be in pursuit.

"Where is she then?"

"In the Barnes and Noble at the mall, with a cell phone and cash. I told her I'd call her or come for her as soon as I could."

I frowned, thinking how desperate a mother must feel to decide her child was safer alone in public than with her.

"Where are we going?" I asked.

"I'm just driving. I figure that if I keep moving, he can't find me."

I decided to offer a note of calm. "Look, give me your phone. We'll get this taken care of real soon. And then you have to take me back to the hospital because people are waiting for me there."

Karen nodded and handed me her phone. I squinted, trying to make out the letters on the tiny keys in order to press 1-888 SHELTER. After two botched attempts, my call went through and a hotline advocate answered on the second ring. I was introducing myself as we pulled up to a stop light. Suddenly, the back door opened and Cliff Morgan slid in and grabbed the phone from my hand in one swift move.

My first impulse was to grab the phone back, but then Cliff pressed the "off" button and with that tiny beep, I suddenly recognized the peril of the situation. My belly responded with a hot, sinking sensation that felt like an attack of stomach flu.

"Drive, Stupid," he said to Karen. "The light's green."

Karen accelerated through a busy Oakland intersection. We were on Fifth Avenue, approaching the University of Pittsburgh and the sidewalks and crosswalks were dense with pedestrians. We would come to another stoplight soon, and I prepared to jump out even if the car kept moving. Traffic slowed as we approached Bigelow Boulevard.

"Turn left up here," Cliff commanded, and Karen obediently crossed into the far left lane and came to a stop. I grabbed and pulled on the door handle, but nothing happened.

"The locks are on. You can't open the doors," Cliff said with a note of impatience. I looked over and said, "Karen!" urgently, expecting her to press a button to release the locks, but she sat motionlessly staring out the windshield, her face a mask with sunglasses. I then tried to pull up the door lock manually, but Cliff had laid his hand over it. "That won't work either." He sounded irritated. "But I don't think you want to get out. I have an offer I want to make to you."

"Get in the right lane and go straight across Forbes, then turn left and go through Schenley Park," he instructed Karen.

Cliff leaned forward and spoke into my left ear. "You know, I can have you killed and I will if you keep making trouble for me." He sat back in the seat and ran a hand through his hair. I turned and saw his jacket fall open. He was wearing a holster that held a gun just inside his armpit. I decided to hear out what he had to say, just in case I wasn't already toast.

The car made its way past the Hillman Library, the Frick Fine Arts Building, the Carnegie Lecture Hall and Phipps Conservatory, all structures endowed by a veritable pantheon of industrial gods. They and their ilk had laid the foundations of the prosperity of the city, and probably all of them had employed the likes of Cliff Morgan.

"You know your friend — what was her name?" Cliff asked.

"Bonnie. Bonita. Taylor." I turned further in my seat to face him.

"I tried to talk sense to her. But she was just determined to make trouble for me. What kind of sense does that make?" He sounded genuinely puzzled.

"You mean, you spoke with her?"

"I tried to make her an offer, but she just flat out rejected it." He shook his head regretfully. "And it would have been an easy thing for her. It was a sweet deal, business I could easily direct her way. She could have become a regular, well-paid expert witness through my connections. Traveled all over the country too. A lot of people would jump at an opportunity like that." He shrugged and pursed his lips in an expression of disdain. "Some people just don't know a good thing when they see it."

"Head toward the Oval," he told Karen. "We'll have us a nice drive through the park."

I watched grassy hillsides and tree-filled slopes go by and wondered if I would get out of the car alive. Unlike the buildings we had passed, Schenley Park was endowed by a woman and featured winding roadways through acres of greenery, with lots of isolated spots. But Schenley Oval offered not only a spectacular view of the city, but also many public facilities, including a track, soccer fields and tennis courts. I waffled between dread that I was about to be shot and dumped in the woods, and hope that Cliff wasn't planning to kill me if they were driving through such a busy part of the park.

"But I've learned my lesson," Cliff continued. I had been afraid to speak, but the silence that followed this statement seemed to require a response.

"Your lesson?" I said.

He nodded, his face a statement of sadder-but-wiser irony. "That's right. It doesn't do any good to try to help somebody out." More silence. I knew it was my turn to say something.

"It doesn't do any good," I echoed.

"I'm glad you're a good listener," he said, "because I don't want you to forget what I'm about to tell you." He waited and I slowly said, "Okay." Karen was driving in silence, climbing the hill to the Oval, past picnic groves and the Veteran's Memorial, maneuvering through the curves like a professional chauffeur, someone hired to drive attentively and ignore what's going on inside the car.

"You saw what happened to Pham last night."

Pham? What's Pham? I shook my head in bewilderment.

"Pham Van Trong, one of my operatives." He sounded utterly disgusted with me for having to explain this. I nodded quickly and made a note to never act bewildered again.

"Pham Van Trong," I said, as if holding up my end of a conversation.

Cliff seemed reassured that I was still paying attention.

"That's his Vietnamese name. Most people just call him Van. Now there's a man who's had some trouble. Had a visa to be here with family — some of his folks had made it here after the end of the war — but then he got arrested for selling drugs and was going to be deported. As it happens, another of my operatives brought him to my attention. Van's a crackerjack martial arts expert, a real asset to the team. And so I made it my business to make sure Van could stay in this country and work for me. Now, he's a U. S. citizen with a wife and a couple of kids and a real nice house in Cranberry Township."

Cliff Morgan seemed very proud of this American success story. I spoke to show I was listening. "Cranberry Township," I said in an approving tone of voice.

Cliff nodded. "Yes, he's got it all." Then his face hardened. "And why do you think a man like that would try to cut his own throat?" He glowered at me.

I didn't know what to say to this, but didn't want to act bewildered. I tried to come up with a response that would keep him from getting more upset with me.

"Because he felt he had to." I said this definitely, as if it were an obvious deduction rather than a desperate guess.

"That's right," Cliff said, like a game show host confirming a contestant's winning answer. "That's exactly right. Because Van is a man who knows that he owes his life to me. And he knows that if he were ever to divulge my business to anyone that it would be very bad for his wife and his kids and that house in Cranberry Township. Could be bad for the rest of his family here too." He'd been brushing the nap of his trousers, but now he looked up, and directed his gaze into my eyes. "I believe you have a lot of family, don't you?"

I felt the blood drain from my head, but I knew I ought to answer. "Yes," I said quietly.

Cliff reached into his inside breast pocket and pulled out a sheet of paper folded in three. He opened it and read. "Your mother, I see that she lives not far from me," he said amiably. "All by herself. And you've got that sister, Mary, staying with you now — that was a surprise. She's in from Texas isn't she, lives in Austin. Quite a town. And she has a boy and a girl who are three and five, and they live on West Lynn Drive and her husband has a dental practice right there behind their house, isn't that right?'

"Yes," I said miserably. Getting myself killed had been my only worry a moment ago, but now I was terrified for everyone I loved.

"I've got more here about your other sisters, and about Leo." He said his name suggestively, like a fourth grader teasing a classmate.

"Leo," I said, "is just my ex-husband." Perhaps I could divert him from Leo, at least.

"He's the ex-husband you sleep with," he said simply. He folded the paper and put it back in his jacket. "In the security business, we call this 'intelligence gathering.'"

"Intelligence," I repeated, feeling utterly defeated.

"Yes, and you can see how valuable it can be. A person in my position requires loyalty, and this is the means that never fails. I can see that you're impressed." He addressed Karen. "You can start heading back now." Then he turned his attention back to me. "I know you're anxious to see your dad. But let me just finish up what I have to say."

I felt deeply chilled, and held my left arm close with my right arm, trying to keep from shaking. "Okay," I said.

"I need you to take back whatever it was you told to those detectives. You never saw Van before, and you don't know a thing about what that Dr. Taylor was thinking about my daughter."

I thought, "Uh-oh, too late! The police already have Bonnie's journal." Should I tell him and beg him not to retaliate? "Look," I said miserably, "I've already given them a statement, and ... some papers."

Cliff seemed unruffled. "But if your memory goes bad and you can't recall the facts, then the case is dead. And I can retrieve papers and statements and such. The important thing for you to remember is that they can't go anywhere without you. Just don't give them anything to go on." He sat back and smirked. "So, you happen to be worth more to me alive than dead. Because you're going to reverse yourself."

I held onto my arm and said, "I can do that." My shivering made me sound eager, even enthusiastic.

"You have to do that." He waited for me to reply.

"I will," I promised.

Chapter 30

I was dropped off exactly where I'd been standing when Karen had pulled up a half an hour before. I clutched my sling to my chest as I made my way through the hospital's automatic door, feeling like I had to hang onto myself. I struggled to organize my thoughts as I tried to figure out where to go next. The elevators? The information desk? A phone booth? The ladies room? I stood in the lobby wondering what floor my mother and father and sisters were on, waiting for me. I thought about terrorism and how effectively it works. It occurred to me that Cliff must have threatened Karen too, but I felt too outraged to forgive her for helping him. What would he threaten her with, I wondered bitterly, canceling her golf lessons? Then I realized that it was probably much more insidious than that, and shuddered.

My mind darted in many directions at once. I wondered how soon Leo could move in with me, and didn't care that having him move back now meant that I was acting out of neediness. I craved protection. I thought about Abraham Maslow's famous hierarchy of needs, the pyramid graphic that always accompanies his theory in psychology text books. The bottom of the pyramid represents basic needs like shelter and safety. Only when those are satisfied do we turn to growth needs, like love and esteem and self-actualization. I thought how true this is and pictured myself as a casualty at the bottom of Maslow's pyramid, flat on my can. I was still standing in the lobby, motionless and distracted, when Trudy found me.

"Where have you <u>been</u>?" she demanded as she approached me. "I was sent down to search for you. And what happened to your <u>arm</u>?" Her voice rose with consternation. She laid an attentive hand on my back, and the gesture made me feel grounded for a moment.

"I was taken for a ride. I mean, I had to step out for a moment."

"Just now?"

"Yes, I didn't expect to. I was trying to help someone." I didn't want to say anything more, didn't want to say who or why or anything that might endanger Trudy or anyone else in my family. I felt fortunate that my sling provided a distraction.

"And this thing," I nodded down at my arm, "is because I sort of dislocated my shoulder last night."

"Now, how in the world did that happen?" Trudy said with a note of disbelief.

"Oh, it was dumb," I said. "Mary was showing me how to do some of her aerobic kick-boxing moves and I got a little carried away. It's fine really, just a little sore still." I marveled at my ability to invent a plausible lie with no premeditation whatsoever, and smiled wanly at this unexpected side effect of being terrorized. "Now, how's Dad?"

"Well, it doesn't look good," Trudy sighed. "We may be at the beginning of the end. Come on, let's go up. He's not in intensive care, because Mom doesn't want them to prolong the inevitable."

"Is it inevitable then?"

"Probably." The furrow between Trudy's brows grew darker and deeper. "Maybe. I'm not sure. Just come up and see what you think."

It was hard to believe that the man in the bed had been raising hell just twenty-four hours earlier. His paleness was accentuated by his white whiskers, and his skin looked waxy. His eyes appeared to have sunk into their sockets, and he made no response to my entry or to the other women in the room. Still, I spoke in a hushed voice, as if fearful that I might waken him.

"Mom, how are you?" I said, putting an arm around my mother's waist.

"How are you?" said my mother with concern as she took in the sling. "Have you hurt yourself?"

"Oh, just sprained it a little."

"Horsing around with Mary," Trudy offered.

Mary shot a look at me and captured the essence of my silent command: Say Nothing.

Mother clucked, "Oh, you girls," in the same muted voice we were all using.

I went to my father's bedside and took his hand. It was warm but limp. I squeezed it anyway.

"No IV, I see," I said.

"Mom's standing firm," said Trudy. "Although there's a nurse here who's pushing for more of what she calls 'comfort measures,' like hydration."

"But once they have that IV in there, then they'll probably ask to give him drugs, antibiotics and things that will only make this take longer." She frowned. "The man's in a coma. How much discomfort can he be experiencing? In the old days, he'd be allowed to just die quietly in his bed without all this rigmarole."

My sisters and I looked at one another with questioning eyes. Was our mother overdoing this?

"Mom, do we know if Dad would recover any useful function if they treated him aggressively?" I asked. "What did the doctor say?"

"Oh, that they can treat him, even though he may never come out of this. There are so many things they could do — feeding tubes and respirators and transfusions. But it's pointless!" Her voice was rising with emotion. "And I don't want to see this drag out, do you? It's just too much suffering."

"Well Mom," Trudy said comfortingly, "he's not suffering now."

"No, he's not, but look at you all. You've been in this hospital every day since this happened. I don't want to see you sacrificing your lives for a hopeless cause. And that's what this is. If he came to and recovered some function, he'd still be paralyzed. He still wouldn't be able to walk or talk or swallow. And that's just misery, for him and for you."

Then she shocked us by approaching the bedside and addressing her ex-husband. "You hear me Stan? For once in your life, try to think about other people. You've disappointed me and these girls in the past, but here's your chance to redeem yourself." Then she leaned down and spoke directly into his ear. "I mean it Stan. Get going to where you have to go."

We stood in stunned silence. I know that people under stress can explode with feeling, but this was utterly unlike our mother, the very model of composure and courtesy. And I also knew that people in comas could still hear things, and feared the impact of my mother's words. I was the first to speak.

"Mom," I said gently, "why not go with Mary and Trudy to get something to eat?" I looked at my sisters, who both looked as stricken as I felt. "I'll bet you haven't eaten all morning."

She stood up and sighed. "And we have to call your other sisters. They need to know what's happened."

"Well, good, you can go down to the cafeteria and find phones and do it all. And I'll sit tight here," I promised, steering the lot of them out of the room.

"Don't you want anything?" Trudy asked.

"I am really not hungry," I said truthfully. The throbbing in my shoulder was growing intense, and after they left, I took another pain pill.

Once alone with my father, I pulled up the nearest chair and sat alongside his bed. The side bars were not up now, the patient no longer in danger of forgetting that he was paralyzed and accidentally throwing himself out of bed. I rested my head on the side of the mattress. His breathing was barely audible; in fact, he seemed barely there. Still, I reached with my good arm and rested my hand on his shoulder, and I spoke to him.

"Dad, it's Willa," I said quietly. " And I want you to know that I don't believe that Mom meant what she said. She's upset." There was no indication whatsoever that he had any recognition of what I was saying, or for that matter, of what Mother had said.

"I do want you to know that things are being taken care of. Mom is sticking up for you. Trudy and Mary are here, and they're calling Marcia and Glad. We're all going to be here for you."

Then I recalled an important factor mentioned in hospice tracts — that often a patient needs to be given leave to let go. Not the way Mother had done it, but with assurances that everything was all right.

"We all want you to know that you've been a good provider and that we're all grateful for that." I knew that he measured his own success by how much money he had made, and at that he had certainly excelled. "And I want to assure you that we will be all right if you need to go." I struggled to find words that would convey ease and comfort, but all the pictures coming to mind were of the strain of getting along with this imperious, temperamental man. Then suddenly it dawned on me that as difficult as he had been, he had not been evil. He wasn't a Cliff Morgan. And I suddenly, urgently wanted to thank him.

"Dad," I continued, "I'm not only grateful for all you've done for us," I began, and finished my sentence inside my head, "but also for all you <u>haven't</u> done <u>to</u> us." I stopped and weighed my options, then forged ahead. "And I'd like it if...if when you, um, cross over, if you would keep an eye on us. I don't know what the deal is over on the other side, but I'm pretty sure there's something. And right now, I can use all the help I can get. Because, Daddy," and my voice cracked on that word, but I kept talking, "there's a really bad man who's come after me. And he'll go after Mom and Trudy and everyone if he wants to. And I'm really, really scared." I felt every bit the five-year-old whimpering over a nightmare, but this one wasn't going to end with a sister in the next bed saying, "You can climb in with me if you want."

I didn't even know I had fallen asleep until I woke up, startled, to my father's voice in its most commanding tone, yelling, "Just shoot the sonuvabitch!" I shook my head and looked over at my father, who lay just as quietly as he had moments before. So, he hadn't spoken for real, but in — well, maybe not a real dream, but in that vivid, falling asleep state that can startle us back to wakefulness. But even as my disorientation lifted and I recognized what must have happened, I reacted to how much my father had sounded like himself, his old self, the man who wouldn't stand for nonsense. It felt exactly like he'd spoken to me.

"Just shoot him," I repeated wonderingly. The old man's breathing remained quiet and steady. There was no response. "That would certainly solve my problems," I whispered to him. I remembered Leo's pistol in the drawer of my bedside table. I knew how to use it, or at least, Leo had taught me target shooting years ago when we were dating and he'd taken me out to the country. If Cliff Morgan showed up at my house and threatened me, I thought, I really would shoot him. Visions of Bette Davis — or was it Barbara Stanwyck? — in a full frontal shot, coolly firing on her mark, ran through my mind. This is what that creep deserved. Certainly, shooting the man was preferable to letting him continue to threaten, abuse and kill more innocent people.

And so I decided right then and there that I would take Leo's gun, drive out to the Mount Clair and shoot Cliff Morgan.

Chapter 31

There was very little that interfered with my resolution and I proceeded decisively. I persuaded my mother and sisters that I needed to run an errand, and that I was limber enough to drive. On my way home to get the pistol, I did think about the consequences, but refused to let them deter me. I would do the deed, then turn myself in. To my mind, I was performing an unpleasant but necessary act for the good of the community. The fact that I would be held accountable was not sufficient reason to fail to act.

I found my house unoccupied, with a note from Leo that investigators had come and gone and we were now free to use the kitchen. I thought about finding my camera and taking pictures of the crime scene, but decided I shouldn't permit myself to be distracted. I climbed the steps, went to the bedside drawer, and opened it.

There it was, a black .32 revolver that had seen better days. It had first belonged to Leo's grandfather, and looked it, where the finish had worn off the barrel from years of resting in its old leather holster. I picked it up and inspected it for a moment, reacquainting myself with it. The metal was pitted above the handle. I pressed the barrel release and looked into its chambers. Three held bullets, the others only lint. The gun had never held bullets when it was stored at home, and I knew that Leo must have loaded these last night. I couldn't remember which way the chamber moved when it was fired, so I made sure to close it with the middle bullet behind the hammer. That way, I could fire at least one shot, and maybe two, no matter what.

I raised the gun the way Leo had taught me, holding it at arm's length and using the site to aim at an electrical outlet across the room. My finger couldn't reach the trigger when I held it by the brown, hatch-marked handle. I'd forgotten that this gun was too long for my hand. Leo had taught me to grip it higher up, slipping my finger comfortably onto the trigger and then choking the handle. I aimed again, and felt ready.

Not once, as I drove to Mount Clair, did it occur to me that shock and pain meds were influencing my behavior. Instead of questioning my actions, I tried to visualize what would happen when I arrived. I'd discovered as I left my house that my sling provided an excellent place to stow the gun, and so I could present myself at the Morgan's front door without appearing to be armed. If Cliff answered the door, well, that would be that. I would draw and fire, point blank. But where? His stomach would be at my arm level. But that might not do the job. I decided to aim higher, at his heart.

If Karen or Stephanie answered the door, I would ask to speak with Cliff privately. That way, I could fire after the door was closed behind us, and minimize the trauma to Stephanie. I didn't doubt that Cliff would agree to see me — he had no reason to fear me, having so thoroughly intimidated me so recently. Unless he somehow read my intent in my face. I'd make it a point not to look at him directly, to appear cowed and fearful.

But I felt no fear as I approached the Morgan's front door, only a sense of purpose. I rang the bell and waited for the melodic chimes to summon the inhabitants. I slipped my right hand into my sling and held the gun loosely. I was ready to fire right away, or in a few minutes.

But no one answered the door. I rang the bell again, and waited. I had been so intent on carrying out my plan immediately that I hadn't considered what to do if no one was home. A wave of anxiety and disappointment washed over me, and I heard myself whimpering as I rang the bell a third time. I waited, but no one came to the door. Just as I was turning away, I thought I heard what might have been a muted shuffle behind the door. Someone watching from the peephole, perhaps? Was Stephanie there alone, afraid or forbidden to answer the door?

"Hello?" I said aloud. "Stephanie?"

There was no response, but I was not about to give up. I walked around the side of the house toward the back, heading for the French doors in the hopes of seeing into the family room. As I rounded the corner onto the patio, I stopped cold. One pair of French doors stood open, and lying across the threshold was the large and inert body of

Cliff Morgan, wearing nothing but a black Speedo. Karen was standing outside the door, trying to get a grip on his arms. Stephanie was inside, with a hand under each of his knees, struggling to move him.

Karen looked at me with an expression of pure terror. "Omigod!" she cried. "Omigod!"

Stephanie's face collapsed and she began crying out, "Mom, it's okay, Mom! Don't cry!"

I took it all in and raised a finger to my lips. "Shhh," I said as I walked toward them. I removed the gun from my sling and laid it on a glass-topped table. "It looks like there's been an accident."

Karen looked up at me incredulously, then back down at her husband.

"I don't know what he was on this time. He gets real coked up sometimes, but this was worse than normal. I let him have it. See?" She pointed to a ruddy spot on the side of his head, and I could see dark ooze matting the hair behind his temple.

"Good for you," I said. "What did you use?"

"A cast iron griddle." Then she looked up at me, dropped the man's arms and sank to the ground. "I'm afraid he's..." and she began sobbing like a child who's cried so hard that she can't get her breath.

"You're afraid that he's dead?" I said.

Karen shook her head emphatically. "No, no, no. I'm afraid he's not dead," Karen groaned between breaths. "If he wakes up, what'll he do to us? That's why we're taking him to the pool."

Stephanie had sat down where she was, unable or unwilling to step across her father, and was weeping angrily. "Mom," she hissed through the doorway, "tell the truth!"

Karen shook her head, and wiped her cheek with the collar of her blouse. "It could easily be a swimming accident. People have been hurt on our diving board before." She nodded her belief in this possibility.

"Dr. Nilsson," Stephanie interrupted in an emphatic whisper. "It wasn't Mom who hit Dad in the head. It was me."

I was trying to assess the circumstances as clearly as I could. I'd been prepared to kill Cliff Morgan myself, so I wouldn't balk at helping them to finish him off. But I was worried about Stephanie, as much now as ever. What would be the best possible outcome under these grim circumstances? What if we called 911 right now and told the police to come? Might that be a better outcome for Stephanie, to have things go through their proper channels? She'd probably be sent to the juvenile detention center, but surely authorities would take Cliff's abusive history into consideration. There might be justice then, which could mean a lot to this girl down the road.

On the other hand, there might not be. What is justice? I asked myself, remembering that this was the same question that provoked Socrates, who hadn't known the answer either. It seemed to me that Stephanie had more character, and certainly more backbone, than her mother, who had failed to protect either of her daughters. Perhaps by taking the blame now, Karen meant to finally intercede on her daughter's behalf. Perhaps Karen would continue to take the blame, and spare Stephanie a journey through the tortuous legal system.

But if we called 911, Cliff would probably survive, and that would be the worst outcome of all. My mother, my sisters, Leo, all of us would be in danger. Now that I knew that Cliff Morgan would stop at nothing, I had to do likewise.

"Okay," I said, "let's get him into the pool. A drowning will trigger an autopsy, and they will find a lot of drugs in his system. That could be the end of it, but if they don't like that injury, they might suspect foul play. If that's the case, tell the truth. Although I'd be glad if you left me out of it." I placed a hand on Karen's trembling shoulder. "Because I'm definitely prepared to help you. I just wish I could lend you both hands."

On my way home, I briefly entertained the idea of telling someone — Leo, Mary, Trudy — of what had transpired at the Morgans' pool, but I quickly rejected it. Sharing knowledge of this crime, however justifiable, would bring nothing but worry and fear and Cliff Morgan had already caused enough of that. I wondered how I would hold myself together while waiting for official word of Cliff's death and the investigation that would be forthcoming. But in the meantime there would be sisters to shuttle from the airport, vigils to keep at our father's bedside and the collective grieving that was already underway. My family emergency meant that there would be few idle moments to ponder what might happen next.

That night, I turned up the fan in the bedroom window so that I could nestle next to Leo in bed. "I took the bullets out of your gun," I murmured in his ear.

"Made you too nervous?"

"Yep."

"Now how am I supposed to protect you?"

"The bullets are right there in the drawer if you really think you need them. But a loaded gun is just too dangerous to have lying around."

"Well, I guess that guy isn't going to try to come after you now," Leo said, "but what if someone else comes?"

"I don't think I'm at risk now that the police know what they know, and have Bonnie's journal."

Leo took a little longer to fall asleep that night, but not much. I lay in the darkness, huddled against his warm flesh, and felt myself connected to life and love. I did not regret my acts of that afternoon, the almost slurping sound that Cliff Morgan's body made when we rolled it over the edge of the pool, but there was plenty to worry about.

What about Pham Van Trong? I did not know whether he had even survived his injury. I made a note to call the police and ask about him, but suddenly realized that any contact with the authorities might lead to questions about Cliff Morgan. The name would be emerging soon enough, and I had no intention of connecting myself with him now. For the time being, I decided, I would limit my conversation with authorities to those that they initiated. If and when I sensed any signals that they were connecting the dots of the crime at my house and the death at the Morgan's house, I would contact Vicki and bare my soul.

The next morning, I was puzzled when Leo presented me with a brief report in the Pittsburgh Post-Gazette. In the second section, tucked halfway down a collection of reports under the title "City," was a short paragraph about "an apparent home invasion" in Point Breeze. An unidentified assailant had broken into a home on Carnegie Place, assaulted a resident and then been injured when discovered by a relative of the resident. It sounded promising to me that the "assailant" was described as "injured" and not "killed." And I was relieved that no names were mentioned. I hoped it meant that the police were protecting my identity. In any event, I was glad that the

wide world did not know of my predicament. Then I wondered —
had Pham Van Trong been able to avoid revealing his identity? He
very probably would have had to, given his mission, and his boss.

Or perhaps they were withholding his name for a reason. I
suddenly remembered what Karen had said about the police, that she
feared their friendships with Cliff. Perhaps that had been a lie, but if it
wasn't, my situation could be more perilous than I already feared.

"What's the matter?" said Leo with concern.

"I'm just remembering that I had a call into Vicki yesterday."

"Did you check your voicemail?"

"No, I will."

Sure enough, Vicki had called back about the same time that I was
driving out to the Morgans to commit premeditated murder.

I grabbed the remote phone and went to my desk to find Vicki's
number. When she answered, I said "Hi!" brightly, then rushed
through the kitchen past Leo to the stairs, and climbed to the second
floor, where I could talk to Vicki without being overheard.

"I have a question for you," I said breathlessly.

"What's that?"

"If I tell you that I committed a crime, are you under any
obligation to like, report it?"

"If I'm your lawyer, I'm not. Unless you haven't committed it yet.
Then I have what's called an 'obligation to warn.'"

"Well, you are my lawyer, that's for sure." I said this so fervently
that Vicki's tone shifted from sarcasm to concern.

"And your crime was...?"

"Um, I'm not sure exactly, but maybe accessory to murder."

"Oh my God!" After a pause Vicki added, "Are you being
serious?"

"I am, and I have a lot to tell you."

Chapter 32

"And do you have a picture of your father?" the funeral director asked.

All five of us looked around at one another, each wondering if this man expected one of us to produce a snapshot at once and whether any of us had one. We were seated in a semicircle around his desk in a tastefully paneled office in one of the East End's most tasteful funeral homes.

"Do you mean, with us?" Trudy finally ventured.

"No, I mean, is there a photograph that you would like to run with his obituary? You needn't give it to me immediately. The newspaper won't run it until just before the funeral." The silver-haired gentleman guiding us through the sad and sorry details of our father's disposition seemed not only patient, but supernaturally wise. Or maybe he was just experienced while we were raw, and, for the most part, hung over, having drunk a good bit of wine together after we got the call that Dad had died shortly after we'd left the hospital the night before.

"Does it have to be recent?" asked Mary. "Because he didn't look so hot recently."

"Mary!" Marcia protested. She was the eldest and perpetually serving *in loco parentis*.

"I have a photograph somewhere of Dad when he was named Man of the Year by the Rotary Club," Trudy offered. "I can bring it in when we bring in his clothes."

"That should be fine," said the funeral director. "Friends and family are usually glad to see pictures of their loved ones in the prime of life."

This left us all quiet again, thinking about our difficult father and all the difficult details that his death was now presenting to us.

Framing his long life for an obituary was already a challenge. Should all the ex-wives be mentioned, or none? With so many children and grandchildren, there wouldn't be room anyway. In addition, we were learning that we had to procure death certificates for every agency and organization, from the IRS to insurance companies, that would require documentation of his death, and for every relative flying in for the funeral. We also needed to pick the dates for the visitation and the funeral, the clothes he would wear and the casket he would wear them in.

We were escorted to a showroom, or rather, two parlors in this former mansion, where seven or eight caskets sat on display. The funeral director waited to be asked for the prices, which ranged from a few thousand dollars for the plain, fiberglass coffin to many thousands for the mahogany sarcophagus.

"Who's paying for all this, Dad or us?" whispered Trudy when the silvery gentleman left the room.

"Dad's estate," said Marcia. Because she's an accountant, we figured she knew best.

"And after this is paid for, do we know if what's left is going to us?" Glad asked.

"I think so," said Marcia. "But we won't know anything for sure until we hear from Dad's attorney."

"The mahogany one is so beautiful," Glad observed wistfully.

"Yes, and it would make a great baby grand piano," said Trudy. "But remember that this is not something Dad is going to get to appreciate."

"Or play," said Mary.

"And it's probably bad for the rain forest," I added.

"We could buy a fully loaded Mercedes for what this thing costs," Trudy noted.

"Dad thought a lot of himself," Marcia nodded, "but I think he'd find this an outrageous extravagance."

"But, wait!" Glad pointed out. "Look at this!" She showed us how the bars along the bottom of the casket, the ones that the pallbearers would use, were moveable, while the ones on the others weren't. We looked on curiously, enjoying Glad's enthusiasm even as we struggled to understand it.

"Honey," Trudy finally said, placing an arm around Glad's shoulder, "it's not as if Dad's going to be taking this through airports or anything."

Glad frowned a moment, but then slowly nodded. "I guess you're right. Its not like we're picking out luggage, is it?"

"Not exactly," said Mary, in a voice that threatened to turn into a giggle. That was too much for the rest of us. Everyone, including Glad, suffered an attack of involuntary laughter, which we all tried to stifle, which only made it worse.

All this — my father's rapid decline into death and my family's peculiar coping skills — I had endured with the threat of imminent arrest hanging over my head. Every time the phone rang, every time someone came to the door, every time Leo handed me a phone message over the last three days, I expected the truth to come crashing down on me. I repeated Vicki's advice over and over, like a mantra: "Don't say anything to mislead the authorities, but whoever wants to talk to you, tell them that you need to speak with your lawyer first. Then call me immediately." When they came to my door, I would be ready.

But so far nothing had happened. The suspense would have been overwhelming if I hadn't had so much else on my mind. Standing there in the casket room with my sisters, I laughed and wept harder than the others, releasing some of the tension that gripped me. I had told no one but Vicki about my predicament, not only because my sisters were upset and grieving, but because, as Vicki had cautioned me, "Loose lips sink ships." None of them would have privilege.

"You mean, if I told any sister, she could be forced to testify against me?"

"That's right. And Leo too, because you're no longer married."

So I kept my secret to myself, to protect myself, my family — and Stephanie.

But I did call Vicki again, as soon as I returned from the funeral home. "Is there any way you can find out what's happening? It's been awfully quiet!"

Vicki said, "Have you seen today's paper? His obituary is in there."

I had a moment of bafflement, thinking about my father's obituary, then caught up to Vicki. "Cliff Morgan's obituary is in today? Hold on!" I ran for the paper, sitting neatly on the kitchen counter, unread. I scanned the contents index on the front page and found the obituaries in section B. There it was, a column of small print tucked in with the rest of the obits, without a photograph, about Clifford Edward Morgan, local business owner and drowning victim. I read as fast as I could, murmuring as I went. "Died suddenly...West Virginia state wrestling champ, graduate of WVU...Owned and operated Vanguard Security Associates...Member of Mount Clair Golf Club, Pittsburgh Athletic Association, Duquesne Club... Preceded in death by daughter Margaret, survived by wife Karen and daughter Stephanie...Services private...in lieu of flowers, donations suggested to the Ferris School."

I fell silent for a moment, stunned and stupefied. "Vicki," I said finally, "what does this mean?"

"It means, I think, that you're off the hook."

"What? How can that be? What about the autopsy?"

"I made some inquiries, and I'm not completely sure — my source is an old friend I knew when we both worked in the DA's office, someone who was, how shall we say, glad to hear from me. He knows people in the coroner's office."

"And what could he tell you?"

"Well, here's the deal. Autopsies are not performed the way they used to be. Technically, anyone who dies without a doctor present is supposed to be autopsied, but that's just not the way it happens any more. Paramedics find an eighty-year-old dead in his bed, he doesn't get autopsied. It's expensive and troublesome. Same with a lot of natural deaths at home."

"But a drowning isn't natural — is it?"

"Well, no, it isn't. But what if someone in authority claims that in this case, it is? Guy was an alcoholic, used drugs, was known to be careless."

"You're saying that someone in authority intervened and prevented the autopsy? Who would do that?"

"Now, that's an interesting question, Willa. Let's think about that for a moment."

"Think about what?" My mind was darting around like a butterfly on speed.

"Think about this — how many people do you know who were better off with Cliff Morgan dead?"

I actually started counting on my fingers. "Three," I said, thinking of myself, Stephanie and Karen, but then said, "No, wait a minute. How many people are better off?" I tried to count all the members of my family that he had threatened. My mother, Leo, my four sisters, their husbands, their kids...

"A lot," I said finally. "More than I can calculate, er, right off the bat."

"Now, think about the people that Cliff Morgan worked for, and how he worked for them. Do you suppose any of them might have reason to welcome his demise?"

I was still baffled, but I was trying to put the pieces together. "The people who hired Cliff Morgan were corporate officials. They were men and women who needed to be protected when they traveled around the world."

Vicki continued her train of thought. "People who needed security personnel they could trust during their day-to-day lives on the road. Corporate executives who might at times be indiscreet, in some way or another, while they're away from home. They might, say, be married people who hire call girls. Or, they might be straight men who prefer boys when they're in exotic locations. Or, a client might have a problem with drugs, or drink, or gambling. Things a security man would observe but would be trusted to keep under his hat."

"Oh," I said quietly. I ran my fingers through my hair, as if combing out my tangled thoughts. "Maybe this means that — I'm not the only person he was terrorizing."

"That's my read on this."

"And somebody on one corporate ladder or another was able to influence somebody in the county government, in the coroner's office, to look the other way?"

"Government by and for the people," Vicki said ironically. "My impression is that someone high up got to someone high up. I doubt we'll ever know exactly who and how."

"Good grief," I muttered. "That's almost as scary as he was." I thought about this for a long moment and then asked, "But, why would some muckymuck, or muckymucks, want to hush this up? Why protect the people who did him in?"

"I don't know that either. The logical deduction is that someone believes that the less scrutiny directed toward Cliff Morgan and his affairs, the better."

"What about the other people in his business? His 'operatives'?"

"Well, I tried to check on this Pham Van Trong person. Neither the police nor the hospital ever knew his name. And you heard that he escaped from the hospital, right?"

"No, I didn't!"

"That same night. They took him into surgery and stitched him up, and then he disappeared from the recovery room."

"What!? I can't believe this!" I gasped. My mind raced ahead. "This is outrageous, and no one told me! I should call the police right now and tell them who he is. I know where he lives too, he has a house in Cranberry Township ..."

"Hold on, Willa," Vicki interrupted. "Think about this now. First of all, we don't know how he got out of there — by himself, or whether someone else participated. And more importantly, you have to realize that anything you have to tell the police about Pham Van Trong is going to be hearsay from Cliff Morgan. Mentioning any kind of conversation or transaction you had with Cliff Morgan on the day he died is something you definitely need to avoid."

"But, Pham Van Trong is a murderer. This is the man who killed Bonnie!" I was shrill with anger and frustration.

"Yes, well, technically, other people are getting away with murder here too, Willa." Vicki paused as her comment sank in, and then proceeded seriously. "You've got to get a grip and weigh what's in everyone's best interests here."

There was silence on the line as my outrage and sorrow escalated. "It's just..." I said in a quivering voice, "it's just so wrong." I let out a strangled sob.

"That is true," Vicki allowed quietly. "And I'm sorry." She sounded so sincere, like such a friend, that I apologized.

"I'm just upset," I said, trying to recover my cool.

"Of course you are. But you're going to have to accept that there's not going to be any public reckoning. You need to banish any thought of involving authorities in any way. You will have to content yourself with the fact that a kind of justice was meted out privately. But that can never be exposed without placing yourself and others in jeopardy. Cliff Morgan is dead, and his minion has undoubtedly left town. That's going to have to be enough for you."

Chapter 33

That evening, we were in Trudy's kitchen, cooking for ten, a fraction of the number that would gather by the time the funeral took place. For now, we were making a vat of chili that would feed Trudy, Ted and their kids, Leo and me, Mom, the other three sisters, and anyone who might drop by.

Ordinarily, Marcia would have taken charge, but instead she sat at Trudy's kitchen table, nursing a glass of red wine and fanning herself.

"Hot flashes!" she wailed. "Alcohol makes them worse, but Dad just died. What's a girl to do?" She took another sip.

"Try yoga," said Glad, slicing loaves of French bread.

"Or drugs," said Mary, chopping onions.

Trudy and I shot each other a look. There was our sibling assortment in a nutshell, or maybe a box of candy. Marcia — pronounced Mar-CEE-a — was a Queen Bee, and whatever was going on with her, it was the worst, or the best, ever. She was growing plump in middle age, but could tell you everything you might possibly need to know about the latest diet, or any other subject that might come up. As the eldest, she was accustomed to being an authority, and she continued that function even as her retinue of clueless little sisters came of age and developed wisdom on their own. She'd be the gold foil wrapped cherry cordial.

Glad was the un-Marcia, the almond with the hard pink coating. She'd gone the farthest of all of us, settling in California, where she'd joined an ashram for a while, studied meditation and yoga and eventually earned a masters degree in comparative religion. I envied her lean and limber body, and appreciated her reflections on leading a spiritual life, except when they strayed into the territory of moral superiority, which they did with some regularity.

But however much we might irritate one another on occasion, we do love each other, and I think we have our parents to thank for that. Mom, by making each of us feel special, and Dad, for creating the hostile environment in which we learned to become allies.

I was thinking that Trudy would be the solid chocolate, no fruit, no nuts, no cream filling, when I noticed that Marcia had stood up and was wrapping her arms around our mother. Mom was wiping her eyes, and as we all looked her way, we fell silent. There is nothing more heartrending than seeing your mother cry.

"I'm all right," she said, patting Marcia's hand. "Sit down." She looked at all of us. "I want to tell you about something."

Trudy turned down the fire under the pot, I stopped washing lettuce, and we gathered around the island that was part work surface and part tabletop.

"You know," she started, "times were different when I was a girl." This was not news. We all knew the story of the Brubaker family's misfortune—her father had been a stock broker when the market crashed in 1929. Her parents' savings were soon gone and they'd moved in with her mother's parents on the family farm in Westmoreland County, where Mom learned to pluck chickens and her beloved father learned to distill whiskey, which he sold to his contacts back in the city. When he was caught and sent to jail, lean times grew leaner.

"We know Mom," Marcia said consolingly. "We were lucky to grow up so comfortably." She hugged her again and said, almost crooning, "And we know that you always appreciated that Dad was such a good provider."

"Yes he was," Mom said, with more steel than nostalgia in her voice. "You have no idea what it's like to be hungry, and you should all be grateful for everything, everything that he made possible for us."

"We are, Mom, honest," said Mary.

"But that's not what I wanted to discuss with you. There was something your father never wanted you girls to know about, but now that he's gone, I feel that you really ought to know."

We all looked around at one another, checking to see if any one of us looked like she knew where this was going. Apparently not.

"You know that I met your father during the war."

"You took care of him in the hospital and that's how you met, right?" said Mary.

Mother leaned her head to one side in a half-shrug. "Well," she said, "not exactly. We knew each other before he went off to war. I don't know how else to say this but directly. Your father and I — I had a baby after your father shipped out. I left my family and said I was going to the city to attend nursing school, but instead I went to a home for unwed mothers, had the baby and gave him up for adoption."

For what seemed like a long time, the only sound in the kitchen was the fan over the stove, humming loudly while we absorbed the shock.

"You and Dad..." said Marcia.

"Poor Mom," said Trudy.

"Him?" said Mary. "It was a boy?"

"Poor Dad," I murmured.

Mom wiped her nose and blotted tears with a paper napkin.. "I don't know why I'm crying now," she said. "It was such a long time ago."

"Mom!" Glad exclaimed. "You gave up your first born child! For heaven's sake! How sad it that?" And with that, Glad, our self-possessed Zen mistress, burst into tears.

That was all I needed to lose my grip on composure, and the consensus was unanimous. There wasn't a dry eye in the kitchen. Eventually, as the nose blowing subsided, I had to ask.

"Mom, I can understand Dad's wanting to keep this a secret when we were little, but why all this time? Why didn't you ever tell us?"

Mom sat with her hands folded in front of her and stared at them. "Your father thought that this was best, and I agreed with him. At first, it was to protect me, and all of us, as a family. You have no idea how shameful such a thing was in our day. Your aunt Aggie — she was the only one who knew what was going on -- she warned me that he would never marry me after this. Of course," and here she smiled, "she also thought he was good for nothing, just a mechanic, a 'grease monkey' she called him." Mother looked up with a grimace. "The Brubakers may have been poor, but we were proud. Our father had been a professional, our mother had gone to finishing school. Or maybe I should say, Aggie was proud, because I didn't much care."

Agnes was my mother's older sister, and the kind of person who was happy to point out the faults of anything or body that crossed her path. She had ended up marrying a Yale graduate who became an insurance executive and a raging alcoholic.

"Of course, I didn't know if your father would even come back alive." Mother sighed. "It was Aggie's idea that I go to the city and give up the baby. She helped me."

We looked at one another with shared sarcasm. Of course Aunt Aggie would help Mom to leave her family and suffer alone in the city. Aggie's prime directive would be to keep up appearances.

"But, haven't you ever told anyone else?' Marcia asked.

"No," said Mother. "I was so grateful when your father came home and wanted to marry me that I was happy to put the past behind us. And what good could it have done to tell you, any of you? How might it have affected your idea of yourselves as women, your respect for yourselves? No good could have come of it." She nodded, as if agreeing with Dad all over again that this was best kept secret, locked away in the past.

"But now," Trudy said gently, "you'd like for us to know." She was stating the obvious, but it was a question.

"I would," Mother nodded. "Not because it could change anything, but because it is the truth. And truth matters."

A lot of thoughts were racing through my mind then, and a lot of feelings were wrestling with them. I realized that this was going to change my understanding of my parents forever, and I also knew that it was going to take me some time to process it. I felt sadness for my mother and my dad, for the son they'd never had a chance to raise, and for us, for the brother we'd never known. And for that aging guy out there with 5 little sisters he's never known.

There was also unexpected admiration in realizing how loyal Stan and Peg had been to one another — she had stood up for him, and he had stood by her. And they had both, in their ways, stood by me and my sisters. They protected us, even from their own unhappy mistake.

My mother was adding, "You know, that's why I wanted to have all you kids. Losing one just made me want to have more."

I thought about those ancient temples, where sex was sacred and there was no such thing as an illegitimate child, because all children belonged to their mothers. Isn't that how it is in nature? How had humans contrived to make it otherwise?

"So, if not for this brother, I might never have made it here?" Mary was saying, sounding more like a petulant child than a woman with two children of her own, and this made my mother laugh.

"Do-do-do-do, do-do-do-do," Glad sang the Twilight Zone theme. "What if you – or me, or any of us, were never born?"

"*It's a Wonderful Life*, with James Stewart and Donna Reed," said Marcia.

"Did you know he made that right after he came back from the war?" said Glad.

"That explains why he was so intense!" Trudy observed.

"But have you seen *Vertigo*? He's like, nuts in that...."

And that's how we recovered our equilibrium, subtly shooing the conversation away from shocking revelation to movie trivia and drifting back to our kitchen tasks.

Returning to the sink, I flashed on a picture in my mind, from a story Leo used to tell about working at a restaurant while he was in college, and how the owner, a big Greek, killed rats that made their way into the kitchen from the back alley, sometimes very dramatically, with meat cleavers. The story had made me laugh with horror in the past, but in this moment, I thought about Cliff Morgan. It was a horrible association, but a true one. I had helped to kill a rat, and this was a secret I would have to keep for the rest of my life. Even more than reckoning with my parents' original sin, and the reality of an unknown brother, was the knowledge that I came from parents who had kept a secret for over fifty years. And that comforted me.

Chapter 34

I sank down into an upholstered wing chair. The stresses of the past week had finally caught up with me. Through the last frantic days and the anxious nights, I had slept badly and felt perpetually wired, and the result was an insidious but insatiable exhaustion. I closed my eyes on the scene of my sisters and their sundry spouses, ex-spouses and offspring, the older ones looking like a grove of trees standing in the plush room of the funeral home. How ironic that this welcome wave of sleepiness was coming at Dad's wake. I wondered for a minute if there might be a place to lie down somewhere. Then I smiled at the only option I could think of — the casket. "Don't mind me folks! I just needed to take a load off my feet. I've just had a really hard week!"

"What's so funny?"

I opened my eyes on Frank Conrad.

"Oh Frank!" I cried, and jumped out of my chair. "Frank! I'm so..." I had to think fast, because what wanted to tumble out of my mouth was forbidden "...glad to see you. It's so nice of you to come." I hugged him, playing for time.

I could never, ever tell him that Bonnie was murdered, or that the killer had come after me, or that the bastard responsible had been killed and that I had helped. All this rose in my heart to be spoken, and then had to be carefully diverted into silence. I deliberately made my way to the surface of things, like pushing off from the bottom of the pool.

I pulled back from him and said, "Have you lost weight?"

Frank, ever the physician, was adjusting his glasses, as if to evaluate my condition. He shrugged and then smiled. "Well, some, yes." He patted his waistline. "Nothing I'm not better off without."

Then he tilted his head and said, "I was sorry to hear about your Dad."

"Thank you. It's been a rough couple of weeks."

"It's been a rough year, let's face it."

I nodded, took his hand, and gave it a squeeze. "You can say that again." I was deciding that, even if I could tell Frank, it would be cruel to do so. How much harder would it be to grieve the loss of Bonnie if he knew her death had been deliberate? What could possibly be gained by this knowledge? Outrage, bitterness, a sense of injustice so vast and painful that it would yawn at his feet for the rest of his life? My silence then would be not only a necessity of self-preservation, but an act of mercy.

Leo came over to greet Frank, and I felt grateful all over again for Leo's presence, for his steadfast willingness to be with me. Perhaps that alone was reason enough to have him move back into my house and my life, but I knew I should not try to force a decision now, and reminded myself that Leo didn't know just how heinous the situation had become, and what I had done. Like Frank, he never would. And I didn't want to think about how Leo would feel about me if he did.

The men's conversation had strayed to the subject of golf, allowing me to plunge further into to my deep and secret thoughts. I remembered how I'd feared that Bonnie's death was no accident long before I'd known anything about Cliff Morgan, and why was that? It was because of a dream. I recollected it as it ran through mind like a sequence in a movie. I was on the phone with Bonnie, who said she was in danger, because O.J. Simpson had bought her a car but she knew that if she came out of the house, he would run her over with it.

The dream caused me to suspect falsely that Frank had a hand in Bonnie's death. But now, looking back, I saw how valid the dream had been. In fact, a wealthy, athletic, abusive man had made Bonnie an offer that she had refused and she paid with her life. In the realm of the ancient Greeks, this would qualify as a dream from the Gate of Horn, a true dream.

And just then an image of Stephanie came to mind, leaning over my book, avidly inspecting the illustrations of ancient Greek temples with clear and curious eyes. It pained me to realize that I might never see the child again. I would try to contact the Morgans and inquire after them both and hope for a chance to see Stephanie, for the obligation the girl inspired in me had only grown over the last days. I felt the need to provide some kind of assistance, to help her to make her way through what she had suffered, including a mother who had failed to protect her from harm. I knew there wasn't much chance, but I felt compelled to at least try to be a support. I shook my head slowly and sadly. I knew that Karen would not want me around and that it was almost as likely that Stephanie would not want to see me either. Both, I knew, would need to cover over the recent past, the truth of their complicity and the guilt we all shared.

"Willa," Trudy came up beside me and took my arm, and spoke quietly in my ear. "There's somebody here who wants to see you. I ran into her out by the parking lot. She's afraid to come in."

"Who?" I said, perplexed.

Trudy shrugged and shook her head. "Some kid," she said, but then brightened. "Could it be Stephanie?"

"Oh!" I stepped quickly out of the room, down the dark paneled hall and out the parking lot entrance into the bright sunlight. There, indeed, was Stephanie, standing near the door dressed in jeans and shifting uncomfortably from one foot to the other. I stifled an impulse to gather her up in my arms and hug her, but I reached out and took both her hands. They felt damp and cold.

"Stephanie, I'm glad to see you."

Stephanie looked both pleased and pained. "I'm not dressed right for this," she said, folding her arms across her T-shirt and looking down at her flip-flops. "So I didn't want to come in. I wasn't sure I could make it here. I got a ride to the mall and then took a bus." She looked at me with a frank expression. "I didn't tell Mom I was going to try to come here. I was afraid she'd freak out."

"How is she?" I asked. "And how are you?"

"Mom is — kind of a zombie." She nodded toward the funeral home. "Last week, we had a funeral and buried Dad's ashes with Maggie." She shrugged. "And since then, Mom's been like, you know, talking about Maggie a lot. And not sleeping. Or eating much either."

"I'm sorry to hear that." I reached for her hand, with its nail-bitten fingers, and held it in both of mine. "You know, Stephanie, when someone is having to adjust to a new loss, it very often brings up memories of past grief. It's as if they have to mourn the other losses they've had in their lives all over again."

Stephanie nodded, as if this made sense to her. "I guess so." She folded her arms across her chest again, but lifted her eyes from the ground, and fixed them somewhere below my chin. "I dreamt about Maggie last night," she offered. "But it wasn't a sad dream."

"Tell me about it."

"Well, she was in the pool and so was Dad, in the deep end. I was sitting on the edge at the shallow end with my legs in the water. I think Mom was sitting on the patio." She squinted off to the left and said, "But I'm not sure. Anyway, Maggie was teaching Dad how to swim. She was trying to get him to put his face in the water, just like he taught us." She smiled and shook her head at the incongruity of child teaching father. "That was weird. And there was something else funny. There was a lifeguard there. She was on one of those high chairs they sit on, along the side of the pool. And she was watching over all this." Stephanie held a hand up to shield her eyes from the sun and peered into my eyes. "She was you."

I'm accustomed to turning up in students' dreams. Over the years I've been cast as a first grade teacher, a nun, a gardener, a race car driver, a cat and a spider, and all had seemed, upon investigation, to represent a student's feelings about exploring dreams. My heart filled with hope that a lifeguard was a good thing to be, but I had to ask Stephanie what she thought.

"In the dream," I asked carefully, "how did you feel about the lifeguard?"

Stephanie cocked her head. "Well, funny, because lifeguards are usually at big pools with lots of people, and I wasn't sure why she was there. But it was nice to feel that we were all safe."

"I'm glad to hear that," I said, and gave her a smile. I wondered if this might have been a telepathic dream, in which Stephanie picked up on my hopes for her well being. If it was, I was gratified that the message had got through. Or it may be that Stephanie had cast me as a helpful watcher because that reflected her real feelings about my part in her life.

"I guess the lifeguard was you because you've sort of been in a position like that, where you've been able to see everything that's been going on."

I nodded silently, considering the metaphor.

"And I was thinking — do you suppose Maggie was teaching Dad to swim because, well, she's been dead a lot longer? It seemed to me that she was like, showing him the ropes."

Out of the mouths, and hearts, of babes, I thought. "That's so interesting," I said, and meant it. "Can I give you a ride back home? We can talk about it in the car."

Stephanie grinned. "Thanks, that'd be great." Then she hesitated. "But aren't you busy here?"

I looked back inside the long dark hall of the funeral home. There was nothing going on in there that was as important as what was going on out here. "I can excuse myself for a little while. I just need to get my keys. I'll be right back."

When I dropped her off, Stephanie had my e-mail address, my phone number and my promise to continue to see her however it could be arranged. I offered to come in and speak with her mother, but Stephanie shook her head. "I don't think so," she said, opening the car door. But then she paused, "Maybe you could, like, call her or something? That might be okay." Then she slipped out of the car and disappeared into the house.

I backed out of the Morgan driveway, leaving that perfect residence that held awful secrets. Now, like it or not, those secrets were mine too. I felt like I'd made a deal with the universe, and had to hold up my end of it. I was spared more of the evil that Cliff Morgan had visited upon me and mine, and I was spared prosecution. But now I was obliged to look after Stephanie and to help Karen in any way I could.

I decided to run an errand before I returned to the funeral home that day. I drove over to the Garden of Eden and bought myself another statue of the Sleeping Goddess. It's as close as I could come to making a concrete appeal for divine intervention. I've made a special place for her on my bedside table, and now every night I look to her for guidance, thank her for her assistance and promise to honor what dreams may come.

About the Author

After earning a BA in English/Writing at the University of Pittsburgh, Cynthia Pearson began keeping a journal in which she would sometimes record her dreams, and thereby hangs a tale. She has written two books, *The Practical Psychic* with John Friedlander and *Parting Company: Understanding the Loss of a Loved One--The Caregiver's Journey* with Peggy Stubbs, as well as a number of articles and papers. She is a longtime member of the International Association for the Study of Dreams, and often chairs panels on long term journal keeping at its annual conferences. She lives in Pittsburgh.

Acknowledgements

In the beginning, there was Robi Bendorf, who first suggested, "Why don't you write a mystery about dreams?" Over the ensuing years, writing group buddies Mary Galtz, Frank Mediate, Evelyn Pearson, David Sanders and Gina Sestak provided ideas, insight and intelligence. When I finally had a manuscript to review, I appreciated feedback from Dianne Diebold, Ed Kellogg, Anita McClelland, Linn McQuiston, Bill Miller, Dennis Schmidt, Peggy Stubbs, and especially, Rita Dwyer. Henry Pearson and Perk Pearson provided graphics help once production got underway.

When I started writing down my dreams in the 1970s, I had no idea that I was embarking on a practice that would amaze and guide me for years to come. This is in no small part due to my membership in the International Association for the Study of Dreams, which has provided me with not only a wide-ranging education through its conferences and publications, but also the stimulating companionship of its many dedicated members.

Finally, I have to credit Gabrielle Reznek, Courtney Turich, Sam Turich and Tom Turich, for providing me with advice and attention whenever I needed it, and enduring with me the long haul of bringing this book into being.

Made in the USA
Lexington, KY
29 September 2010